C&RPr

# A Den of Foxes

# STUART HOOD
# A Den of Foxes

Methuen

First published in Great Britain in 1991
by Methuen London,
Michelin House, 81 Fulham Road, London SW3 6RB
Copyright © 1991 Stuart Hood

The author has asserted his moral rights

A CIP catalogue record for this book
is available from the British Library

ISBN 0 413 65110 x

Typeset by Deltatype Ltd,
Printed and bound in Great

For Michael

*Pater filio amicus amico*

# PART ONE
# Games of Love and War

La Volpaia
San Vito
Provincia di Siena
13 June 1987

Dear Peter Sinclair

I am writing to you at the suggestion of a good friend of
yours and mine – Will Brodie, a wargamer like myself who
spent Easter here with his wife.

I am not aware that you are a wargamer – ours is a circle
of enthusiasts and as a player of many years standing I can
claim to know most of them by name at least. But the way
Will talked of you, with great warmth I may say, has
encouraged me to write to offer you a position in my very
own wargame. I have two reasons. One is that you have
apparently taken early retirement and so may have some
time on your hands. The other is that I understand from
him that you had what people call 'a good war' not
unconnected with this part of the world. If you joined the
club I think I can guarantee that you would find it
interesting.

I have been wargaming for a good few years. I find it
better than correspondence chess because it takes one into
history, geopolitics, military archaeology etc. Last year I
tried to launch a campaign set in the time of the Roman
Empire and specifically centred on the Parthian wars which
were in my view fought for control over the trade routes
between the Roman Empire, Asia Minor, Central Asia and
China. Unfortunately this project failed to attract any

attention, partly because most of my network are less interested in economics than in military tactics, the use of terrain, questions of logistics, march distances etc – there was even a player in Milwaukee who accused me of trying to foster a Marxist view of ancient history although, in fact, I tend to be greenish in my politics.

I hope that my new game may be more successful. I have already made informal contacts with a couple of wargamers in Europe and elsewhere (including one in Israel who with any luck will be coming to Tuscany this summer) and I feel I have enough players to make it a viable proposition and very much hope that you may be tempted to take part. Let me say at once that my reason for running this game is entirely for my own enjoyment but naturally I do not wish to remain out of pocket. To get the sordid details out of the way then, I shall expect players to use either a self-addressed stamped envelope, or an International Reply Coupon and a self-addressed envelope, or to deposit with me a small sum from which I shall deduct my postal costs. I shall also want a deposit from players whom I do not know personally to prevent players from dropping out of the game without giving proper notice and without returning material necessary for their role.

This time the game will be called ANDROMEDA. The situation is as follows:

In the 2060s Tellus (Planet Earth) was clearly faced by an ecological disaster brought about by a number of factors. They included the accelerated dispersal of the ozone layer with resulting tree- and plant-death; worldwide desiccation that left the Alps as bare of snow and as arid as the highlands of Ethiopia; inundations (caused by the melting of the polar ice-caps) that not only threatened to overwhelm such great estuarine cities as London, New York and Buenos Aires but led in Europe to the flooding of the North German plains and the Po Valley and in the Indian sub-continent to the submerging of much of Bangladesh – not to mention the salinisation of great rivers like the Nile, the Ganges and the Mississippi. A colony of Tellurians (earth-dwellers) has therefore been established on the planet Andromeda to determine its suitability as a site for colonisation. By the Eighties of the 21st century it has successfully constructed its own stable ecology using advanced methods of plant propagation developed earlier in the century in the sky-labs of the superpowers: the United States and China. The colony

4

is now well established. Its Control Commission, however, is exercised by the possibility – given the deterioration of conditions on Earth and the wealth of Andromeda (derived from mineral deposits) – that other colonists may arrive from the few remaining centres on Tellus capable of operating launching-pads (or indeed from elsewhere in the universe) and attempt to found rival colonies. There have been indications from the Commission's extremely accurate signals intelligence unit that the arrival of a reconnaissance in force can be expected shortly. In that case there is, they argue, a real danger of clashes with the newcomers.

In the event of your deciding to take part I have generated the following character for you:

Your PC (Principal Character) is the only surviving child of a scientific family. His parents, who were among the first colonists, were lost in outer space when their shuttle broke away from the gravitational field of Andromeda. He is above average in constitution, strength, dexterity and agility, but not much more than average in intellectual abilities.

Should you wish to play, may I ask you to decide on the basis of the above information:

1. The age of your PC when the game starts on 21 June 2087
2. His function in the colony
3. His interests
4. His emotional attachments (if any)
5. His name

Looking forward very much to your reply – which I hope may be a positive one.

Regards
Christopher Williams


PS. For the purposes of this game I shall call myself Urizen – a name you may recognise from Blake's prophetic books – and you may wish to accept this convention. The view that Urizen represents restrictive morality and can possibly, I believe, be identified with Jehovah seems to make the name an appropriate one for a games master.

PPS. I needn't tell you, I'm sure, that Volpaia means 'the foxes' den'. But don't let that put you off!

The wind puckered the face of the loch but under the lee of the clumps of wooded islands there were glassy patches of calm. Beyond the end of the quay – not so much a quay as a long narrow wooden landing-stage that ran a hundred yards or so out into the water – some small yachts clustered. Their metal stays struck bell-like notes from masts. A bird gave a high whistling call and came in to land at the water's edge with a sudden, accurately judged inclination of its swept-back wings. It was nearly eleven o'clock but the north-western sky was still bright where the setting sun back-lit the green and brown hills. A little up from the loch and set side on to it stood a low red sandstone cottage: what would once have been called a 'butt and ben' but was now defined in the Holiday Homes catalogue in more acceptable terms:

### The Fisherman's Bothie, Lochmore
A fine old stone cottage – single storey S/D K sbs shwr DB heating by open fire and electricity – beautifully situated by the side of Lochmore. This property lies within the policies of historic Lochmore Castle. The Castle was for hundreds of years the family seat of a branch of the great Campbell clan. The present proprietor is Major Campbell-Swinton, DSO MC. The Castle garden is famed for its rhododendrons brought back from China, Tibet and India by the present owner's grandfather and father, and for its views of the hills and bens of Lochmore. Fishing permit available on application. Rowing boat or sailing dinghy can be hired by arrangement with the factor.
  Pets absolutely forbidden. No children.

The factor was a despondent-looking Pole who introduced himself with a slight inclination of the upper body as Garlinski. He had a crinkled face and a yellowish complexion. In his speech Slav intonations were curiously overlaid by those of Lowland

Scots. He was quick to establish his authority by requiring Peter to move his car to a patch of gravel at the side of the cottage where it would be hidden from 'the Big House' by a clump of rhododendrons. The Major, he explained, did not like to have parked cars in his line of vision when he looked out of his windows towards the loch. There was a picture of the loch in the Big House. There were no cars in it. The Major wanted it kept that way. When Peter pointed out that perhaps cars hadn't yet been invented when the painting was made, Garlinski gave him a quick sideways look but said nothing.

Selecting a couple of keys from a large bunch he wore at his belt, he unlocked the door and proceeded to decipher the coded message of the advertisement. This, he explained unnecessarily, was the sitting/dining room with kitchen area. It was, in fact, a rather small square room, with furniture that appeared to have come from an auction: a low formica-topped table set between a couple of armchairs of a dismal brown, a bulky settee that no doubt contained the single bed, against one wall a gate-legged table; along another a set of white-painted bookshelves.

Beyond, an extension housed modest kitchen facilities and beyond that again were what Mr Garlinski called 'the usual offices', which included a somewhat primitive shower. On one wall was a map of the loch and its surroundings showing the depth of the water and the areas where tenants of the cottage might fish. A stern note said that 'any person may be prosecuted for poaching' adding that the capture of smoult spawn was illegal and that trout under 8 inches in length were to be returned to the water forthwith. On the other walls hung foxed engravings of gentlemen in full Highland fig grouped round freshly slaughtered deer, of picturesque ruins and picturesque peasantry in bonnets and plaids. The Major, Garlinski explained as he took his leave, would no doubt call in the morning. He liked to know who was using the premises.

Peter unloaded his suitcase from the car, carried it into the bedroom and dumped it in the curtained recess that served as a wardrobe. Then he fetched his lap word-processor and radio, his binoculars and cameras, and debated where to place them.

Eventually he laid them in a haphazard way in the living room. His books, files and research material, he decided, could stay in their cardboards boxes in the boot of the car till next day.

Meantime he cleared from the bookshelves the literary detritus of successive tenancies. It ranged from thrillers and blood-and-guts war books through a biography of Lloyd George to a thick paperback, bought no doubt in some airport lounge, on the cover of which a lady with a deep cleavage offered herself to the reader's gaze; food for the erotic fantasy of businessmen, diplomats, journalists and international sportsmen on inter-continental flights. Flicking over the pages he found sex on page twenty and assumed that it would recur at regular and predictable intervals throughout the novel. He added it to the pile he was constructing in the far corner of the room beside the box where, to judge by the layer of sawdust and scraps of bark, Garlinski (who else?) when the cold weather came would stack the day's ration of logs.

But long before that weather came Peter would be gone. Travelling again. On the move once more, as if trying to shake off a pursuer. Perhaps even to San Vito which he had known when engaged in other, grimmer wargames.

In the west the light was fading and to the north clouds stood black over hills that were like a stage set or a diorama. The sight drew him down to the water's edge. The loch was very still and dark. Looking back at the castle he saw its crenellated outline and the high windows, where a light suddenly sprang up. Had the Major been studying him from one of these windows through his old service binoculars? Then the midges drove him indoors.

Lying in bed he watched the gloaming thicken to dark and wondered about Christopher Williams, who had written to him from a countryside of hot enclosed valleys where the broom grew impenetrably over forgotten wartime graves. What could he be like? Well-heeled presumably, one of the rich international jet-set who were colonising Tuscany. And how should one reply to the letter, which on some impulse he had not thrown out with all the junk mail but had brought all the way from

London? Curiosity almost drove him to rise from his bed and look for it in his briefcase but he was too comfortable and warm. Under the duvet his hand moved unerringly to find a spot just above his right nipple where a dark stain of pigment had slowly, almost imperceptibly, developed over the last year, spreading, darkening, itching a little, the site and focus of fears which he must sooner or later confront, while lacking the courage. Soon – in the autumn maybe – at all events once he had settled down again in London, he would do something about it. Ring Will Brodie and ask him for the name of a good consultant. Confront the truth whatever it might be. He turned on his side and took up his accustomed foetal position, drawing the clothes higher to shut out the midsummer twilight. In the long light northern evenings of his childhood the corncrakes, deep in the hayfields, had driven sleep away with their relentless, rasping call. On such an evening he had stumbled on the idea of his own mortality and started up in childish terror. There were no corncrakes any more, either here or probably anywhere else in the British Isles. But there was the constant 'wheep' of waterfowl – oyster-catchers probably – to keep him awake as he lay and attempted to master his childhood fear.

I have generated the following character for you as readers:

> Your PC is called Peter Sinclair. He is the son of the editor (deceased) of a local newspaper in a small town in the east of Scotland. He has (until recently at least) always been secure in the soundness of his constitution, to which his medical records (so far) bear testimony. His intelligence (see various IQ tests to which he has been subjected, eg in the army) is something above average; his analyst however is of the opinion that she has seldom seen anyone so appallingly stupid when it is a question of his own emotions, his deep compulsions, the motives he so carefully conceals even from himself.

9

You will wish to know the answer to the following questions:

1. The age of your PC
2. His CV to date, ie when the game starts in June 1987
3. His emotional and other attachments
4. The reason for his return to Scotland

Since this may be the first time that you have taken part in a game of this kind let me set you on the right path.

1. He is sixty-four. He has taken early retirement from his college and might therefore plausibly be intending to work on a book long promised to his publisher, his colleagues in academia and himself
2. His CV includes what is called a 'good war'
3. He is almost certainly, as the saying goes, unattached but has been married twice. By his first marriage he has a daughter who lives in Canada with her mother (now remarried); there is no longer any contact with either. From his second marriage he has a son who – through his mother, Orna – has Israeli citizenship: a problematic relationship with both, a source of pain, sorrow and nostalgia
4. He has spent much of his life 'in the South'. You may therefore wonder (particularly if you are Scottish) why he has chosen to return to the North and will no doubt dismiss this as a silly question deserving a silly answer; will find sufficient reason in the fact that, crossing the Border on his way to Lochmore, he had found himself recalling some lines from Scott – but from which of his rum-tee-tum poems? – that ran: Lives there a man with soul so dead/ That never to himself has said/ This is my own, my native land/ Whose heart within him ne'er has (burned?)/ As homeward journeying he has turned/ His footsteps from a foreign strand? Or words to that defect
5. He would define himself as a person of the Left who, given his generation, has followed a familiar political

trajectory from the romantic communism of the Thirties and the Popular Front through the agony of the defeat of Republican Spain to an anti-Fascist war, disillusion with Stalinism and the long painful search here and there on the Left for a group, a party dedicated to socialism. He is at present – and has been for some time – so to speak politically unattached

**6.** Where his physical and mental state is concerned you may find the following definitions relevant:

  **a** Melanoma (malignant), a malignant tumour, usually developing from a nevus and consisting of black masses of cells with a marked tendency to metastasis

  **b** nevus, a circumscribed new growth of the skin of congenital origin

  **c** metastasis, the transfer of a disease from one organ or part to another not directly connected with it

**7.** You may wonder to what extent his nocturnal terrors are due to hypochondria, to vague memories of conversations with his doctor friend, Will Brodie, to a more or less furtive thumbing of medical dictionaries in university bookshops

**8.** If you have the answer to this question you may surmise that his Highland trip is less a return to his roots than a fugue – a flight from the terror made suitably manifest by a black spot

The morning was moist. The bens and hills were veiled. In a piece of parkland bordering the drive to the Castle a troop of girl guides went damply about the business of beginning the day. There was, as far as Peter could see, no one around the Big House or about in the policies where the rhododendrons dripped in gentle imitation of their native forests; but when he got out of the car to open the gate, he thought he saw Garlinski's crumpled face at the leaded window of the gatehouse. The village was a handful of anally tidy houses whose gardens appeared to have been colonised by rhododendrons from the Major's plantation: a tobacconist and stationer's, a general store and a shop offering tartan scarves, ties, bonnets, along with Celtic brooches, expensive pots of jam laced with whisky and calendars featuring Highland cattle.

Having stocked up at the store and ordered his papers, Peter drove back to breakfast in the Bothie. As he sat over his coffee a firm rap on the door and a loud voice calling his name announced the Major. There he was, in green wellingtons and knickerbocker suit, dark against the pale filtered light, tall, red-faced, with a slightly slack underjaw, blue bloodshot eyes, leaning on a crook with a ram's-horn handle, hail fellow and conventionally well met.

'Morning,' he said. 'Just going round the policies. Thought I'd see if everything was in order. Sinclair, isn't it? Any relation of Waldo Sinclair, the rugger blue? Anything you want, ask Garlinski. Fishing permit. Hire of rowing boat or sailing dinghy. A good chap, Garlinski. Was my batman when I was liaison officer with the Polish forces in '44. Training for Arnhem, they were. A marvellous bunch, the Poles.'

Peter decided to play the army card. 'Yes, I came across them in Italy.'

'Did you now? What was your outfit?'

'Actually I was on the staff then. I'd been on special ops for a while and as a result I'm afraid the army quacks downgraded me to B.'

'Is that so? You must come up and have a dram and a chat one evening. By the way, the cottage is for yourself. No lodgers. You never know these days. Had a couple of queers once but Garlinski sent them packing. Well, good day to you. Take a walk through the rhododendrons, they're worth a visit.' And he was off, calling to heel a spaniel that had been examining tufts of grass on the other side of the path and setting down damp markers of his territory.

There could be an alternative scenario in which Peter Sinclair, instead of playing the old boys' army card, mentions his grandfather (another Peter Sinclair), blacksmith in a cloth-mill (owned by the Swinton family who may or may not have married into the Campbell clan), stone deaf from the din of the machinery, silent behind his great white moustache, retired without a pension after sixty years of service, presented with a silver-handled walking stick on which his initials were engraved and which he accepted impassively, took home and calmly smashed with an axe. But for one reason or another it is not one Peter Sinclair followed; you may wonder whether this was due to: the convention of good manners sweeping awkwardnesses under the social carpet, the craven desire for a quiet life, or a kind of exhaustion of the spirit.

Next morning Peter carried his books in and stood them in the bookcase. Those he could not accommodate there he ranged along the wall; others still he stowed in the recess in the bedroom beside his walking shoes and wellingtons. It was strange to see them in this new setting – an experience, he reflected, similar to what the Russian formalists called *ostranenie*, that sensation of seeing familiar objects clearly, distinctly, for the first time, as it were – a moment which, he believed, vital art and writing recorded, allowing us to look at things with momentary pristine innocence so that we see the world around us afresh and understand it differently (and better) from that moment on. It might, he reflected, be a nice point to make in his introduction, although the book was still to be written. He had read once – or perhaps had merely imagined it – that Mozart had been able to hear a whole symphony in his head in a moment of time; he fully believed it, for in his own mind he could run through the argument of the unwritten book with the speed and facility of a computer: from the provisional (boring) title *The Failure of the Avant-garde* to a demonstration that avant-garde art, which had once seemed to threaten tyrannies, had become not only political but anti-political, an expensive form of interior decoration produced for wealthy patrons, for the proprietors of art galleries and the directors of the museums of modern art.

The trouble was that he could not bring himself to accept the burden of putting pen to paper or rather finger to keyboard. The thought of the labour involved paralysed him; the idea of rehearsing arguments he had reiterated in lectures and seminars, in common room discussions, on radio and television over the last ten years or so, was quite simply too boring to contemplate. In that sense, too, the journey north was a fugue – if a flight into the past could be so described – and the whole idea of hiring the cottage for the three summer months (interpreted by his excolleagues as a sign of his determination) was perhaps merely an escape into a lair like the lairs of the foxes and wild cats (were there still wild cats?) away at the head of the loch.

When he sat down at his word-processor and made the screen come alive, what he proceeded to inscribe on it was:

The Fisherman's Bothie
Lochmore
June 1987

Dear Urizen
You see that I have used your *nom-de-guerre*, which means that I am already hooked and prepared to take part in ANDROMEDA, although I have to confess that I have certain problems with SF. But before I set them out – and as a gauge of my interest – let me answer the questions you set me in what seems to me a slightly more logical order:

1. The name of my PC is David Balfour
2. He is a plant-biologist and a space-scout
3. His main interest is wargaming
4. He is thirty
5. He has a companion five years older than himself called Catriona Cameron, an electronics engineer and, like him, a space-scout. An orphan, she has been brought up in institutions as 'a daughter of the state' (of which more some time).

Now for my problems with SF, which you may feel are pedantic ones. But here goes. First of all the names: these in my experience are often banal inventions. I do not believe that by the year 2087 the kind of name we are familiar with will have been replaced by numbers or what sound like bits of Esperanto. I have therefore chosen perfectly ordinary (Scottish) names for my PC and his companion. Some people will detect in them an ironical reference to the hero of Stevenson's *Kidnapped* and the heroine of its sequel *Catriona*. If they do make the connection it will be a slight bonus. If not, no harm is done. I hope however that my David Balfour will not prove such a prig as Stevenson's and that Catriona will be sexier than the original.

My more fundamental problems are connected with the social and economic presuppositions of such SF as I have read. What I miss is any convincing account of the modes of life and social organisation of the communities of the future. Take your colony on Andromeda; what is its economic base and what its social structure? What about the material conditions of life, not to mention its practicalities? – to put it crudely, what do they do with the urine lakes and the mountains of shit they must produce in the course of twenty-four hours? How do they dispose of their dead?

From this you will have gathered – I hope the discovery doesn't put you off entirely – that I would describe myself as an historical materialist; which is the shamefaced way in which Marxist academics describe themselves in these days of rampant conservatism. It follows that I want to know how the colony is funded, what the social relations are between the colonists, what power structures obtain in the community. Are its members differentiated by function, by rank, by wealth, by – dare one ask – class? What sort of ideology do they have? Who elaborates it? Is it enshrined in codices or constitutions? Have they a religion? How do they regulate their lives? In what kind of assemblies? Are all men and women given an equal voice? Until I have some sort of societal model I shall find it very difficult to proceed.

Then there is the immensely important question: how were they chosen in the first place? If Tellus (our old Earth) was threatened by global catastrophe, who allotted the places on the space-ships that took the founders of the colony to Andromeda? Did the great and powerful of the Earth gallantly decide to stay behind and share the fate of their fellow creatures in the face of a catastrophe which they had watched over the years with amazing complacency, dimissing the campaigners for a cleaner, healthier earth as at best eccentric and at worst subversive, until not only were the Sahel, Ethiopia, the Sudan and large tracts of the Indian sub-continent affected but America's Middle West too was

**15**

burnt to unreclaimable desert? It would, I feel, be surprising if the great and powerful did so sacrifice themselves.

You will have noticed no doubt how deeply I am already being pulled into the game. In fact I have plunged in head first for reasons which I believe I can detect but which are irrelevant to anyone else.

How odd that you know Will Brodie. He was physician in the college where I taught, counsellor to students and staff and friend to me – a shoulder to weep on. Odd though how he, the most pacific of people, can be hung up on war and the history of war. Maybe it has something to do with a sense – in my view quite unjustifiable – of having missed out on an important experience. As you will know he was declared unfit for military service – some heart condition, I believe – and spent the war in a teaching hospital. Which may be why he took to wargaming and kept pumping me about military matters and my own experiences in Italy. Incidentally, I have half a mind to visit Italy this autumn. If so I shall certainly look you up. Yours is a part of the country I got to know well under peculiar circumstances during the war. I haven't been there for some years. I would find it quite disturbing to return. But perhaps time has been able to exorcise certain spectres and bad memories.

So, on reflection, count me in on the game. *Ci sto* as the Italians say. I look forward to hearing from you. Wargaming will be a welcome distraction from the boring business of producing an academic work, which is what I am supposed to be doing in this Highland retreat.

Sincerely
Peter Sinclair


To walk up the drive, past the Big House on through the long avenue to the gatehouse where Garlinski sat like a spider in its hole and so on to the post-office was another stratagem to escape from work – a further evasion. The day was grey but warm. An occasional fine spray of misty rain was pleasant on the face. The girl guides were tending smoky fires. Beyond their camping-ground he was aware for the first time of the small river that ran through the flat meadowland in loops that threatened to become ox-bows. Here and there the black cattle had trampled down the banks to get at pools where they splashed with their hooves and drank, looking round at his passing with vacuous eyes. Strange, he thought, that it was as 'ox-eyed' that the ancient Greeks had described the goddesses on Olympus. As he crossed the humpbacked bridge at the junction with the main road a heron gave a preliminary flap with its wings and slowly lifted into the air. If there was a heron there were presumably trout. Maybe he would ask Garlinski if he could borrow a rod. He walked slowly, taking time to stop and to reflect, to examine a clump of speedwell on the side of the road and to think about Andromeda.

You are to imagine that once your PC has posted his letter to Italy and made himself known to the postmistress as the temporary tenant of the Bothie, he returns to his base, eats oatcakes and cheese, drinks coffee and proceeds to sit again at his word-processor. What is he writing on the screen?

David Balfour woke in the sleeping cubicle when the centrally controlled alarum went off. It was 0430 and time for the morning shift in the hydroponics lab. Outside the constant daylight would be relentless, as it had been for three months, and would continue to be so until the planet slowly turned its face away from the sun and the long night began. As he rose he covered Catriona from whose back and legs the coverlet had slipped. Raising it for a second he kissed her at the base of the spine. She responded with a slight sound and an almost imperceptible twitch of a muscle. She did not have to rise till 0700 when she had to prepare for the daytime shift at the electronics centre where the hardware that controlled the colony's delicately balanced ecology, its communications systems and its weaponry, were constantly checked and new systems designed and tested.

She had met David when they were both posted to a detachment of space-scouts, sharing the exhilaration and dangers of sweeps over the grey dust-deep surface of the planet; on their return to base what more natural than that they should unwind together in a cubicle in what were called the 'recreation

17

facilities'? It was a relationship that gradually became more than a sexual one. In normal life – if that expression was applicable at all in the colony – Catriona was a grade 2 electronics engineer and therefore on a higher social wage than David; it was her status that had got them the sleeping cubicle with the attached living-space. Otherwise they would have had to live in one of the segregrated communal dormitories and clubs where sex was strictly forbidden.

Admittedly there were 'the recreation facilities' in which they had first made love – facilities for marital (and non-marital) sex, in a honeycomb of horizontal cubicles which formed a sort of annexe to the dormitories. More or less permanent couples or transient consenting pairs, provided always that they were heterosexual, could book cubicles by the half-hour or hour. There was no danger of AIDS, which was rampant on Earth, for all colonists had been tested for HIV; nor was there any danger of unwanted conception, for birth control was strictly enforced and abortions compulsory except with special permission of the Control Commission by which the colony was governed. In any case women found it difficult to conceive on Andromeda – a phenomenon which was attributed to exposure to a constant if low-level amount of radiation.

The installation of the facilities for 'recreation' had been fiercely resisted by some of the founder members of the colony, who had brought with them a relentless puritanism; but they had been overruled by more pragmatic members of the Control Commission who argued that sex was bound to assert itself and that the facilities could be so managed, with such bureaucratic precision – a careful log was kept of names and identity numbers – as to positively discourage their use. For a couple of years before Catriona was allocated living-space David and Catriona had learned the inconvenience of having to book a cubicle, the frustrations of tenderness restricted in duration by a timing device, the experience of emerging to the smiles and jokes of their colleagues.

When he walked out under the high overarching roof, tinted to mitigate the cloudless ferocity of the light, David passed between the blocks of living quarters and the block of communal centres; the canteens and services, the recreation hall from which there came the cries of the basketball teams and the thud of the squash balls. On the white concrete paths men and women crossed each other as the shifts replaced each other, some moving awkwardly in their space suits to go out beyond the protective walls to inspect the drift mines where rich lodes of uranium and caesium were exploited; others were bound for the centres where they monitored the performance of remotely controlled machinery for getting ore far out near the greyish-white horizon. The hydroponics lab where David worked lay beyond the communications and administrative building with its array of aerials and dishes, the Fortress, where the Control Commission had its headquarters and managed the colony.

Not that the Commission was necessarily felt as oppressive. David was part of the consensus which held that, if they were to survive, there had to be central control, strict discipline and repression of the individual will for the general good. It was one of the few and as yet only vaguely defined tensions within his relationship with Catriona that once or twice she had hinted at the possibility – indeed the need – for dissent, for alternatives. Not that she could claim to be discriminated against. As a skilled technician she was highly regarded; but she maintained that the men and women who sat in the Fortress were more repressive than necessary, that discipline had been exalted into an end in itself, which brought in its train a blunting of the feelings and a tendency to inflict punishments too grave for the offences.

The hydroponics lab was a long vaulted construction of transparent plastic. In it the runnels were alive with colourless liquid, the refined and purified, recycled urine from the colony's cesspools, just as the rich compost on which the dwarf fruit-trees, the tomato-vines, the thick plots of salad and soya beans flourished greenly was treated sludge. At one end stood the great vats in which a slurry of microscopic plants was swirled round until it turned into a thick suspension of proteins. Called botanically *fusarium graminearum* it had grown naturally in the soil on Planet Earth – and no doubt still did, in spite of the

**19**

climatic changes. It had been brought in a culture in the first ship to land on Andromeda, carefully nurtured and bred until now it provided the staple fibrous diet of the colony.

The atmosphere around the vats was heavy with the smell of fermentation; sometimes David would come there just to inhale the sweetness with its edge of corruption. The foreman on duty welcomed him in a friendly way; he was a decent man shaped by long service on Earth in the presidential guard units before he was detailed to the advance party that had founded the colony. Now considered too old for military duties he had been semi-retired to personnel management of the hydroponics lab to which he brought obsessional concern with tidiness and with unvarying routines. Thus the gardening instruments, although they were made of untarnishable high-grade metals, had to be wiped and polished redundantly. He watched carefully as David fed his indentity number into the computer and so logged the time when he joined the team of controllers who monitored the flow of the clear rivulets that ran down carefully calculated gradients to the beds and on to the recycling tanks.

The morning passed quietly. David's task was to watch the monitors and check the input of nutrients to the irrigation canals; an undemanding job but less boring than one on the assembly line in the electronics depot. After a couple of hours he was relieved and went off to the beds where plants grew and flowered. Part of David's work was the tedious job of pollination by hand of tomato plants and dwarf fruit bushes, apples, plums, pears; but he preferred to work on propagation by layering and grafting, the patient business of hybridisation – skilled jobs that would go on through the long winter when the ecology was kept stable by artificial heating systems fuelled by methane gas from sewage, and the crops followed each other regardless of the seasons.

At 1200 he was free to break. In the canteen the men and women of his shift sat waiting for a meal in which the protein fibres would be flavoured as meat, fish or chicken according to the menu of the day. Their talk was trivial and good-humoured but with a ground of uneasiness, for recently there had been constant untraceable rumours about the future of the colony, rumours which were passed, discussed, whispered over in corners out of range of the ubiquituous and highly sensitive listening devices. The rumours, Catriona asserted in the privacy of their sleeping cubicle, were deliberately put about by the undercover agents of the Control Commission – of course there were agents, what did he think? – to test opinion in the colony, to discover how people reacted, who discussed them and how they were interpreted.

The latest batch was to the effect that there was to be a crucial change in demographic policy leading to an enlargement of the colony or even the establishment of another colony beyond the horizon. The reason? That the colony was threatened by invasion from Planet Earth or from elsewhere in the universe. The antennae that rotated slowly on the roof of the Fortress had picked up signals to this effect. If this were true, David knew he and Catriona would both be involved for they were trained to scout and manoeuvre one of the rocket-propelled scout-capsules. So far their sorties had been confined to the immediate vicinity of the colony and they had never lost sight of the high translucent dome with its moveable shutters which, when the great storms of solar wind came, shielded the inhabitants from radiation. Practice sorties of this kind had with time become a routine experience for them both; but David could never quite banish from his mind the memory of how his parents on just such a reconnaissance had lost power and been sucked into the dark of space. It was their deaths ten years before, when he was in his teens, that had made him eligible for a place on the shuttle to Andromeda – a replacement of human resources with the right to permanent residence.

On the monitor which covered one wall of the canteen there was a stream of imploding and exploding abstract, electronically generated patterns, accompanied by gentle sequences of chords and a low pulse like the beating of a heart as heard by a foetus in the womb: a combination of shapes, colours and sound, calculated to soothe anxieties, to relieve stress, to relax men and

21

women whose lives were of necessity claustrophobic, whose tempers might – and sometimes did – flare in bursts of anger.

Suddenly a long frequency modulation broke into the low-pitched sounds. On the monitor there appeared a close-up of the commander of the month; a middle-aged man with a moustache, widely believed to be descended from the old British royal family which had retained extraordinary influence even after the founding of the Federal British Republic and its absorption into the American state. His announcement was brief: Isabel Dufy, a communications specialist Grade 1, had been found guilty of conduct calculated to destroy the equilibrium and safety of the colony. She had therefore been condemned to extrusion. Sentence would be carried out forthwith.

The picture cut to the face of a young woman, one that David knew from the days just after his arrival on Andromeda, for it was with her he had first used the 'recreational facilities'. Now she was escorted by a group of guards who handled their weapons with strange, archaic conventional gestures; behind them a couple of technicians carried a perspex capsule. Bringing up the rear was a priest of the strict Christian rite that been brought by the first colonists and carefully preserved on Andromeda. He intoned a prayer in a text used only by the adepts. It was in a language which David experienced as at once very beautiful and almost totally incomprehensible. The woman was pale, upright and already remote. When she stumbled a couple of guards caught her but she shook their hands off and continued on her way which led to the point in the transparent outer wall where an entry and exit port with its airlock protruded.

The priest continued his litany, raising his voice as if to hide the sudden scurry as the perspex capsule was brought quickly forward and the woman unresistingly fastened down. The lid snapped shut. The commander stepped forward. The priest chanted a last phrase. The capsule was inserted in the airlock, the door closed behind it and the outer door swung open. There was a sudden flash of propellant and the capsule shot vertically

upwards leaving a slight trail in the planet's thin atmosphere. She will be dead already, thought David, as the trail dispersed into a wisp and the capsule was lost to sight, dead without mask or radiation suit. She will drift through space for ever.

Peters first walk into the rhododendron garden took him up along the side of the Big House and through a gate in the garden wall. He had to pass the kitchen premises, which he imagined as stone-floored, with a great Aga range on which pots and kettles simmered constantly, supervised by Mrs Garlinski from whom her husband had learned his Scots intonations. Did she keep a spotless kitchen or was it more likely to have mouse-droppings in the stone-floored larder and behind the dresser? Did the Major eat well or was he more interested in his cellar? Peter could imagine him, bowl in hand, consuming his porridge *ambulando* in the traditional manner, though whether there was always a jug of real cream to dip the spoon in at each mouthful was doubtful – top of the milk, more likely. And did he eat alone? Was there a Mrs Campbell-Swinton, and who were the Swintons anyway? Were they indeed the mill-owners he had so often heard his mother talk of who had employed his grand-father, the white-haired old man he remembered sitting by the fire within the silence of his deafness, waiting for death?

Looking back he caught sight of an elderly woman with a nice face and a pile of untidy hair at a back window. She bobbed out of view when she became aware of his gaze: Mrs Garlinski no doubt. Then the thickets of rhododendron bushes received him, stretching out their dark shiny leaves and long trumpet-shaped flowers. He bent low under the heavy branches to read the tin labels on the trunks but they did not enlighten him much for he had never been 'a great gardener' – a series of London flats had not allowed much scope and when there had been a garden it had been the province of his wife, Orna, who had maintained that he had the botanical taste of a municipal park-keeper. *R. fortunei* (China) he read on one label. On another – the shrub had immense trusses of white sweet-scented blossoms – *R. campbelli*

(Bhutan – 9000 ft – Lt-General Campbell 1926). In a clearing among lower shrubs, which he took to be azaleas, a cluster of little headstones: Jackie, good dog, Rover, old pal. A little apart from the rest, a memorial with a lumpy cat fashioned from soft stone that had weathered away over the years.

As he turned to push further into the undergrowth a woman appeared crossing the grass of the glade. She was perhaps in her late fifties or early sixties dressed in a curiously old-fashioned and somehow girlish way: sturdy shoes, a long tweed skirt, a knitted jacket. Peter smiled and said 'Good afternoon.' She looked at him vaguely, smiled a little and walked on towards the house.


At this point I want to say something about Vladimir Propp, who has no place in my narrative although he is, I believe, very relevant to it. As his name indicates he was Russian. In the 1920s he elaborated a theory about the morphology of folk-tales, that is to say the structures and formulae that recur in these ancient stories.

Naturally what we are working on – you as readers, I as author – is not a folktale, but I incline to believe that some of the patterns he described apply more or less to most fictional narratives. This seems an appropriate moment to consider how far the present narrative conforms to Propp's analysis.

The initial situation, Propp states, is that one of the members of a family leaves home – what he calls in a useful kind of shorthand 'absentation'. This would apply to Peter Sinclair. Query: Where is his family? Who is it composed of? Does it exist? 'Home' may, of course, be a purely metaphorical term that could cover 'base', 'normal place of work', 'institution'. In this case the college, presumably, for our PC seems to be unencumbered by family ties – indeed by chance or by purpose, or as a result of the hidden logic that governs his life (as it does yours and mine) he is a solitary being.

An interdiction is then applied to the hero on the lines of 'Don't do X'. See the Major's injunction: 'No appendages'.

Alternatively, (for Propp, like Freud in his interpretation of dreams, likes to have things all ways round) there can be 'an inverted form of interdiction' – that is to say a positive instruction to *do* X; for instance, to walk up and see the rhododendrons. The next stage begins when a new personage appears. This personage is usually the villain of the tale. It seems unlikely that either the lady in the garden or the woman at the window is that villain. They feel more like secondary figures in the margin of the narrative with roles that are not yet established.

The fundamental question, Peter reflected as he sat once more by the window in the bothie and watched clouds stir and shift on the shoulders of the hills, is whether the practices of avant-garde art, avant-garde theatre or avant-garde writing were ever in any demonstrable way politically effective. The fact that the great tyrannies of our time have persecuted the avant-garde in the name of socialist realism or Aryan aesthetics, did seem to demonstrate that authoritarian political systems feel threatened by representations of our world that subvert our perceptions of reality by breaking the accepted canons of taste. But when had any piece of modern painting, architecture, film or writing for that matter, had a crucial political effect? What had all these fine inventive minds in Russian – people like Lissitsky, Rodchenko, Tatlin – been able to oppose to the philistine cruelty of Stalin? Or Brecht, for that matter, effectively done to halt the rise of Fascism? Put it more broadly: was the avant-garde in the arts or literature ever an effective political force?

What had Peter himself, to be brutal, contributed to instilling critical attitudes in the students who had heard him propound the need to demystify the concept of high culture, to place cultural production in its social and economic context, which required an understanding of society and the springs of power within it? He recalled a bright young man with a marvellous grasp of radical theory, fluent in discussion, original and acute in his essays, who was now a speech-writer for a Tory minister, intelligent, cynical, on the way up. Perhaps his efforts had been pointless; hewing against the grain of the wood, pissing into the wind, in a world where politics was dissolved into the discourse and the play of signs was proclaimed to be more important than the politics – not to speak of the class-struggle. In short, he was increasingly isolated, obsolescent in an order of things where the multinationals were the lords of the universe, rulers over societies lobotomised by consumerism.

Peter turned away from the window and sat at the table. In the small old wooden bowl he had placed beside his word-processor there was a handful of marbles, small and variegated or large and transparent, threaded miraculously (or so it had always seemed to him as a child) with strands of colour. He took a couple in his hand and rocked them to and fro on his palm. His worry-beads, Orna had called them. She had guessed their childish fascination for him and had tracked them down in a junk-shop off the Portobello Road. Now as he listened to their gentle clicking sound, Peter remembered her with sorrow.

They had met at a conference on The Russian Avant-garde in Tel Aviv attended by extraordinary survivors who had worked with the agitprop trains and seen Mayakovsky plain. She it was who had been his guide through the contradictions of her society – about which he had vague and sentimental notions – revealing to him how it was caught between the empty slogans of socialist utopias and the realities of colonial practice, enmeshed in East European bureaucracy and religious fundamentalism and to be saved (perhaps, if there was time) only by the rebellious spirits of which she was one who dared to challenge the orthodoxies of Zionism. As they drove to a kibbutz on the frontier with Jordan she had shown him the vestiges here and there of deserted Arab villages and how in Hebron – on the newly conquered West Bank – a Zionist community was installed armed and led by a rabbinical zealot.

When they parted they were lovers. Within a year she turned up in London working for an Israeli documentary producer and brought to Peter's flat her passion and political energy. Then more – as she pointed out later in bitterness – to overcome his insecurities than for any attachment to such formalities on her part they had got married. It lasted five years, till her discontents with life in Britain had extended to envelop not only the British Left but Peter and his political attitudes: the fastidiousness with which he and his friends debated what faction, clique, sect or tendency they could bear to associate with; the inconclusive debates about whether or not to join (enter) the Labour Party; a certain daintiness which was she alleged an excuse and justification for inactivity. Not that her fellow anti-Zionists in real or imaginary exile were much better, bickering and feuding, strong on theory and analysis, weak on effective political action, paranoid, convinced they were the targets of Mossad which had, she maintained, more important things to do.

So that the day came when in an angry debate about some irrelevant trifle Peter said: 'Why don't you go back to Israel then?' She had taken him at his word and left with Yoram their three-year-old son. It was a break that had caused a long internal haemorrhage in his heart. He had not seen her since. Once he had thought to recognise her in a newscast in the forefront of a demonstration against Israeli army brutality in the Gaza Strip. But he might have been mistaken. Just as he might be mistaken in imagining that Yoram might be one of the troops who hustled blindfolded Palestinian boys off to interrogation, beatings, prison without trial.

Peter laid the marbles back in their bowl, took the disc out of his word-processor, covered the keyboard and went to bed where he lay in the long twilight and could not sleep. As the light died at last he turned on the lamp by his bed and followed the adventures of the lady with the cleavage as she passed from lover to lover, from stud to stud, in Beverly Hills and Malibu.

La Volpaia
San Vito
Provincia di Siena
2 July 1987

Dear Peter

I was naturally delighted to get your positive response.
Welcome to the ANDROMEDA wargame. Your definition
of your PC is fine.

Your thoughts on SF are interesting but only relevant in so
far as they condition your own moves which will, I think, be
concerned with action rather than social theory, if I may put it
that way. But it will certainly be interesting to see how
historical materialism rubs off on wargaming!

Did I explain that every move will take up a 28-day month?
This means that a game-turn should be completed roughly
every five weeks. So I should have two weeks to process the
turn, the players one week to ponder their next step and the
post two weeks to convey the letters from me to the players
and back.

For your first move I have to tell you that an advance party
of intruders has landed on the planet. They must be presumed
to be aiming to establish themselves there. Your PC has to
embark on a recce to discover their size and intentions. He and
his co-pilot in their two-seater scout- capsule will be armed
with the conventional weapons of the colony: laser guns with
computerised range-finders and sighting mechanisms. They
will face a force with the same sort of weaponry, but Mark II.
It's your move.

Looking forward to
hearing from you
Urizen

PS. May I in this age when – as I hear – the hoarding of trivial
information is publicly celebrated on the television screens in
Britain, offer you this useless but curious scrap: Did you –
perhaps you did – know that the Duomo in San Vito contains a
shrine to Saint Vitus, son of a Sicilian patrician and martyred
under Diocletian, who is especially invoked in cases of chorea,
the disease known as St Vitus' dance which, if I am not
mistaken, afflicted George III.

Dear Urizen

I have been mulling over the situation you presented me with in your last letter and wondering how to respond. So far I can give only the following reaction:

Following on the unmistakeable intelligence that 'intruders' have landed on Andromeda David and his co-pilot, Catriona Cameron, are detailed to carry out a reconnaissance to just within the operational radius of their capsule, which is 100 kilometres. They are to take with them the normal armament of laser weapons and concentrated rations in the form first used for space exploration in the previous century. Their capsule carries high-resolution video cameras which will transmit a constant signal to Control in the command room in the Fortress. They are not to stay away from base for more than twenty-four hours. Their regulations forbid them to exchange fire with any unidentified forces without prior clearance from the Commission.

The scout-capsule is fuelled and brought to the exit port. The two scouts take their places, the capsule enters the lock. When the pressure has been equalised the retro-rockets start up, the outer port opens and they are propelled out and across the chalky grey and white face of Andromeda. They throttle back and fly close to the surface, relying on their radar to guide them. They reach the limit of their operational radius very quickly. At Herringbone Ridge, a feature they have recced many times before, they land their craft in a slight depression where it will be out of direct sight. They then proceed to unload from the capsule two small snow-cats (the archaic name persists) and push forward a couple of kilometres until they have a clear view over the territory beyond.

About ten kilometres away they spot a small force reconnoitring in highly manoeuvrable vehicles, which use bursts of rocket propulsion to jump over obstacles, rocks, chasms. They are pursuing a course which will bring them within range of the weapons of David and his co-pilot in under an hour. Catriona reports to the Fortress sighting strangers, gives their precise position and a bearing for their line of advance together with her own map reference. The Fortress instructs the scouts to take up positions about four hundred metres apart so as to cover the flanks of the intruders' advance. David notices that the Fortress does not use the neutral word 'strangers'. Catriona signals him and they move into positions near the crest of the feature. There is no sign so far that they have been detected. Over to you.

So far, so good. But shall I tell you what this wargame reminds me of? For four years I was caught up – as perhaps you were too – in what we foolishly still call the last war (as if there hadn't been a few hundred other wars since 1945). If you were you'll no doubt recall sand-table exercises with little houses and trees pinched from some child's innocent farmyard set and laid out in an improbable landscape of coloured sand (not unlike how I imagine the landscape of Andromeda) on which we officer cadets studied the siting of the heavy machine-gun in defence or the tactics of the platoon in the attack and so on and so forth. We had a colonel- commandant, more than slightly touched, it seemed to me, who had a wooden rattle (the kind they issued to air-raid wardens, do you remember?) with which he simulated machine-gun fire as he walked up and down the classroom. In reality it sounded rather different.

So, a sand-table exercise on the barren face of Andromeda! But at the back of my mind there is still a niggle: I find it difficult to engage in a situation which is not fully conceptualised. I mean by this that I have no clear idea of the global or should I say cosmic situation against the background of which events in Andromeda are supposed to unroll. For example: there must be launching pads on Earth. Where are they? Who owns them? Who controls the launching programme? What has happened to the world economy? Do the poor and dispossessed, fleeing from the floods and the drought, dying no doubt as in the great floods and famines of the past in India and China (how many millions were drowned in this our 20th century by the Yellow River, what about the one-and-a-half million souls who perished in Bengal in the great famine of 1943, how many in Ethiopia in these present times?) who find shelter of a kind in the streets and hovels of those great cities that still survive – do these wretched men and women supinely accept that some people (how chosen?) can be launched into space to colonise Andromeda?

I have been working on a scenario that sets out my view of the future a century from now. It leaves open a host of questions but it will do for the moment. I enclose a first draft. I'd be grateful for your comments. Meantime, *ciao*.

Yours<br>
Peter Sinclair

PS. When I fidgeted unbearably as a child my father, a staunch Presbyterian, used to ask if I had been afflicted by St Vitus' dance. How is that for a transcultural curiosity?

PPS. Sorry to be pedantic but the disease that afflicted George III was actually porphyria, one symptom of which is red discoloration of the skin.


## A Scenario for the Year 2087

Perestroika came too late to save the Soviet Union from fragmenting into a number of secessionist republics – the Ukarine, White Russia, Russia proper, the fiercely nationalist Baltic states, the feuding republics of the Caucasus where old animosities of religion and race were acted out in blood, rape and massacre. These succession states were deeply penetrated by Western capital and exploited as a source of cheap labour and raw materials by what had come to be known as the Fourth Reich. Over the first quarter or more of the 21st century their governments were right-wing, chauvinistic, dominated by the military, by industrial managers and religious zealots. In Central Asia the Muslim fundamentalists, following on the collapse of the Russian Empire, installed their ferocious regimes as part of a confederacy that stretched from Pakistan through Iran and Uzbekistan to the Middle East, a confederacy armed with atomic weapons and so powerful that the United States was forced to abandon its client, Israel, to its fate, which it hard-headedly accepted – that of a tiny Middle Eastern state on the edge of a power bloc with which it must live in peace or perish. It continued to survive by becoming the arsenal of the Muslim bloc, furnishing it with advanced scientific technology in much the same way as in the late 20th century it supported and armed the white dictatorship in South Africa before the bloody War of Liberation at last freed that country. Thereafter its secret service,

Mossad, was deeply involved alongside the CIA and the Chinese intelligence services in the systematic and largely successful campaign to destabilise the uranium-rich South African republic, Azania.

In Eastern Europe (including the Russian republics) the memory of Stalinism's bloody tyrannies had led to the abandonment of socialism. This in turn has given rise over the years to an economic and ideological convergence with the capitalist West, with which they now shared a culture based on self-enrichment and the single-minded pursuit of profit: paradigm of what the ideologues of the West called a 'free market economy in a free society'. Its workings have led over the years to the almost terminal despoilation of the planet. Western Europe, for its part, has declined into becoming a vast, decaying cultural museum in which the artefacts have deteriorated physically from over-exposure to the breath, the shoes, the hands, of multitudes of cultural pilgrims and dazed tourists. Fortunately they have been persuaded to be content with reproductions; for originals of works like the Botticelli Venus in the Uffizi, the Judith and Holofernes by Donatello from the Loggia dei Lanzi or Rembrandt's self-portrait in the Rijksmuseum were long ago replaced by copies remarkable for their faithfulness and apparent texture (the result of research into holography and photo-reproductive techniques), the originals being kept in suitably regulated conditions and exhibited only to a limited public of scholars, connoisseurs and members of the ruling circles or 'clans'. This, is of course, was before the rising waters flooded Amsterdam and the Rijksmuseum

By 2087, which is the year that concerns us, the world has been divided into two huge spheres of influence that recall the division of the world between the Portuguese and Spanish empires in the 16th century. The United States and China are still great rival powers but Germany is the heartland of a third economic and political system. Africa, South America, the Indian sub-continent, South East Asia, the Islamic republics of Central Asia, Australasia, the Siberian republic with its immense mineral deposits, have been for many years the sites of intense rivalries between the superpowers.

These rivalries have constantly threatened to explode into war, and indeed have frequently done so; but the wars have been fought not directly by the USA and the Chinese People's Republic but by surrogates whose enmities are fuelled by their rival intelligence agencies; systematically and cynically they have fomented the jealousies, the competing claims, the prejudices of the poorest and most exploited social and ethnic groups throughout the world, till they have erupted in pogroms, civil wars, frontier disputes, guerrilla movements, terrorism and counter-terrorism, bringing in their train poverty, economic collapse, depopulation and hordes of refugees. The violence of despair has been channelled into aggression that serves the interests of the military-industrial complexes which for so long have dominated the world economy. Its centre of gravity has shifted to the Pacific where Australia and Japan (both dependent on China) and New Zealand and Chile (both clients of the United States) vie with each other for financial and economic control.

There came a point round about 2060 when the superpowers were forced to listen to the scientists and ecologists and admit that the future of Tellus was limited – that a long terminal sickness could be diagnosed. The generals of the Pentagon, the industrialists of America's silicon valleys, lobbied the United Nations and with the votes of their client states pushed through a programme which aimed to colonise space and specifically to plant a settlement on Andromeda. The shuttle that carried the first settlers was called the Mayflower; the colonists who were in command of the flight were the Founding Fathers. They represented the harshest and most authoritarian elements in what was still anachronistically known as the Western World, who hoped on another planet to erect a society based on 'traditional values' and a fundamentalist religion. When the shuttle was launched from a pad in the Arizona desert – the old launching sites at Cape Canaveral having long been submerged – David Balfour's parents were on that flight, tolerated (although not true believers) as leading experts in exobiology and extra-terrestrial ecology.

Question: Did Peter Sinclair come to formulate this scenario overnight? Did it take shape during the first couple of weeks spent by Lochmore? Was it the result of long sombre brooding over the last decade? What had led him to doubt the possibility that in the future some form of socialism might be established, 'with a human face', as an alternative to capitalism? Judging by this scenario how would you describe his political profile?


Garlinski ships the oars and says: 'Here.' They have rowed for about half-an-hour to a stretch of water at the tail of an island where birches grow, pale and drooping, down to the water's edge. On the way over Peter had seen the trout raise dimples on the grey surface. Now, under Garlinski's sceptical gaze, he picks up the rod and casts the line with reasonable success over the face of the water. Garlinski sits and smokes silently. Once or twice there is a slight flurry where the cast slants from the water but when Peter strikes, the line comes back in slack.

The whirr of the reel recalls how he fished with his father on a day when the sky was patched with cumulus clouds that swept shadows over the hills. Near the head of the river the water spilled, white-flecked, over stony reaches to settle in peat-brown pools. In each lay at least one trout, effortlessly keeping station in the rush of the water, moving with a quick flick of the tail to intercept some morsel of food and then returning to its post. When a fish tugged and took the bait Peter whipped the rod wildly. The sunlight flashed on the golden-brown belly of the trout as it swung on to the bank. The hook had gone into the lower jaw and the pale flesh tore as he pulled it out. After a moment's hesitation he grasped the fish as it flounderd gasping on the turf, stuck his fingers in the gills and pulled the head back with a quick jerk to kill it. Then he opened the wicker creel that was slung over his shoulder, pulled up a few handfuls of grass for lining and on it laid the trout, still supple, not yet fixed in rigour. On the hillside, among the birches, a cuckoo tossed its call across the glen. Farther down the river his father, that grim, taciturn man, stood deep in the water in his waders and changed a fly. It was one of the rare occasions when they were at ease in each other's company and perhaps happy together.

What, he wonders, as he draws the line gently in towards the boat, were Garlinski's boyhood memories? Some of his life he could imagine: captivity and hungry despair in Russian prisoner-of-war camps after the partition of Poland in 1939, transfer to Central Asia and from there eventually – the wait must have been endless – down through Persia to the Gulf. Then came the long voyage to Britain to train and wait, train and wait, and court the local girls till he and his comrades were dropped to hopeless combat in the fields around Arnhem. But what had been the landscape of his youth? Peter found it difficult to imagine.

'Did you fish when you were a boy?' he ventures to ask and suspects that he is merely exposing himself to Garlinski's scorn.

'No,' Garlinski replies and is silent.

The boat drifts a little as a slight breeze springs up. Garlinski directs it into more sheltered water. Peter changes flies, marvelling (as he had as a boy) at the delicacy of the feathers and the contrast with the cruelty of the barbed hook they concealed. He does not know how long they have been on the loch. No doubt Garlinski knows, for the boat is hired by the hour, over and above which there is a fee for Garlinski's services as ghillie. Garlinski has just looked significantly at his watch when the fish takes the fly, the reel whirrs and the line tightens. Carefully Peter plays the trout until, looking over the side, he can see its silvery darting body close by the boat. He draws it safely in and with the skill remembered from his boyhood pulls back its head to break the verterbrae. It lies limp in his hand. Death will soon dull its brightness. A couple of pounds, he reckons.

Garlinski says, 'A bonny fish,' unships the oars and begins to pull back to the jetty.

Peter waits till he has made the boat fast. 'Will you take a dram?' he says. Garlinski agrees readily. In the cottage he stands deferentially until Peter indicates a chair.

'Malt,' says Peter, 'the only whisky worth drinking. What's your favourite drink?'

'Vodka,' says Garlinski, 'but whisky's fine.'

'Tell me,' Peter goes on, seeking to profit from the moment of intimacy, 'who was the lady I saw in the garden the other morning?'

'Miss Grizelle,' Garlinski replies, empties his glass and rises to go, cutting off further conversation. Peter pays him for the hire of the boat and his services as ghillie and adds a tip. Garlinski gives a formal inclination of the upper body and turns towards the door. 'The Major told me to remind you that you are expected for dinner tonight.'

Peter nods and watches Garlinski go up the dirt road towards the House with a slow upright gait that recalls the soldier who had jumped at Arnhem and survived.

In the hour till dinner – seven-thirty prompt, Garlinski had said – Peter gutted the trout and laid it on a plate in the fridge. In the morning he would go down to the village for oatmeal. For lunch he would eat the fish fried and sprinkled with the meal. Then he sat down at his his word-processor and began to write about David Balfour.

What is it that causes grown-up men and women to yield to compulsive day-dreaming and set their fantasies down in black and white as fiction? What triggers, what impulses set off the process?

The narrative you are reading grew from an obsessive memory of an estate by the shores of Loch Lomond, visited half-a-dozen times, site of academic occasions; meetings with old friends, a pleasurably-painful encounter with someone loved and lost, surprising acquaintance with persons previously known at most by name or reputation or even with total strangers who in the pale northern evenings talked with extraordinary freedom – like fellow-passengers on a trans-atlantic flight – about themselves, about their work, about their institutions, gossiped, were spitefully amusing, instructive, safe in the knowledge that, the weekend over, there would be no need to face their partners in conversation for weeks, months or indeed ever again.

The scene from the House, looking across the darkening islands of the Loch towards Ben Lomond, drew from these clever, articulate women and men from London, from the States, from Europe, cries of surprise and pleasure when after dinner they strolled out on to the drive or standing on the steps above the drive chatted, laughed, drank their brandies. The memory of the site is insistent. It has formed a nucleus round which other memories have clustered and along with them conscious and half-conscious thoughts. It has left on my memory an after-image that refused to fade, that has been drawn into my dreaming-in-broad-daylight which is Freud's definition of fiction. Sometimes as I confront the vacant page which challenges me with its emptiness, like the silence of the analyst sitting beside the couch, there rise to the surface from unconscious depths formulations, images, memories, fantasies, that surprise, delight or frighten me.

That is how I imagine Peter Sinclair in the cottage by the loch, sitting at his word-processor, as I am now, and this is what he is writing, not knowing precisely what he wants to say, following the development of his own narrative with a certain surprise, answering promptings over which he has not full control but which, had we the key, might tell us great deal about him.


When the extrusion order had been carried out there was a silence in the mess. Extrusions were not a frequent occurrence. They took place normally at most once a year at the midpoint of the long winter night when morale was at its lowest and the strains latent in the community manifested themselves in ill-tempered petty quarrels, brawls, or in more serious incidents leading to confrontations and defiance of authority at various levels. Then at a meeting of the entire colony one person was named – the nomination usually came from an ordinary member

37

of the colony who had, in fact, been prompted by the supervisory agents of the Control Commission – and accused of having incurred the general disapprobation of his or her fellows, for laziness, for failing to conform to the rigid codes of the colony, for lowering morale, for neglecting the routines on which they all depended for survival, for causing tensions. The choice was confirmed by a show of hands in the great assembly hall. (There was no memory of the vote going in favour of the accused). Then the chosen victim was led – just as Isabel Dufy had been – to the exit port and despatched into space.

It was a grim custom which the authorities justified in the archaic language of a text known obscurely as Leviticus Sixteen, which was read out by a priest as part of the ritual when the victim was chosen. Like all members of the colony, David could remember it word for word although there was much in it that he did not understand. This was how it ran: *And Aaron* (which presumably meant some sort of official or priest) *shall lay both his hands on the head of the live goat* (but this was a man or woman not a goat) *and confess over him all the iniquities of the children of Israel* (who were they and what was their relationship to the Israelis whom he knew of chiefly as anti-terrorist experts, advisors on security and arms-dealers?) *and all their transgressions in all their sins, putting them upon the head of the goat, and shall send him away by the hand of a fit man into the wilderness.*

Once the offending element had been removed from their midst there was a sense of relief among the victim's fellows, a feeling that they could confront the long night more easily. It was noticeable that the leisure facilities were used a great deal in the next twenty-four hours or so.

But the fact that the present extrusion had been ordered out of season, as it were, pointed to some offence of exceptional gravity against the laws of the colony. So it was some time before the colonists gathered in the mess began to speak – but not about the scene they had just witnessed – to rise and move away alone or in small silent groups. Meanwhile the gentle sequence of chords with their accompanying heartbeat, which was the normal background to their lives, had begun again;

shapes followed each other in the monitor in an unpredictable succession, constantly renewed, never apparently repeated. They soothed and fascinated with their flux and motion, with their colours, so striking in this landscape of white rock and grey sand. Soon it was time to go back to the hydroponics lab where the plants, their flowers and seeds had a strength and brightness more vivid and interesting to David's mind than the patterns on the great screen.

At 0800 the shift was over and David did not return to his living quarters. There was a wargame session he wanted to attend; part of the course that would hasten his promotion in the colony's defence force. As a scout Catriona should by rights have been there too, but of late she had avoided coming with a series of not altogether convincing excuses: shift patterns, extra duties, pressure of work. It was not an important issue but David was beginning to feel it as a slight irritant that disturbed their relationship, raised questions he felt diffident to ask, awoke doubts he did not wish to express even to himself.

The wargames tutor was a man in his early fifties, with thinning blond hair, quick and almost birdlike in his gestures, fit from the jogging that took him faithfully round a track of his own devising that circled the Commission's headquarters and the hydroponics lab. He had planned, it was said, the logistics of the launches which had brought the earliest colonists to Andromeda and had negotiated with the multi-nationals which had funded them over the number, social extraction and specialist skills of the pioneers.

As usual the wargame session was held in a classroom so arranged that those who attended could be disposed in two opposing sides. A partition guaranteed secrecy for their conferencing as they worked out their reactions to the enemy's moves. It was, their tutor explained to each new course, immaterial in which historical era the particular wargame was set. It might refer to the campaigns of the Hundred Years War; to the little wars of the Crusader states against the rising power of the Arabs; to colonial wars like those waged against the invading settlers by the Maori warriors of New Zealand, who had forced the British authorities to negotiate a settlement; to any number of engagements in the Second World War or Vietnam; or indeed to the long drawn-out war of attrition in the Urals between the Siberian Republic and Germany's Fourth Reich. Not that these examples would say much to a generation whose knowledge of history, military or otherwise, was astonishingly vague.

Never mind, the point was that certain basic rules of warfare had not altered across the centuries. They had to do – within the framework of a larger strategy, of course – with logistics (the organisation of supplies), intelligence (accurate information about the estimation of the enemy's strength and intentions) and tactics (the management of the forces under one's command in a given engagement, judgments about when to commit one's reserves, the importance of creating a concentration of power at a crucial point to overwhelm and defeat the enemy). These fundamental principles of warfare they would apply to the situation which he would now expose to them.

It was, he explained, clearly, pedantically, a military situation dating from the last phase of the Second World War and related specifically to the campaign in West Europe against the forces of Germany. In other words the date – not that it would mean much to them – was early 1945. The exercise was based on a situation map brought back from that war by his grandfather, called – as he himself was – Peter Sinclair. Peter Sinclair had been a staff officer attached to a headquarters in the South of Holland, a part of the world which, as they might just conceivably know, was now totally submerged but at that time was still above sea-level, although it had to be protected by a complicated system of dykes. He pressed a button to switch on the monitors and brought up a map. It showed a wide river – actually the Waal – but that was unimportant; what was important was the deployment by either side of their resources in terms of men and equipment, to which one had to add certain imponderables: combat experience and morale.

To the north of the river lay Holland, occupied by the German army. On the German side the forces committed to the defence of the Waal, a token holding operation, were a collection of training battalions and reservists, stiffened by some front-line infantry who were resting after recent heavy losees, among them some Russian units; which they might perhaps find curious because the Russians were fighting the Germans. But these were Tartars from central Russia – from the Volga – who had deserted or been taken prisoner by the Germans and were now incorporated in the German armed forces. All this, however was by the by. A long way to the south the allies – that is, British, American and, being himself a Canadian national, he was proud to say Canadian forces were pushing through Germany's fortified frontier zone towards the Rhine. That was the main thrust. Here, to the north, on the Waal, relatively weak allied forces held the river-line to contain the enemy in Holland and act as flankguard to the main offensive. These forces included a brigade of infantry – three battalions of largely untried troops.

'You are to imagine that the local brigade commander has decided to make a reconnaissance in strength across the river, which is about a kilometre wide and, if successful, to exploit success.' They had enough landing-craft for a crossing at about battalion strength. He ought to remind them of the weaponry available. It included primitive bolt-action rifles, light machine guns called Brens capable of firing up to 800 rounds a minute. In support there were two troops of artillery, each of four 25-pounder guns – so called because they fired a shell weighing approximately 50 kilos. If necessary, fighters from the tactical air forces could be called up for air-strikes. In terms of armament there was more or less complete parity except that the German machine-gun had a somewhat higher rate of fire. The German artillery consisted of 50mm guns and a few of the very versatile and highly accurate 80mm dual purpose anti-aircraft/anti-tank gun. The first move was up to Team A of which David was leader. They sat at a long table and began to discuss their aims and method. Beyond the screen there was a low hum of voices as the 'enemy' began to make its dispositions to meet the attack.

Peter Sinclair, having switched off his word-processor, put on a shirt and tie and walked up the steps of the Big House. Garlinski opened the door and showed him into a drawing room where under the tall portraits of his ancestors the kilted Major waited and with an 'Ah there you are!' poured him a large whisky. Peter drank and looked up to where the men in their silver-buttoned coats and tartan trews, with their claymores and dirks, posed against dusky landscapes in which there was sometimes the confusion of battle, sometimes pastoral calm with a classical ruin to close the vista. Completing the line was a more modern painting, a bright slick portrait that might in its day have been hung in the Royal Academy summer show and featured in *The Tatler* or *Illustrated London News*: a heavy face above the red tabs of a general staff officer, three rows of medals, in the background a suggestion of mountain peaks. The little copper plate said Lieutenant General Sir Hector Campbell, KBE, KCSI, DSO, MC.

'My father,' said the Major. 'Bhutan, you know, rhododendrons, that sort of thing.'

If the men had the Major's slack jowl the ladies tended to be pale, sharp-nosed and chlorotic (though that might well be a result of the dirt of the years) with a look that reminded Peter of the woman he had met briefly in the garden, who now entered and sat down quietly in her long grey dress and tartan sash without any greeting, so as not to interrupt the Major, who was explaining how in the Fifteen an ancestor – depicted with a long-barrelled fowling-piece in his hand and a brace of pistols in his belt – had led his tenantry to battle on the side of the Hanoverians and for the Protestant faith.

Perhaps her silence was merely due to the fact that she had heard the Major's stories innumerable times and preferred to remain with her own thoughts; but what if she had turned inwards because the world outside was supremely uninteresting compared to whatever it was that made her from time to time smile to herself and move her lips or give a little laugh at which the Major said firmly as if to a child: 'That's enough now, Grizelle.' Then almost as an afterthought he said: 'This is my sister. Say how do you do to Mr Sinclair.' The woman rose, plucked nervously at the tartan sash she wore over her shoulder and held out a hand that was small and soft and nerveless.

There were no other guests. Garlinski announced that dinner was served and they moved into a dining-room where the windows gave on to the loch. The Major sat at the head of the table, his sister faced him with her back to the window and her hands folded in her lap. Peter sat on the Major's right. The meal bore the mark of Mrs Garlinski's hand; it was Women's Rural Institute cooking, solid, homely – very Scottish, thought Peter. There was little conversation. The Major was a good trencher-man and ate with concentration, seriously. After the apple with Dunfillan crust Grizelle rose and with a little curtsey retired. She had not spoken thoughout the meal which she had eaten with the anxious care of a little girl fearful of committing some breach of grown-up conventions.

Garlinski brought in the port. The Major relaxed and began an interrogation for which Peter was prepared and to which he decided to respond goodhumouredly. Slowly and accurately the questioning established Peter's social background, his army career (which was commended – the Major, it emerged, had been 'chewed up a bit' in the last great assault across the Rhine) and his academic one (which was dismissed as mostly a waste of time and tax-payers' money). The bottle went to and fro between the two of them as they talked and the light faded a little. Now the questons were directed at Peter's personal life. Married? Divorced? The Major shook his head over a mixed marriage – he didn't believe in mixing the breeds – not on racial grounds, Peter must understand, for he had any number of Jewish friends, but because there were all sorts of problems about behaviour and language, ways of dealing with life. It didn't really work. He knew what he was talking about. '*Je parle en connaissance de cause.*' (The French gloss was delivered with surprising confidence and with an almost perfect accent).

There was a silence and the Major pushed over the port bottle. As the wine worked the Major relaxed and his jaw seemed to become even looser. Any minute now, thought Peter, he will start 'talking dirty' as they used to say in the days when the Major's ancestors were ten-bottle men and drank themselves under the table nightly. So it was no surprise when the Major asked with a flash of his bloodshot eyes: 'What about sex? Now, I mean. D'you still get it or are you past it? I've really more or less given it up,' he went on without waiting for an answer. 'My wife and I – she was French by the way – split up years ago and she went back to France. No divorce – she thought marriage was for life. Died ten years ago, poor thing. I never got hitched again though over the years I've naturally had the odd girlfriend. But it's not worth it, in my view. All that effort – phonecalls, meetings – especially if the girl's married . . . And once you've shot your bolt they expect you to talk to them and listen to stories about how horrible hubby is. The game, my dear Sinclair, simply isn't worth the candle. Not that there isn't the odd sexy moment. These young girls who come here and tie up their dinghies at the jetty now. Showing everything – more or less. Not like it was when we were young eh? Not easy to get though. But wonderful to look at. I sometimes just sit upstairs with a good pair of field-glasses. It comes under the heading of what I call *les menus plaisirs*. Ever heard the expression? From the French court at Versailles. Little pleasures. Little indulgences. Little complicities. Sometimes you'll find a young woman who's prepared to play games. There was an actress once came to dinner – wife of of an old army friend – much younger than himself . . .'

The door opened and Garlinski came in quietly, bent over the Major and whispered in his ear. The Major rose and excused himself.

'He'll be a while,' said Garlinski and began to clear the table, 'I wouldn't bother to wait.'

So Grizelle is not the villain – a victim rather, a woman apparently helpless in front of life. Brain-damaged? Drugged? Or a fugitive from the world who has withdrawn from the struggle with unhappiness, the hopes deferred (that notoriously make the heart sick) retreated from a society, a class, a family that denied her in some fundamental way until she turned their denial against them as her surest weapon? Or a woman traumatised by some experience – far back in her girlhood or youth – which had driven her into silence? I do not know where I found her, what her role is to be in the story, nor why she should be so strongly present in my daydreaming, in those thoughts and images that present themselves, often between sleep and waking; eidectic images that are with me insistently when I wake or, as now, sit at my word-procesor and know what she looks like, the feel of her hand, see the little bob of a curtesy with which she leaves the room. Yet I do not know her, do not believe I ever knew anyone like her. Perhaps she lives somewhere in me – a repressed memory, a projection, an anima. I do not know.

'Sorry about last night,' said the Major, knocking at the door round about midday. 'My sister, you know. She has a sort of turn now and then. Nothing to worry about really. But I have to deal with her. You must come up to the House again.' And he was gone.

For the first time Peter noticed that he had a slight limp, the result no doubt of 'being chewed up a bit' at the Rhine crossing, the real one, not the botched business on the Waal that had concluded Peter's own war.

You may think it was a good question – the one posed by the Major over the port – potentially encompassing as it did Peter Sinclair's marital status, his attachments, past or present, his sex-life, erotic propensities and practices, and one permitting an answer that addressed itself to all or any one of these topics. He had been saved from having to provide that answer by the Major's revelation about *les menus plaisirs* and by Garlinski's entrance; but it still stands. You may wonder, given your knowledge of Peter's past, his formation, his undoubted tendency to moralising, what the answer to it might be. Did he, for instance, being 'unattached' (no longer married), use his position and authority as head of liberal studies in his South London college (it is, after all, fairly common for this to happen) to obtain sexual favours from women students? Or is it more probable that he had a long-standing relationship with the assistant librarian, a married woman now in her late thirties?

Over the years he had developed the habit when he took a book from the library of stopping to chat for a little to this serious woman with her soft dark-brown hair drawn back in a floppy bun. Her way of dressing was neat, slightly formal and ambiguously modest; thus she favoured a severe dark skirt with which went a variety of thin blouses through which, when she stretched up to take a book from the shelves, one could see the modelling of her arms and which, when she sat at her desk and bent over to stamp a book, revealed her shoulders and amid a whiteness of lace the subtle shifting hollow beneath her collar-bone where her breasts rose perceptibly. Her face was rather square with a strong jaw and would no doubt thicken with time but she had a pleasantly attractive look; a quizzical glance, a slightly mocking expression of the eyes and mouth when she discussed the latest college gossip, interdepartmental feuds, reported the bickerings and professional jealousies at the last faculty meeting or commented ironically on the facility with which yesterday's young radicals turned their coats when the Warden, protesting his devotion to liberal ideals, declared that the criteria of the market must determine the future of higher education.

On the wall behind her was a large map of the British Isles on which she had marked with small coloured pins, using an elaborate code, holy wells, fountains and springs, by which the superstitious still left offerings of scraps of clouts on hedges, on branches of trees or on the fencing that surrounded the muddy source where the water sprang from the earth. To her delight he was able to tell her of one such 'cloutie well' not yet on her map, in a little glen near his birthplace on the east coast of Scotland. Fenella's Well, named, it was said, after some Celtic or maybe even Pictish princess. From there they had gone on to discuss the

Celtic cult of severed heads and the probability that they had belonged to victims sacrificed to the *genius loci*, the deity or nymph or other supernatural creature that caused the water to flow from the darkness with a gentle pulse like that of blood from an inexhaustible vein: one that had to be replenished with the blood of human beings or (next best) of horses, proud beasts worthy of sacrifice and inhumation along with the great chiefs of the tribes.

When she spoke she became animated, erudite and poetical, citing rare texts, quoting as a possible memory of these ancient practices lines by a minor Elizabethan poet: 'Gently dip but not too deep/For fear you make the golden beard to weep/Fair maid, white and red/Comb me smooth and stroke my head/And every hair a sheave shall be/And every sheave a golden tree.' There was, to his mind, a curious contradiction between the feeling with which she quoted the verses, her passionate attachment to legend and speculative archaeological theory and her sceptical appraisal of the events around her in the college: a contradiction of which her bearing and dress were a metaphor. It was something that continually suprised and intrigued him.

Then one evening, knowing him (as she later confessed) to be alone in his office, she entered with great composure, shut the door and said very simply: 'I'd like to make love to you.' It was not long after his wife, Orna, had left him and gone back to Israel. In that sense he was free; but was she not married? It was an unspoken question. She guessed at it from his hesitation and replied to it with one of her most quizzical looks, saying that she considered herself to be her own woman, that she had certain rights over her own body and inclinations. She would be disappointed if he said No but would understand. Men were easily frightened.

Thus began an affair consummated and continued in a curious block of flats on the edge of South Kensington. In its long corridors, where it was rare to meet any of the inhabitants, the paint flaked on the walls and the skirting boards were loose, the carpeting worn. Peepholes in the doors suggested the eyes of call-girls and dubious masseuses looking out suspiciously or expectantly onto an atmosphere of decay and decadence. The apartment she brought him to belonged, she explained, to an old friend, an airline pilot who was away a lot. He had certainly left little trace on the apartment, which was tidy, decorated (appropriately) with airport art from Africa, South East Asia and South America: folk artefacts degraded by mass production. It was curiously impersonal – a stop-over where a bachelor might rest for a couple of days, drink from the well-stocked cupboard and entertain girlfriends. She kept the key (whence this trust? out of what relationship?) in the drawer of her desk in the library.

No further explanations were forthcoming either about this friend or about her husband, except that he was a Treasury solicitor. Her love-making was marked by on the one hand frank, almost matter-of-fact instructions on how to explore her body and give her pleasure and, on the other, by warmth, laughter, jokes and fun. At college they began to eat together in the refectory, to walk together to the tube, to be seen on some occasions (her birthday perhaps) eating in a little Italian restaurant down the road. They became – as it were – an official couple, accepted as such by colleagues and even by the Warden. Their public behaviour gave no offence, being on the face of it that of friends whose offices were in the same corner of the rambling building and whose interests seemed in some curious way to coincide.

Once he invited her to his own flat overlooking Regent's Park, but she refused. Nor was there ever any question of his being invited to the address she lived at in Wimbledon. Having discovered it from an envelope on her desk, one Sunday morning in the summer vacation when she was far away on a Greek island, he drove down the long curving street of semi-detached houses and searched for the number as if, finding it, he would magically detect some tiny testimony to the fact of her existence or at least some aura she had left in the car-lined streets of South London. Drawing up a little way from her address he walked back and into the little front garden, its mountain ash tasselled with red berries, and up to the green-painted front door.

Peering through the letterbox he could see little except a table with on it a Victorian basin and ewer decorated with sprigs of roses. The jug held an arrangement of dried grasses, teasles, poppy-heads and immortelles. The stairs had a dark blue carpet and bright stair-rods. At the far end of the lobby a curtain of some Indian stuff marked the entrance to the kitchen. The venetian blinds on the bow windows were closed shut, the curtains on the bedroom above drawn against the sun.

He turned away into the empty Sunday morning street and drove off disconsolately. He did not tell her of his visit when she returned and demonstrated, when next they were together in the flat, how her whole body had been meticulousy exposed to the sun. And to whom else? he wondered, but repressed the prick of jealousy.

In his last couple of years at the College, as his position was gradually eroded by a faction in the faculty, which in the name of realism called for more studies in business management and less talk about theory, aesthetics and the place of the arts in society, she risked the displeasure of the Warden by the sharpness of her interventions against Thatcherism in Academia. When Peter decided to take early retirement she was typically stoical but on their last visit to the flat he felt her tears falling on his chest. When the flat door shut behind them she said simply, 'Well, it was good while it lasted. Something to remember. I like things I win from life, don't you?'

In the two years from that day they had kept in touch – which is the negation of touching – by an occasional postcard: from holiday on Santorini, at Knossos, in Siena on her part. From Upper New York State, Vancouver, Kingston, Ontario, according to where his peripatetic conferencing and lecturing took him on his. Exchanges of formulae and banalities. Her name was Anna.

The Fisherman's Bothie
Lochmore
12 August 1988

Dear Urizen

The twenty-eight days aren't up yet so I have no real excuse for writing to you except that I have been worrying away at the wider scenario of our wargame. What is becoming clearer to me is the probable state of Tellus in the year we are talking of: 2087. Enclosed is a short paper setting out my prognostications.

What is it like in your part of the world these days? I remember the nightingales that used to keep me awake in early summer. The darkness was spangled with the cold light of the fireflies but they seem to have vanished from the Italian countryside – there's a marvellous essay by Pasolini, which you may know, lamenting their disappearance – and in any case they were over once the wheat was cut in June. Simply writing to your address tempts me more and more to visit you. Looking forward to the next move.

You will have noticed the date. Grouse shooting starts today. My landlord, of whom more some time, is off with his ghillie, a Pole called Garlinski, believe it or not, slaughtering the birds.

Sincerely
Peter Sinclair

## Peter Sinclair's Prognostications

By the Sixties of the 21st century power in almost all societies, but especially in the most advanced countries, lies in the hands of the clans: power-groups of financiers, industrialists, great landowners, military men and scientists, masters of computers and lords of artificial intelligence. The wealth that sustains them derives from two sources. One has been that great industrial boom and expansion of trade which followed on the opening up of the republics of the Soviet Union and – with more difficulty –of the great Chinese republic to capitalist trade and development in the first decades of the century – a goal achieved not by invasion or covert operations (long abandoned as costly and

50

ineffective) but by the potent ideology of consumerism and the seductive images of greed, sex and power beamed in by satellite television.

But there are other powerful dynasties which have arisen more recently by controlling the cultivation, production and distribution of drugs, in particular cocaine. Too important in terms of their financial reserves and private armies to be excluded from power they have gradually intermarried with the clans, often buying alliances with the beauty of the young brides they offer to the young men (but not just the *young* men) of the old dynasties. Like them they have constructed their great fortified centres proof against flood and tempest where, protected by guards recruited from among the most brutalised children of the *favelas* (the word was been adopted universally and is applied indifferently to the shanty towns that ring like scabs the old metropolitan cities like Peking, Chicago, Berlin, Melbourne, and whose inhabitants constitute what is called 'the sub-class') they live behind electronic fences secure from the attacks of the *jacqueries*. Their lives and those of their dependents are eased by the ingenuity of scientists, ergonomists and designers, and embellished by the work of skilled artisans, creators of splendid décors no sooner installed than they are obsolescent, inventors of subtle mechanical toys to fill the mansions and offices and clubs of the powerful.

In their artefacts, which combine film, photography, holography, video, with the older medium of paint and pigments, daring of invention goes hand in hand with ironical triviality. Not only the homes of the clan members and the new dynasts but public places, institutions and art galleries, are repositories of cultural bric-à-brac – pieces that have survived natural disasters from disparate ages and cultures. Wrenched from all context in history or society they are indicators of the flux of taste. Thus, at the auctions where the sunburnt potentates and their fragile women contend for them, a plastic Mickey Mouse from the 1940s will go for a price as high as that of an Anglo-Saxon ivory diptych or the solemn image of a mother-goddess stolen from some site in Iberia or from a museum in the days of the great inundations when bold thieves risked instant execution to plunder the deserted cities.

Performance flourishes: young boys and girls of great beauty, intelligence and skill, are lifted out of the *favelas* to be models, singers, musicians, acrobats, dancers, strippers, whores; like exotic flowers they spring from the shit and rubbish dumps which ring the fortified cities of the clans. Sometimes they too contrive to insert themselves by marriage – or more often by liaison – into the hierarchies of the clans and it is noticeable (though it is not something publicly acknowledged) that some families have members whose skin colour or hair texture betray an admixture of blood from the subclass; often they bring with them the hidden threat of AIDS. For this reason – and for considerations of security – as in Spain at the height of its Catholic power, there is legislation to prevent anyone with any such genetic admixture from reaching a position where they might have access to commanding power in finance, industry or the army.

From the *favelas*, too, come the witch-doctors; men and women who are credited with extraordinary powers and who supplement the counsellors, therapists and psychoanalysts that practise so lucratively in the clans. Soothsayers, necromancers, chiromancers, casters of bones, readers of Tarot cards, inter-preters of I Ching, they live on the fears, lusts and jealousies of the men and women who visit their huts deep in the *favelas*, not entirely clandestinely, for they arrive with bodyguards, but at least anonymously, for their faces are veiled or obscured by dark glasses. These healers and soothsayers are experts in potions, philtres, and aphrodisiacs, concocters of magic oils to banish age, to attract lovers, to ensure fidelity, skilled dispensers of hallucinatory substances derived from mushrooms like *Amanita muscaria*, grown illegally – an offence punishable by death – as is *Strychnos toxifera* from which they extract the swift-acting, bitter, blackish-brown poison: curare.

In both the superpowers religion flourishes although China, while tolerating a variety of beliefs from Christianity to Islam and Buddhism, is officially wedded to a residual form of

Marxism, a sterile assembly of texts which the young learn as a duty and which have no apparent relevance to the society in which they live. The United States prides itself on being a country where Christianity flourishes in a variety of forms, their litanies and rituals often overlaid with elements absorbed over the years from the more ecstatic worship of the *favelas*. To counteract this contamination of the true faith is the aim of a strong group among the conservative clergy. They attribute the spread of the rituals and enthusiasms of the sub-class to certain deviant priests who from time to time disappear into the *favelas*. There they join forces with the tiny nuclei of men and women who denounce the immorality of post-industrial society, proclaim the possibility of a juster, more humane world and are willing to sacrifice their lives for its attainment.

The conservative clergy, while equally critical of social decay, see it only as the result of a decline in individual morals – an increase in sinfulness – and call for spiritual regeneration, for repentance to turn aside the just punishment God is visiting on the earth in the shape of disease, hunger, ecological disaster, on a scale unknown since he scourged the children of Israel for their transgressions. They were the inspiration of that highly organised group of scientists, military men and intellectuals drawn from the traditional clans and proud that they have never had links with the coca-millionaires, who in the seventies contrived to take over the project to explore Andromeda and, calling themselves 'Pilgrim Fathers', to set up a colony there.

Over the first half of the twenty-first century the population has been reduced immensely by terrestrial disasters – floods, hurricanes, tidal waves – leading to crop failures and famine. Add to these the ravages of disease, in particular AIDS, which is by now endemic, if not pandemic, and welcomed as such by many leading figures in the hierarchies of the superpowers who – according to their respective ideologies – see it either as a God-sent scourge or as an agent of natural selection which will reduce the population level to a point at which the resources of the planet will once more be adequate to sustain human society. It is a powerful instrument that usefully culls the masses of the subclass. But although weakened and reduced by disease its members can still present a threat to their rulers in their closely guarded fortresses for whom they provide labour, servants and soldiers. Control over them is still uncertain. It is at its most effective in the factories where selected women and girls from the *favelas* assemble the circuitry for the electronics and rocketry which the clans have developed to dominate space and control information.

Surveillance extends naturally to other important centres of production: the mines where increasingly scarce and precious metals are extracted at perilous depths, or the agro-factories and hydroponic installations where basic foodstuffs and synthetic protein grow under artificial conditions together with the inert, deformed meat-producing beasts evolved by genetic engineering: the so-called transgenic animals. In such production centres discipline is severe and is reinforced by rituals like the mass induction of new workers, who take an oath of obedience of their employers and have read out to them the consequences to indiscipline, slackness, and the formation of unauthorised groupings. Punishments range from humiliation – the pillorying of offenders with a placard slung round their necks spelling out their offence – to periods of unpaid labour with reduced rations. In very serious cases there are public beatings and imprisonment in the private jails attached to places of work. For cases that come under the definition of social subversion there is the death penalty.

There are, it is true, regular occasions on which the social controls are relaxed. Chief among these are the great games and sports festivals, which are still called Olympic Games, where the competing athletes belong to a ruthless, and conspicuously wealthy elite; they are often drawn precisely from the most disadvantaged but toughest, most resilient children of the slums. The games are frequently accompanied by riots involving the supporters of rival teams or athletes, which while not officially sanctioned, are accepted as an inevitable concomitant of the games. They are the expression of traditional enmities based on pigmentation, language, dress, eating habits etc. The roots of these differences lie too far back in history to be any longer disentangled. The fear of the rulers is that this violence may one day be diverted into other channels by 'deviants' and 'anti-social elements' – subversives who from time to time emerge from the *favela* to preach a mixture of evangelical Christianity and utopian socialism based on rare, highly corrupt and half-understood texts by 19th century political theorists. Theirs is a tradition of millenarianism which experts claim can be traced back across the centuries to the Middle Ages and beyond.

The ringleaders of the riots are dealt with severely, their executions being shown live simultaneously on all television channels. The rank and file undergo rigorous conditioning in military training-centres, which have their own highly effective methods and an equally high success rate, for it is precisely from among the ex-rioters that the army and police draw their best and most ruthless recruits. Other troublemakers – evangelists and utopians – also enter these establishments as prisoners but rarely re-emerge. They are said to be missing.

Deviance among members of the clans is more difficult to detect than among the preachers and priestesses of the *favelas*, for it is not usually expressed openly, nor is it necessarily linked to violence. One symptom is 'compulsive writing behaviour', which is sharply repressed. Other symptoms include the tendency to question the justice of the harsh regimes of the superpowers, which is interpreted as an inability to adjust to society. Such deviants – a rare but important category – are controlled in various ways: dreamers of alternative societies receive psychoanalytic treatment to help them to adjust to reality or – should that fail – are administered psychotropic drugs ranging from sedatives and tranquillisers to (in stubborn cases) chlorpromazine, the 'chemical straitjacket'. Habitual offenders and recidivists are forced to have a chip implanted subcutaneously which contains the circuitry for a small computer capable of regulating cerebral functions and thought patterns.

Alternatively, their movements are tracked by a transponder

surveillance system – an externalised conscience, as it were, which checks their drug levels by telemetry and decides whether they may continue to move about freely or require to be brought in for medication. Hardened or impenitent cases who do not respond to treatment also 'disappear'. Their children, if young, are offered for adoption, if older brought up in closed and closely guarded institutions where they are taught that theirs is the great good fortune to have the state as father and mother. Educated to be high-grade technicians and moulded to their role they are expected to become faithful servants to the state. But others retain a deep unspoken resentment of life in these closed and closely guarded institutions or are old enough when 'orphaned' to wonder at their parents' fate.

Such is Catriona's case, for she has all her adult life secretly nursed suspicion and anger over the helicopter crash that killed both her father, a specialist in exobiology, and her mother, his colleague, who was declared posthumously to have been in touch with radical deviant priests working in the *favelas* – a fact of which her husband must have been guiltily aware.


It was Saturday – a day of patchy skies. Squalls of rain ruffled the loch and scribbled grey slanting lines across the hills. Peter Sinclair walked up to the village, bought a paper, bought more supplies to tide him over the weekend and submitted to interrogation by Mrs Fraser, the storekeeper's wife, a process which, over time, would allow the village to establish to its own satisfaction his identity, his motives for coming to the bothie and his business there. Yes, he was enjoying himself. No, he came from over on the other side, Edinburgh way. No, he hadn't any folk left in Scotland. Yes, the rhododendrons were wonderful. Was it the Major's father or grandfather, he asked disingenuously, who had brought all those plants from India?

As he walked back to the bothie he wondered whether he had been imagining a slight constraint when he tried to discover more about the General. What he did gather was that the General had been very strict; you had to mind your p's and q's with him.

Mrs Fraser knew because her mother had been in service at the Big House between the wars. Very strict. The Major, now, was much more easy going than his father had been. And what about Miss Grizelle? At this point Mr Fraser called from the back of the shop from which he exercised his authority, and the conversation was broken off. Peter walked slowly back. Sitting for a few minutes at the window he looked out over the loch and ran a couple of marbles to and from in his cupped ahands. Then he began to write.

David was pleased with the outcome of the wargame. He had been a divisional commander in the sector where the crossing was to be made. When the infantry landed he provided not only artillery support but air-cover in strength so that a foothold was gained with acceptable losses. Then the director of the exercise intimated that elements of a German armoured division had unexpectedly entered the combat zone; but David rustled up a squadron of tank-busters which came in low and dealt with the armour, which was in any case in a bad way with many of the tanks still on transporters and in need of repairs. Exploiting success he reinforced the landing till a proper bridgehead was established with a serviceable pontoon bridge. Whereupon the corps commander ordered the division to enlarge the bridgehead from which the armour and lorried infantry would break out and execute a turning movement round the northern flank of the German forces on the Rhine.

The game ended with the bulk of the corps over the river, its armour poised to strike east and north across the plains of North Germany. It had been, the director said, a well conducted game in which the tactics employed were a good deal more intelligent than those that history recorded; a frontal assault by the British, American and Canadian forces across the Rhine complete with gliders and parachutists. A great set piece. There was a well-established story that the British prime minister of the day had watched the crossing from a chair not far back from the Rhine – literally a ringside seat. But David found it hard to credit.

Peter Sinclair switched off his word-processor and busied himself with the small chores of life in this room which was gradually becoming his own familiar space. What he remembered, thinking back to those distant days when the armies in north-west Europe ground their way across the borders of the Third Reich through floods, forest and deep concrete defences, was how surprised he had been to be able to drive his jeep into a deserted hamlet – Gertruidenberg said the map – within a couple of kilometres of the River Waal, and park it behind the church without a shot being fired from across the water. The door of the church was open and he walked in, found a door and climbed up into the belfry by stairs that smelt of dust and pigeon shit. His footsteps on the wooden stairs disturbed a chattering jackdaw and a couple of pigeons, which took off with a clatter of wings.

At last he stood behind the parapet, his back to the steeple. Suppressing a hint of vertigo he looked out over the polders of occupied Holland. It was strange to see laid out before him, green, patched with shadow, untroubled by movement, a landscape he had studied for days on the maps. There were the dyked islands with their reed beds, from which at night the Tartar deserters came swimming across; dazed boys speaking a few words of German, hopeless and lost, unable to tell where they were, why or whom they were fighting. But no different in their peasant stoicism, he reflected, from the Gurkhas he had known in Italy and of whom they reminded him, for their faces too were of the East. A boy with a bullet-hole just above the wrist cradled his arm. His face was pale with pain and with fatigue from the swim across the river, pushing before him a bundle of reeds as a precarious raft. But he made no sound and accepted with a slight smile the cigarette Peter offered him.

Peter scanned the landscape with his field-glasses and saw here and there little heaps of spoil from weapon-pits, tracks across the fields from forward troops to a company or battalion headquarters but little movement. No trucks, only a couple of horsedrawn vehicles, field-kitchens perhaps. Otherwise it was as peaceful as a Dutch seventeenth-century genre painting, had the same light, the same illusion of tilting slightly up towards the horizon. All that it lacked was a rainbow to demonstrate the artist's virtuosity. What it had instead – away to the east as he was turning to climb down – was a trail of white vapour that suddenly rose and hung in the upper air where it lingered until a current of air teased it apart. Another rocket, he thought, a V2. Hitler's last desperate weapon.

Then he drove slowly back through the fields to the brigade headquarters commanding this, the most inactive sector of the front, to which he had been posted as staff officer on his return from Italy: a slight, tiresome limp – the result of a shrapnel wound – had meant that he was still downgraded medically. In this military backwater he passed the time by keeping the situation maps up to date, wrote intelligence summaries which no doubt someone read somewhere, interrogated the occasional prisoner or deserter, and quarrelled ridiculously with the Dutch liaison officer, a major who ran agents across the river and stubbornly refused to share whatever intelligence they brought back with them. Far away one could sometimes detect the roll of artillery or bombing. But down here by the Rhine the freshfaced boys straight from England sat in their weapon-pits and were content that – cold and wet apart – theirs was a cushy war.

Then came a conference at brigade HQ to which Peter had to explain the enemy situation, which he did, stressing that while some identifications of enemy units were clear from prisoner's statements others were less certain – indeed it was difficult to know what kind of unit they represented or what strength they were in. No, he had no information of any movement of fresh troops into the area. There were no reports of activity from Corps HQ and none from aerial reconnaissance or the fighters that daily overflew the roads and railways deep into enemy territory. The brigade commander gave a little sceptical grunt. Was that all? he asked. Peter looked over to where the Dutch major sat; but he was silent and merely shook his head. It had to be said, Peter went on, that enemy units from the front were from time to time brought back to refit and reform in Holland.

This was most likely – given allied air superiority – to take place under cover of darkness and at short notice; but he could not be more positive than that. The brigadier heard him out and commented that he had better be right.

Then, turning to the commander of the infantry battalion that held the river line: 'All right then, Henry,' he said, 'you will let me have your plan of operations in time for a final conference twenty-four hours from now. Operations to begin at first light the day after tomorrow.'

Then they were dismissed. 'What was that about?' asked Peter of a staff captain, a sharp young barrister whose ambition (which he would no doubt realise) was to sit on the bench at the Old Bailey.

'Oh don't be naïve. It is about the fact that the brigadier and the CO of a second-rate battalion know the war is almost over, know they haven't a hope in hell of being involved in any serious operations and so have decided to have a little side-show of their own. Who knows, they might pick up a gong for it.'

In the event the colonel's gong was posthumous. The enemy allowed the raw troops to land when they attacked at first light under cover of mist thickened by smoke from the twenty-five pounders. Peter watched the attack from his observation post in the church tower: the landing-craft breasting the current like water-beetles, the troops landing and climbing up the dyke that lined the bank, the way they went scurrying across the field beyond with the curious crouching run of men under fire. As the smoke lifted and thinned something moved beside a shed in a field beyond the polder where the troops were deploying. A tank poked its gun round the end of the shed, then further over another and another again. The tracer from their machine-guns drew bright lines and arcs in the morning air; ricochets spun lazily over the water. Damn, he thought, they must have moved in overnight. There was nothing he could do but watch how the infantry halted, rose again, moved on, faltered, lay pinned in the enemy crossfire. Then, as the sun rose, the smoke cleared altogether to show them falling back to the landing-craft in little groups, too bunched together for safety, stumbling and dying in

60

the flat meadows. The bullets pelted in sudden squalls on the water as they straggled back in boats, swimming, sinking, drowning, while the artillery laid down another protective screen of smoke that drifted and thinned in the breeze.

Then the fighters came in low, lower than the church tower, and gracefully, almost nonchalantly, hit the German armour and self-propelled guns with their rockets. It was over in a couple of hours. Peter climbed down from the tower and drove back to where the landing-craft were ferrying the survivors back, whitefaced, drained, not talking much. Fortunately he had warned that enemy troops could move in at any time; formally therefore he was in the clear and the brigade commander would have enough troubles of his own explaining away at Corps this 'reconnaissance in force' as the day's communiqué would call it. But Peter carried with him the memory of a boy at a forward aid post weeping, calling on his mother as he watched the blood pump from his shattered leg and knew he was going to die. Did the Major, he wondered, share that kind of memory?

He was interrupted in his own memories by a motorcycle that came up the drive from the gatehouse, fast, with a long low roar and skidded to silence with a skillful flourish at the foot of the steps. The rider seemed to be cased in black leather and casqued with a black helmet; not very tall, slim; was busy for a moment about the machine, then ran up the steps and in at the front door without apparently ringing. Peter had not connected the Major with motorcyclists in black gear. Unless it was a courier of some kind – which seemed unlikely. From time to time he looked up at the House from writing his letter to Urizen, to see if the machine was still there, and even went to the door drawn by vague curiosity. It was perhaps half-an-hour later that Garlinski came slowly and deliberately down the long curving unmetalled road from the Big House and turned towards the bothie. As he approached at his measured pace Peter finished running off the last page of his long – too long? – paper for Urizen, removed the disc from his word-processor and switched off the power. Then he waited for the knock.

I have to confess that just as Peter Sinclair is using his wargaming, his speculations about the state of Planet Earth in 2087 and the story of David Balfour as an excuse for not working at his book on the politics of alienation or to occlude other more heavy thoughts, so I too have been postponing a turn in my narrative which cannot any longer be delayed. You may guess from this that the messenger coming down from the Big House to the bothie brings us to another stage in the development of the tale. To recapitulate, what we have had so far – using Propp's schema – is absentation (Peter Sinclair leaves 'home'), an interdiction – 'no appendages' as the Major put it – which (always according to Propp) should now be broken by the appearance of a new personage: the villain who disturbs the peace of a happy family (violation), makes an attempt at reconnaissance, receives information about his victim and attempts to deceive him in order to take possession of him or of his belongings.

My problem is partly that while the narrative seems to be moving in accordance with Propp's morphology I am not yet sure that the new personage fits the bill. But problematic she certainly is: which may account for restraints and hesitations. These have nothing to do with literary techniques or the patterns of storytelling, but with deep fears, desires, fantasies which I am loathe to express. But the author is falsely shamefaced; such resistances are in the long – or not so long – run overcome in an uneven struggle within the author's heart, mind, psyche or whatever you care to call it. The itch to write – *cacoethes scribendi* – is a tenacious affliction.


'The Major's compliments,' said Garlinski when Peter opened to him, 'and could you step up to the Big House for a few minutes.' Together they walked up to the House although 'together' does not not quite convey the way in which Garlinski contrived to be marginally behind Peter, keeping his distance, respecting his station, ready to draw abreast only if addressed. At the foot of the steps the motorcycle sat at an angle in the gravel, a big, powerful looking light-blue machine with bright exhausts. On the petrol tank was the name Triumph.

'The 650cc Tiger 110 regularly clocked a speed of 117.2 mph during tests in 1954. The Ton-ten, as it came to be called later, was a sports version of Thunderbird, the first post-war Triumph, launched in 1949. It shared the Thunderbird's ultra-modern polychromatic paintwork in a new shade – Shell-Blue Sheen – as well as the four-barred chrome embellishment on the petrol tank and the characteristic headlamp nacelle. Phased out in 1961 the T110 set a standard for combining speed and reliability with up-to-date looks. It was not an unmanageable beast either. It had versatility and comfort and a miserly fuel consumption of 62–70 mpg. Having been primarily a flag-waving machine for export, the Tiger 110 is comparatively rare on British roads today.' (*The Classic Bike*)

The Major, said Garlinski, was in his office, which was a room by the front door where he sat in a battered leather chair behind a wide desk on which were some correspondence files and a box of cartridges; in one corner, green wellies and various other boots; in another, fishing rods; on the wall behind him a couple of doubled-barrelled shotguns.

The Major rose: 'Nice of you to come up. Care for a drink, or is it too early for you?' Peter accepted the whisky. The Major sipped at his and began to discuss the relative advantages of fishing the loch with fly, with a spoon or with an artificial minnow; the last two, he always felt, being a bit unfair to the fish – rather like using a pump-action shotgun for pheasant shooting – and in any case not really suitable for taking the sort of fish in the loch, although he could remember his father – mind you, this was before the last war – landing a nice five-pounder at the tail of the island opposite the bothie. Peter listened and wondered at the purpose of this elaborate gambit.

At last, after wagging his jaw a few times, the Major came to the point, which was that he had had a most unexpected visit from a sort of second cousin whom he couldn't decently send away. Peter would no doubt have seen her bike in front of the house. From which he might have gathered that she was a bit unconventional. He would be most extraordinarily grateful if Peter could put her up for the night on the sofa-bed, the point being that the guest rooms hadn't been used for ages and Mrs Garlinski, who was a treasure but could be a little difficult at times, had said flatly she couldn't get one of them into a fit state at such short notice.

The Major stopped with his long jaw dropped and looked at Peter, who almost without reflection said naturally he would be delighted to help, whereupon the Major got up, went to the door and shouted, 'Lucinda.'

It was a family name he explained, as they waited for her to appear, but her friends called her Lucy, who was suddenly, quietly there. About thirty. Ginger hair almost punkish in its cut and a transparent skin. She was not in her gear, unless her miniskirt counted as gear.

She shook Peter's hand firmly and looked at him with amusement. 'So he's persuaded you,' she said as she picked up her glass. 'It's really very nice of you. I shan't impose myself for long. And I am quite house-trained.'

'I was telling him,' said the Major changing the subject, 'that it was your bike outside there.'

'You're supposed to say,' she went on, looking at Peter mockingly, ' "Do you really ride a bike?" and then – just to show that you're with it – you add, "You're not by any chance one of these Hell's Angels we've seen on television, are you?" ' She ran her hand over her stubbly hair. 'Or else that you find the gear kinky. Do you?'

Peter reflected and said he didn't think so. 'Actually, I was wondering about the bike. I rode a Norton 500cc briefly in the army. I remember racing another officer – he's a bishop these days – along the Hog's Back on one.'

'Go on,' said Lucinda.

'That's about all I know about bikes,' he said. 'What else can I say? Except that yours looks pretty powerful and a bit of a rarity.'

'People who are into bikes call it the Ton-ten. It's a marvellous thing to ride. You're supposed to laugh and say: it must be great with all that power between your legs.'

'My mother,' said Peter, 'thought it was indelicate for women to ride anything other than side-saddle and therefore had her doubts even about push-bikes.'

'I see you're more used to talking to today's young people than I am,' said the Major, intervening abruptly as if he found the conversation slightly distasteful. 'Well, here's to your good health, Lucinda. Sliant.'

'I hope,' said Lucinda as she sipped her whisky, 'that we're not going to have much of that Highland stuff – Gaelic and pibrochs. Aunt Clotilde used to say the noise of the bagpipes starting up always made her want to pee.'

Peter laughed and excused himself. He had to tidy up a bit.

'Not for my sake,' said Lucinda. 'I hate obsessive tidiness. It reminds me of my convent school. Nightdress folded thus and tucked under the pillow so each morning. Skirt draped on the back of the chair at night. Pleats straight. And so on and so forth.'

In the bothie Peter tugged at the sofa-bed, which unfolded reluctantly, got blankets and sheets out of the cupboard in the bedroom and made up the bed. Then he lay on it for a moment and found it hard but not uncomfortable. Should he, he wondered, sleep on it himself and let Lucinda have the double bed? But given the geography of the place that might be complicated, so he decided to leave things as they were, grilled himself a steak and sat down at his word-processor to pass the time till she should come. As he waited he wrote.

★

It had been a long session. The wargame had been prolonged; the postmortem detailed and contentious. So it was no surprise for David that Catriona was in their living-space by the time he returned. She was lying on the bed. Behind her a monitor was switched on but she had turned down the sound. The lips of the speaker – one of the founding fathers – moved noiselessly, but David could guess that he was reiterating the need for discipline, for self-control, if they were to survive on Andromeda. He sat down on the bed. Catriona still wore the overalls that were obligatory in her workplace. He ran his hand into a gap just above the waistline and felt the familiar smoothness of her skin which had that transparency that can go with a certain colouring: red or rather pale ginger hair, grey eyes. His hand moved over her belly and his fingers entered her light, silky, reddish fuzz. She put her hand on his arm and drew his hand out gently but firmly.

'Did you see it?'

He nodded. 'Did you know her?' he asked.

'Isobel Dufy,' she said, 'of course, I knew her. We used to eat together in the canteen. A wonderful person. They repeated it again just now. They'll show it over and over again just in case someone missed it. Did you see how brave she was? I hope I'd be as brave as that.' She got up, undressed quickly, turning her back to him, and lay down again in their sleeping space.

David was puzzled and, as often when there was tension of some sort between them – a misunderstanding, a difference of opinion – tried to circumvent it by changing the subject. 'Did you hear? They're saying there's going to be a magnetic storm, like after we just got together and there were those amazing auroral displays. They say it's going to be like that again. We're going to have to be careful about radiation. So don't forget your counter tomorrow.'

Catriona said yes, she knew but she seemed preoccupied with other matters. She had retreated further from him, pulling the coverlet over her head. David undressed and lay beside her. The soothing softness of her skin and the smell of her hair on the pillow were unchanged. She was there, familiar, close with her back to him as she often lay. He put out his hand and slid it down over her belly, expecting to feel her muscles relax as she offered him access to the spot where the skin was smooth, silky, tender, the flesh split and pink. But today her legs locked all away. He moved his hand up till his arm was round her waist and asked what was wrong.

'What is wrong,' she said, 'is that a sister is dead and you think you can make me forget it by fucking me. Like *she* said – give them the chance and men will use sex to flush away our fears and anxieties, as if orgasm were some sort of anaesthetic. I'm telling you it isn't.'

'Right,' he said, 'let's talk about it tomorrow.' And cuddling close into her back he fell asleep.

But Catriona lay and thought of the capsule drifting away through space beyond all hope of re-entry. Would the body be uncorrupted, the face she remembered unspoilt, the features relaxed in death which she remembered passionate and lively in argument and in the quick secret meetings at which she and a handful of others had discussed Andromeda, its future and how to change it?


Peter looked at his watch. Eleven o'clock. He decided to stop – as he often did – in the middle of a passage. This, he had discovered to his surprise, made it easier to take up the thread again; for curiously it remained unbroken – indeed seemed to grow in his mind or (more likely) in his unconscious – until next he sat and fed the paper into his machine. In bed he lay for a little and reflected with surprise that whereas before Catriona had been little more than an idea, a character that had not yet acquired a clear image and a personality, she had now un-mistakeably taken on the physical characteristics of the young woman with the Ton-ten bike, who would sleep a few feet away from him. When he thought of her he felt the first movements of desire.

He fell asleep before she came down from the castle. When he woke in the morning he lay and wondered whether to go through to the shower and risk waking her, but when he opened the door he saw a note on the table: 'Thanks for the bed. See you again perhaps – I hope. I'd quite like to have a talk. Lucy.' Lucy not Lucinda. Her friends call her Lucy.

So Lucy/Lucinda is not on the face of it the Proppean villain, who should in any case perhaps come in a different guise. More like Mephistopheles – as in a nineteenth-century illustration to Gounod's *Faust* – with a pointed beard and a feather in his cap, chewing a straw, a dagger stuck in his belt. In order to take possession of his victim's belongings the villain may, says Propp, attempt to deceive him (trickery); the victim, for his part, submits to the deception (complicity). He would even more plausibly be a young man in his late twenties, good-looking, with a beard (which may or may not conceal a weak chin) and a jaunty air: an ex-student of Peter's – gifted, wayward, but above all paranoid. His name is Duncan Hogg.

Peter had been up at the village to buy eggs from Mrs Fraser at the store and to expose himself to further cross-examination, bartering some scraps of information; about his birthplace, about his status (divorced), in return for clues about the Major and his family history. Such as that the money really came from a marriage two generations back to a Miss Swinton, daughter of a millowner and a little heiress in her own right; her son – the General – had been abroad a lot of the time between the wars; that his wife, who had been one of the MacDonalds of Sleat, had died shortly after the girl, Grizelle, was born so that the poor lassie never really had a mother; that he had been too old for the last war but had been active in the local Home Guard and was forever parading them up at the Big House or running about on the hills. Mr Fraser – he was in a reserved occupation as postie at the time – had just about died of a cold he caught on one of these daft manoeuvres as the General called them, though Mrs Fraser thought they sounded more like boys playing at Cowboys and Indians.

Peter switched the talk to the Major and his wife. Yes, said Mrs Fraser, she remembered the Major's lady fine – French she was and didn't take to the country life that much. She went away to some place in France where she was supposed to have a big house of her own, a château. The next they heard she was dead. No, they had no bairns. Very sad because the family would die out with the Major. Miss Grizelle? A douce creature but she'd been like that ever since she was in her teens – not the whole shilling, you might say. But real nice. Very sad for the Major, very sad. And he was that good to her. No, he'd never remarried. Oh there had been rumours and some folk said he'd been a great one for the ladies, But she didnae ken about that. Maybe Mrs Garlinski knew but she wasn't one to gossip.

Miss Lucinda? There used to be a lassie came to visit when the Major's lady was there. But she didn't know that much about her. 'John,' she shouted through to her husband who was as usual hidden away behind the house, 'do you remember a Miss Lucinda up at the Big House?' John, she explained parenthetically, used to do a bit of work in the shrubberies until it got over much for him. But John's reply was a muffled negative. Peter paid for his eggs, promised not to drop them on the way back and set out for the bothie.

He found him sitting at the table examining the word-processor. 'Duncan,' he said between laughter and annoyance, 'where the hell did you spring from?'

Duncan, bearded, broken-nosed, looked up and mustered him calmly. He had Peter's marbles in his hand and was making them click together. 'Nice bulls,' he said. 'Marbles, I mean,' he went on, 'we must be careful to use received standard Southern English, mustn't we, old man? When I was wee my mother made me a cloth bag to keep mine in. Did yours?' Peter nodded and waited. 'I heard you were hiding in some swanky country cottage, the young man explained, still playing with the marbles, 'so I thought I'd look in on you. I got the address from your girlfriend in the library – the married one, Anna what's-her-name. Come on, don't say she isn't your girlfriend, it's common knowledge. All right – was. I told her I needed to see you about my future. She came clean and I hitched. The proles hitch – other people have cars.'

'I should throw you out,' said Peter, 'but sheer nerve always wins, doesn't it? How are you planning to get back to Glasgow?'

'Oh, I'll get back. But I thought maybe I'd stay for a couple of days and go over this idea I have for a Master's. It's a study of the other self in Scottish literature.'

'But Duncan, you haven't even got a first degree. Can I remind you why? Because you said it would have meant complicity with the system.'

'That's right,' said Duncan, 'no way was I going to put myself on the line along with all these petty bourgeois creatures parroting about deconstruction and the mirror phase, throwing about gobbets of Lacan and Derrida. Derrida? Of course I've read him. What d'you think I do with my time in the squat after I've been and cashed my giro? I read. I study. Listen, I'll tell you what I think about Derrida. When it comes down to it, what's he saying? No, listen. He's saying that we canna mean what we say or say what we mean and there's no world out there in any case to talk about. Nothing outside the text. I hope he remembers that when the bomb drops on him in Paris or wherever. But he was always on these reading lists of yours at the beginning of term. Peter Sinclair will lecture this term on structuralist, post-structuralist and post-modernist thought. I never saw Lenin's *Materialism and Empiriocriticism* on any of your wee lists. Did I now?'

Peter came back from the stove with a pot of tea and set it on the table. He didn't happen to think, he said, that Lenin was the world's greatest or most original philosopher and *Materialism and Empiriocriticism* was, philosophically speaking, fairly crude and secondly, while he had problems with Derrida, Derrida was someone one had to take seriously, tackle intellectually and not just write off in a phrase.

'But he's shite, Peter, he's pure shite. And you're behaving like a fucking liberal as usual.' Duncan poured himself a cup of tea and lapsed into a disapproving silence. 'Well, never mind Derrida and the rest of that trendy bunch,' he resumed when his tea was finished, 'I'm working on a book about the split in the Scottish character – ever heard of the Caledonian antisyzygy? It's a grand word. It means that we're a nation of schizophrenics and that that's our strength. Not like the fucking English. Or the French for that matter. You know me – I'll be drawing on Freud and Marx. You'll remember what Bettelheim said about the concentration camps; and he was a shrink himself when he was put in Dachau. That it was the ones with a good healthy neurosis who survived. I have a synopsis I want you to read. Of course you don't have to. No doubt it's not up to your intellectual level.'

Peter replied tangentially that there was another more urgent problem. Which was that he had rented the cottage on condition that he didn't share it.

'Oh,' said Duncan, 'that's all right. I saw himself – the laird or whatever he is – and explained I was your nephew. He hummed and hawed but said that if you were happy he was. There's a bed-settee, I see. I bet you've put up a girl-friend or two, you old libertine.'

Peter was silent. He knew from long experience Duncan's tenacity, his sudden flaring enthusiasms, his deep-seated lack of confidence which made him at the last moment draw back from submitting to the judgment of any authority, intellectual or institutional, but he knew too the courage with which this autodidact from down the Leith Walk had bludgeoned his way into higher education as a mature student with behind him a history of odd jobs: construction worker, barman, holiday camp steward, sparring partner in a boxing academy down the Old Kent Road. What drove him on was the need to assuage an insatiable hunger for knowledge, which – as Anna used to say – was almost pathological, a kind of intellectual bulimia. For three years Peter had encouraged and shielded him while Duncan like a wild-cat prospector hunted the vein of originality that ran through the chaotic faulted geology of his mind.

'All right,' he said, 'but only till Saturday – three days. Then it's down the road, comrade.'

'Don't you go calling me comrade. I've no time for parlour lefties like you. Nor for any party I've seen yet. Forget the CP or the SWP or the so-called Revolutionary Communists. I tell you, though, when the time comes I'll be there. One day you'll hear of me.'

So he settled in; which meant that work was impossible. It was not merely that he was physically large, with his bruiser's physique, his massive head and thick bush of reddish hair, but that he also annexed a great deal of space pacing up and down, gesticulating, spreading his typescript on the table. In truth what annoyed Peter most was that he could not progress with the story of David and Catriona (that resentful daughter of the state) although he had thoughts about how it might develop. Instead there were arguments with his guest, ritual exchanges of jokes and abuse behind which there lurked on both sides deep ambiguities of feeling, emotional stresses, rivalries. These led to re-runs of old fights over politics in which Duncan accused Peter of being irrevocably marked by the romanticism – not to say sentimentality – of the Popular Front against Fascism and basically a liberal, whereas he himself espoused an uncompromising model of Marxist-Leninism which was, he claimed, the modern expression of the political essence of Scottish Calvinism.

'You mean,' said Peter, 'that there are the chosen few and the rest of us are to be cast into outer darkness.'

'Something like that,' Duncan agreed. 'Class is, you might say, the mark of the beast or of salvation. There's no way you can escape your class formation, man. I've told you often enough you're just a wee petty-bourgeois intellectual. And not even up-to-date – not really with it. Still stuck with ideas about alienation and Brechtian stratagems. Well, it'll be interesting to see which way you jump when the cards are down.'

In between times there were discussions about what Peter had been up to in 'the people's war against Fascism' – his fingers flickered the quotation marks – which, for Duncan's money, had been an old-fashioned imperialist struggle in which no thorough-going left-winger should have been involved.

'You know perfectly well what I was up to – as you call it –I've told you often enough.'

'Special Operations – what did that mean?' asked Duncan, disregarding the refused gambit, 'because that's where they spawned the SAS. Don't deny it.'

Special Operations, Peter explained patiently, had meant in his case being dropped into enemy territory – Tuscany – near San Vito to be precise, to make contact with and support resistance groups. When he came back he had been posted for medical reasons to Intelligence, the mention of which made Duncan look sideways at him and stroke his beard.

'Aye,' he said, 'we all know what that means.'

It meant, Peter explained patiently, collating information from a variety of sources – prisoners-of-war, captured documents, and hush-hush stuff that came down from higher echelons and had the stamp of authority. Enigma, ultra top secret material, actually, as everyone now knew. Keeping a situation map of enemy dispositions, reporting the identification of new enemy units, briefing the brigade commander on the strength, movements and probable intentions of the enemy. Sometimes we got it right. Sometimes not. And that was the long and the short of it. 'But I still worry about the times we got it wrong. Because a lot of people lost their lives.'

Duncan grinned his disbelief. What lay behind his grimace, Peter knew, was a scenario in which Duncan cast him either as an MI5 officer pretending to be a left-wing socialist and operating in academia or a trendy radical received into the Establishment because of his intelligence background, which might come in handy for keeping a finger on the pulse of student politics. It was a double bind from which no protestations could deliver him, so Peter was relieved when Duncan asked him to teach him how to use the word-processor; which kept him busy and quiet.

On their second day together, desperate to curtail the dissection of Duncan's twenty-page synopsis (each page contested) which he found dense, convoluted and wayward, Peter sought out Garlinski, hired a yacht, took Duncan on board and sailed far out towards the islands at the head of the loch where, tradition said, the laird's ancestors were buried. He loved the feel of the rudder in his hand balancing the forces of wind and water, the moment of hesitation when the sail fluttered at the mast-head and he put the boat about. Then the boom came over smartly causing Duncan to duck and break off his exposition of his namesake Hogg's *Confessions of a Jusified Sinner* as a paradigmatic case of the split personality in Scottish literature and its relevance to the problem of Scotland's unresolved national identity.

Across the lake, under Benmore, a squall drew a black line across the face of the loch. Racing towards them over the water it drew behind it a veil of rain. Peter held the boat as close to the wind as possible so that it heeled over until Duncan, bracing himself against a thwart, burst out to accuse him of doing it on purpose; which Peter did not bother to deny.

Thereafter Duncan refused to set foot in the yacht but wandered off by himself, striking up an unlikely acquaintance with Garlinski whom he visited a couple of evenings later in the gatehouse and came back having – as he put it – the drink taken. 'Interesting man, Garlinski,' he said. 'Did you know there are fourteen kinds of vodka. You did – you didna tell me though about the young woman on the motorbike. Garlinski said you put her up. I bet him you fucked her.'

'Duncan,' said Peter, 'tomorrow's Saturday. I'm going to Glasgow to do some shopping – get new ribbons for the word-processor, look in the bookshops. See a museum maybe. Can I give you a lift?'

But Duncan said he'd maybe stay a wee while longer – have another go at the word-processor. In any case he wasn't interested in the artistic loot of Glasgow industrialists. When Peter drove off in the morning Duncan waved to him from the door and then turned back into the bothie. To the word-processor, no doubt, which he was close to mastering.

To visit Glasgow for Peter, the east-coaster, was to explore an unfamiliar city, site of political legend and folk history, where by the dead quays a giant hammer-head was now merely a massive sculpture, a piece of industrial archeology. In a museum

74

a group of tourists wandered through elegant rooms furnished with delicate spindly furniture among which he recognised the wardrobe and dressing-table in his parents' bedroom, purchased in that other world and time before the first Great War. He bought his ribbons, looked in a couple of bookshops, had tea in a tea-room with scones and sticky cakes that brought back memories of shopping trips with his mother, and drove back quietly along the motorway towards the hills which showed their peaks to the north.

As he came slowly down the gravel drive he saw them, sitting side by side on the jetty, their feet dangling over the water. They were smoking, passing a joint to and fro. She was listening with her face towards the land; Duncan was talking hard. When she saw the car she raised her hand to wave and Duncan looked round for a moment then turned away without a greeting.

'Hi', she said when Peter came down towards the water's edge, 'I was passing and thought I'd look in. Duncan here kept me from being bored.' Would she like to come in? Have a drink or a coffee? Peter asked. 'Just for a minute though,' she said. It was getting late and she had to get back to Glasgow. She was giving Duncan a lift. Over her head Duncan looked straight at Peter and smirked.

In the house Peter busied himself making coffee in the kitchen and strained to catch the sound of her voice, but all he could hear was Duncan's steady drone, her occasional laugh. He was, he recognised with considerable astonishment, prey to jealousy and frustration such as he had not experienced for many years. By the time the coffee was ready he had mastered himself sufficiently to go through the ritual of hospitality, which was soon over. Peter watched as Lucy got into her gear.

By the time she had zipped up her leather jacket and Duncan had picked up his canvas holdall from the bothie door, he was collected enough to produce appropriately neutral formulae, saying to Duncan that he expected he'd see him again one of these days and to Lucy, 'Take care,' – which she might read as she wished.

'You too,' she said with a smile which was probably merely

polite. Then she drew her helmet over her head and kicked the motor. Duncan got up behind her with his holdall in his lap and put his arms round her waist. She opened the throttle and they were off. At the bend Duncan gave what could only be a mocking wave. They disappeared up the avenue, with a change of gear and a new note from the engine, towards the gatehouse where Garlinski no doubt would mentally record their departure and draw his own conclusions. 'Shit,' said Peter out loud. He walked down to the loch got into the yacht, ran up the sail, and reached far out across the water.

Propp says the villain appears twice during the course of the action. First he makes a sudden appearance from outside and when he departs takes away with him a magical agent belonging to the hero – 'the object of seizure fluctuates to an enormous degree' – and then disappears. It would be interesting to guess which, if any, of Peter's possessions Duncan (if he is indeed the villain) might have purloined. Propp has nothing to say about the young woman who spirits Duncan away. She could, of course, be the princess whom the hero marries in the end, thus winning a throne and her virginity. You may like to speculate on the probability of such an outcome. You may on the other hand dismiss it on the grounds that she is hardly likely to be a virgin.

Peter knew of the fantasies of jealousy and how they are spun from when he had been in love with, indeed infatuated with Orna. In those days when she first came to London and they were not yet 'together' he had worked on scenarios of revenge for being slighted, jilted, undervalued, neglected – the litany of self-pity was endless – scenarios he had run and re-run in his mind, improved, elaborated in a process that was uncomfortably close to a writer's daydreaming. Thus, when Orna one day announced that she had half-promised to go on a trip to France with a TV scriptwriter, he imagined himself pouring sugar into his rival's petrol tank so that the whole engine gummed up and the car with the guilty (why *guilty*?) couple inside, complete with bag and baggage, came to a humiliating halt among hooting buses and taxis – or, better still, just as they were driving up the gangway on to the cross-Channel ferry.

Even more satisfying was the scenario of an encounter at a party where words were exchanged and he (Peter) threw his rival (notoriously not an athletic type) over his shoulder with a cunning judo hold. Not that Peter knew anything about judo, so maybe it had better be a throw he had learned all those years ago when his rival was still at prep school and he (Peter) had been training in unarmed combat for special operations; but the point was that (in his daydreaming at least) the matter was settled once and for all.

Later – when they *were* together – Orna had coaxed him into relating his fantasies and rolled about in bed laughing; but there was also the reality of the day, not long after she announced she was going back to Israel when he had smashed chairs and mirrors while Orna stood sadly in a corner and let his fury expend itself. Her last words as she left for the airport with Yoram had been: 'I think you should see someone before you do someone an injury.'

He had 'seen someone' and believed he had progressed a little towards a wiser conduct of his emotions since those days of infantile rages and macho imaginings; or perhaps it had merely been a question of age, of maturity as people say. But now, as the boat reached out towards the centre of the loch and he thought of the pair sitting on the pier chatting quietly, sharing more than the joint – or so it had seemed to him – he had to admit to serious doubts about the permanence of his cure, the famous talking cure; which was why, as the loch darkened and he turned the boat's head round towards where the lights had come on in the Big House, curiously handsome in the dusk with its Gothic air, its make-believe battlements, absurd turrets, phoney crenellations and Scottish baronial towers, there ran through his mind certain insistent queries. Where were they now? Why had she offered Duncan a lift? Duncan who was not only personable but thirty years younger than himself, who could turn on the charm – had indeed had once propositioned Anna – and had a penchant (for all his Marxism-Leninism) for delicate upper-class girls on whom he depended for subventions and the frisson of sexual contact with class enemies he despised and would in due course abandon abruptly, brutally, to punish them for being what they were.

Peter dropped the sail and let the boat lose way until it came alongside the jetty, tied it up in the last pale light and went into the cottage. He stood at his table for a moment debating whether to switch on his word-processor. It was then that he became aware that something was missing: his favourite coloured glass marble. In a fury he picked up the remainder and threw them at the wall.

It will depend on your age whether or not you accept as plausible this picture of jealousy. Young, you may optimistically imagine that, with age, life – emotional life that is – becomes easier. All passion spent and all that shit, as Duncan might say. If you do, bear in mind Goethe at the age of seventy-three consulting his doctor on the matter, enlisting the help of his patron, the Duke of Weimar (with whom in their young days he had galloped about the ducal territories in search of sexual adventures), to further his suit with a nineteen-year-old girl, then making a formal proposal of marriage to her embarrassed parents and as he drives off, rejected, in his travelling coach, composing verses to express his pain that the gods, who had blessed him so greatly in life, had brought him 'to those lips so rich in blessing' only (so he wrote) 'to tear me from them to my destruction.'

Which might lead one to wonder about 'love', whatever that word may signify; its nature, its impermanence, its destructive quality as a devouring selfishness which lulls its victims with a show of kindness and affection; about the extent to which it is a self-centred need, about the possibility that it is merely a social construct, defined in terms of age and heterosexuality, which we incorporate in our psyches in childhood and childishly apply to certain relationships for the rest of our lives.

It was late when he went to bed. In the meantime to overcome his rage he had written steadily, losing himself in his Andromeda fantasy in which Lucy/Lucinda had come to merge with the young woman called Catriona.

The friendship between the two women had begun during just such a solar flare as the Commission's forecasters were predicting. At such times when the risks for energetic particle radiation were high – up almost to the danger limit of 200 rem – the women of the colony were required to take shelter in special accommodation to reduce the risk of acute body doses leading to sterility, although why that should worry the authorities puzzled many of them; for only a handful of women had been specially designated as genetically suitable for 'the replacement of human resources'. When necessary they would be impregnated with frozen sperm from the Founding Fathers.

The solar flare lasted two weeks. Catriona found herself in the company of a young women, dark haired and dark complexioned, who displayed a capacity for laughter and a certain mocking disrespect for authority. Together they played at backgammon and chess and draughts, not against computers, as was the normal practice, but against each other; laughing, pretending to quarrel, eating together and choosing to share a sleeping space.

It was on the second week that Isabel said as they showered together: 'You haven't said anything about my colouring.'

'Why should I?' was Catriona's reply. 'You must have been checked out before they let you on the space shuttle to Andromeda. So you're dark. I'm ginger. What difference does it make?'

Later, as they lay under the coverlet in Isabel's living-space, feeling the warmth grow, holding hands, cuddling together, Isabel said, 'My mother was from the *favelas*. Her name was Alita. Ever heard of her?'

'Yes,' said Catriona, and remembered how even in the

institution where she had been reared stories had circulated, whispered, embroidered, officially denied, only half-understood by a young and lonely child, of a woman called Alita, soothsayer, reader of hands and cards, who had used her skills to gather precious intelligence about the clans, their arsenals and treasure houses. Some of this, the whispers said, she had acquired by taking into her bed young and impressionable guards or men from the elite of the clans who came to her for her magic and the sexual skills with which she bound them to her. There was a story that she had had a child by one of them before the great failed rising of the 2060s after which she was captured and then publicly and barbarously executed. But how much was truth and how much legend Catriona confessed she did not know.

Stories, most of them, Isabel explained, encouraged to make Alita into some sort of evil witch with sexual powers no men could withstand – victims of an irresistible natural force. Like the young man from one of the clans who fathered her child, a deviant who had cut himself off from his roots, and thrown up a research post in astrophysics to work in the *favelas*, organising protest, deeply involved in planning the great revolt of which Alita was the political leader. Arrested along with her he had 'disappeared' to avoid the embarrassment of even a sham trial.

'He was my father,' said Isabel.

A young woman, rich, lonely in a dynastic marriage, childless, had adopted his year-old child and brought it up as her own. So Isabel had grown up in a closely guarded villa with its electric fence, its swimming pool, its patrolling sentries with their dogs, and the bullet-proof limousine that took her to school by a route that skirted the *favelas*, where she remembered seeing scrawled on the side of the shanties the strange name Alita. Once it had even appeared on the walls of a villa opposite her own home only to be quickly scrubbed out and painted over. It was her nanny, an old family retainer and herself a woman from the *favelas*, who, looking at the girl's growing body, claimed her as one of her own people. It was from her that she received her secret name of Alita.

By the time the solar wind had fallen and the authorities deemed it safe for the women to emerge Catriona and Isabel had laid a sure basis of trust and affection on which to continue the discussions they had begun quietly in bed together and now pursued in low voices as they strolled among the rills of the hydroponics laboratory, walked together to hand in their washing to the communal laundry and be issued with fresh overalls, underwear and bed-linen, or wherever there were least likely to be listening devices. What they questioned over the weeks and months were matters fundamental to the nature and running of Andromeda.

Thus, why, although women's skills as high-grade technicians were recognised and there were no discrepancies in the levels of their social wages compared to men, yet were there only two women on the council of the Control Commission? Why were women inseminated only with the seed of the Founding Fathers? Why could they not choose their own partners if they were allowed to become pregnant? Why were relations between members of the same sex severely forbidden by the authorities, chief among them the priests who traditionally had a strong voice in the Commission? Was it right that a scapegoat should each year die for the good of the people, as the priest put it during the ceremony that preceded the extrusion of the victim? Must the community be run on lines that denied to most of its members any say in the pattern of their sexual behaviour, of their lives and the social structure in which they lived them? Was it true that evidence had been picked up of attempts to found other colonies on Andromeda? Who was behind them? Was it inevitable, as the authorities suggested, that any other settlement must be hostile and therefore resisted and if necessary destroyed? Was there no possibility of peaceful cooperation between different groups on the planet? What was to be the fate of the sub-class in the *favelas* if the decision were taken by the clans to abandon Planet Earth? Dangerous questions, to be spoken of quietly and not discussed with others unless one was very sure of where they stood.

It was some considerable time after the solar storm had passed

– an interval in which the two women had become used to meeting regularly for sport, at meals and to talk in quiet, dead corners – before Isabel revealed that her work (she was attached to the communications centre of the colony) involved monitoring transmissions from Planet Earth. Recently there had been very heavy traffic to and from Earth in the colony's most secret code. There was no doubt in her mind that there was some sort of a crisis. It could merely be to do with the launch of the spacecraft due on Andromeda in the next few months. That was always an operation surrounded by secrecy and security. But it could be that rumours of a landing by 'intruders' had some foundation. In which case the heavy signals traffic pointed to a crisis – an emergency. She had a woman friend in the deciphering department who might be prepared to talk.


He was still writing when he thought he heard the sound of wheels and then of footsteps on the stones outside the bothie. There came the unmistakeable slight noise of metal scraping against the outside wall. A couple of steps took someone up to the door to knock. When he opened it was with a sensation of joy that he saw Lucy standing in the light from the room, taking off her helmet and brushing drops of rain from her gear. Of course she could come in – no she wasn't disturbing him – did she want a coffee, a drink? She settled for a whisky. He said, 'Cheers,' and waited for her to speak.

'He's quite a character, Duncan,' she began. 'Look what he gave me,' she went on and produced from her jacket pocket the bright coloured glass marble. 'Isn't it beautiful?'

'Yes,' said Peter, 'he pinched it from me,' and burst out laughing. Lucy/Lucinda apologised, protested she hadn't known. Finally she fell laughing herself. 'Very significant, a therapist would say. Tell me – why do you put up with him? Are you a masochist or something?'

'I put up with him, I suppose,' said Peter, 'because I know what makes him tick. The weight of an ideology that says you have to excel or be classed as a failure. Drummed into him by his

82

parents. By his teachers. So he takes his revenge. He's the artisan of his own defeats. What they call a failure neurosis.'

'Well, he's at least interesting. Not a wimp, shall we say.'

'I think,' said Peter, 'he's looking for a fight – in general, I mean. A sword for hire, you might say. The Scots were always great mercenaries.'

There was a long pause during which Lucy rolled the marble to and fro in her hand reflectively before laying it down. 'What makes you think that?' she asked.

'Look at him. Very macho,' said Peter, 'totally unreconstructed. Politically charged. No place to go.'

Lucy looked at him seriously. 'I see,' she said thoughtfully; then with a change of tone went on, 'In Glasgow he insisted on taking me to a pub and proceeded to get very drunk and very argumentative. Eventually he got into a fight over whether someone called John Maclean had been a Bolshevik or not. That was when I slipped away and drove back. I freewheeled past the gatehouse and down the drive. So here I am. Can you put me up?'

From the motorcycle she brought in a travelling bag and going into the back of the house changed into slacks. 'I suppose I could have gone up to the House. But it's late and they go to bed at sundown more or less. To save electricity. Very Scottish. I'm sorry. Is that racist? But it's true. He can be so mean – my uncle. And then I'm not sure I want to repeat the experience of my last visit.' She looked at Peter as if expecting him to question her but he said nothing.

Over supper she talked about how she had used to come and visit Aunt Clotilde. 'She wasn't really an aunt but what else could one call her – it was all too complicated. She always spoke French to me. She was a terrible snob really – so proud of her accent – she came from the Île de France and thought they didn't talk proper French anywhere else; certainly not in Paris. And then she had these ideas about how to dress. A young woman must be always be *bien chaussée, bien gantée* and then she could get away with a dress or suit that wasn't perhaps *de première qualité*. Can you imagine – in the seventies!' All this so that one could find *un bon parti*, settle down and be a good wife and mother.

Grizelle? Aunt Grizelle had been away a lot, in various nursing-homes. When Lucy was about fifteen Grizelle had actually been there most of the summer. One morning she had come looking for Lucy and taking her by the hand had drawn her into a dark corner under the main staircase where she began to whisper in her ear some urgent, incoherent, incomprehensible warning. Lucy was frightened because Grizelle was holding her very tightly by the wrist and she didn't like the way her warm breath tickled her ear. She tried to break away but Grizelle told her not to be stupid and listen. At that moment the Major had come out of his study and caught sight of the pair of them in their corner. He came up, told them to stop this whispering and ordered Grizelle to get back to her room. Lucy should pay no attention to such silly behaviour. Pay no attention at all and let him know if it ever happened again.

Next day the Major had driven away with Grizelle, who did not return. So in a way it had been rather lonely for a young girl to spend long stretches of her holidays in the Big House; yet it had been a sadness when Aunt Clotilde went back to a dilapidated château in the Île de France with amazing plumbing and eccentric electric fittings to die quite soon. Of what? No one seemed to know or perhaps didn't want to say. So there had been no *bon parti*. After her aunt's death she had stopped coming till now: a kind of sentimental pilgrimage to Lochmore. But maybe sentimental pilgrimages weren't a good idea.

Peter assented and wondered as he watched the play of her features what sort of *parti* she had made on her own. Or rather what sort of partners she had chosen for herself in the fifteen or so years since her aunt attempted to prepare her for the marriage market. In the silence that had fallen he wondered where the conversation was heading or indeed why she should have come back for shelter.

It was with a sharp look that she suddenly asked how long he had known the Major. He explained.

She considered for a minute and then asked; 'Have you been

84

on a conducted tour of the House? There's a place called the shrine. The sword his father wore when he was commissioned, his own sword. I didn't know they still had swords. Did you? A plaque with their regimental badges. Medals. Photos of himself in regimentals, in mess dress, buttoned up to the chin. In baggy shorts. North Africa, I think he said. Reviewing troops with the Queen Mum and with Queenie. Regimental groups. Boring,' she said. She paused and inconsequentially, as it seemed to Peter, asked: 'Have you ever heard of *les menus plaisirs?*'

Did she mean historically? Peter asked, falsely naïve.

She shook her head.

Yes, he admitted he had heard of them and felt something like a change of gear in their dialogue. The Major, had used the expression, he added, but hadn't had time to explain it.

She laughed, said Peter was very canny – was that the right word? – and asked what he thought the Major meant?

Peter considered for a few seconds and said it seemed to him that they might cover a number of activities.

'Such as?'

'Such as voyeurism. Watching young women on yachts through field glasses.'

'Anything else?' Peter hesitated before venturing a further move in the game they had seemingly begun. Said at last that if he added anything to the list, it would be pure speculation, which might say more about him than it did about the Major. If she saw what he meant. Lucy laughed again and said she had a pretty fair idea. From this point on, Peter felt, their talk and what lay behind it might take unexpected directions, confront them with surprises.

'The other evening,' she said, 'after dinner, Grizelle got up from the table – you know how she does – like a very well-bred little girl. It makes me so angry – no, not angry, sad to see a grown woman carry on like that. She was hardly got out of the room when my uncle asked if I'd like to go next door into the drawing room. All leather sofas and leather easy chairs. Turkish carpets and a smell of tobacco. Garlinski brought in the port and whisky and was dismissed. I had a glass of port and then I said I though I'd better get back to the bothie and not keep you up. But he insisted I couldn't go without a glass for the road. He used some extraordinary word for it –'

'A *deoch an dorris*,' said Peter. 'Gaelic for one for the road.'

She nodded. 'That sounds right. Quite suddenly he said he had a favour to ask of me. So, innocent like, I asked what it was. Do you know what he did? He actually got down on all fours and said would I mind sitting on his back while he took a turn or two round the table. Said if I really liked having something between my legs this was my big chance. Or was that all talk on my part?'

'So?' said Peter.

'So I didn't quite know what to do – or say. Did I just burst out laughing? Did I tell him to be a big boy and stop playing silly games? Did I tell him off for putting this ridiculous role on to me? In the end I simply held out my hand, helped him to his feet, thanked him for the dinner and said I'd let myself out. Can you understand it?'


Peter could remember sledging in the fields outside the town and how as he lay belly-down on his toboggan a girl from his class came and sat astride his back. The feel of her bones and muscles. Her warmth and softness. The excitement and con-fusion that landed them both in a heap in the snow at the bottom of the hill. It had been an experience repeated over and over in the gathering dusk of mid-January. Then they had gone chastely home, dragging the toboggan behind them along the windy streets of the town, where the powdered snow whirled at draughty corners. She left him casually at the end of the road where his father had built the new bungalow, symbol of his status in the community as editor of the weekly paper, with its central heating and wide windows behind which he now stood and watched his son's return.

'Who was that girl you were with? Don't tell me, I know her. And I know her family. From that housing estate. She's not the kind of girl you should be seen with. There will be no more gallivanting about with girls, do you understand?'

The gallivanting had come later but he could still remember the girl's name. Jeannie Wilson.

He said nothing of all this, being too intent on following the way their relationship – their acquaintance, if relationship was too strong a word – might be changing, becoming more intimate as they discussed the nature of pleasure. So he found himself saying; 'I can understand that he gets some sort of erotic buzz out of it. That's not terrible in itself. But I'd be worried – if I were him – if that was the only thing that gave me a buzz.'

'You mean an erection?'

He admitted this as a possible reading but not a necessary one. Lucy laughed and said that was a very academic way of putting it. Peter said he was, after all, an academic of sorts. If she wanted an academic explanation he'd say that it was a clear case of a fixation – the persistence of an anachronistic sexual trait whose origins can be traced back to some specific occasion in the sexual life of the subject's childhood. Wow, she said, that was a mouthful. Some people, he believed, Peter continued, were turned on by rubber aprons because they reminded them of being bathed by Nanny.

'What about you? Have you a fixation?' she asked teasingly.

He said he thought sexual behaviour was very complicated and compounded of many things – some derived from far back – but a fixation, as he understood it, was when one got stuck at some infantile stage.

'What about leather gear?' she asked. 'Does that turn you on?'

'You asked me the same question – in a sort of a way – when we met. I don't think so. Anyway it doesn't strike me as odd, the gear I mean; it's very practical. I think I prefer you in slacks though. But I'm not fussy – as they say.'

Did he really mean he found nothing – but nothing – erotic?

He thought for a few seconds before saying; 'The skin on a woman's leg just above the top of her stockings. The ante-chamber to sex, you might say. It stirs my tactile imagination.'

'Some people are easily pleased,' she said and laughed. There was a silence. 'I think I'll just bring the bike in,' she said. Peter made no objection so she wheeled it in and placed it in front of the window. Together they pulled out the bed. When he said goodnight she kissed him lightly on the lips.

Like Peter lying in bed and looking back over the evening, you may be wondering about Lucinda, her background (her class origins are fairly obvious), her profession (if she has one), her *curriculum vitae*, which should include more than just her schooling and further education (if any), her emotional life, attachments, marriages, children, present status, sexuality. A number of possibilities present themselves, all of them open to permutations and combinations:

1. She is the only daughter of a UN diplomat. Has been to a series of expensive schools – including a finishing school in Switzerland – where she learned little except good manners, tennis and self-assurance. Shortly after leaving school she was briefly married to a merchant banker who was, to quote her considered judgment, 'an upper-class twit'. Is now divorced and living on alimony
2. She is the only girl in a large and disorderly family. Her father, a television producer, never ceased to lament that she was not a boy although she could for instance run, swim and climb trees as well as any of her three brothers. Using a Christmas present of a cheque from her French 'aunt' (who was married to a Scottish landowner) she acquired a secondhand motorbike the moment she could legally do so and, androgynous in leather gear, rode all over the Home Counties. When the girl was sixteen her father abandoned her mother – who had the French connections – for a plump, white-skinned, red-headed actress. Leaving home, the girl went to art school and took up photography, working in a successful commercial studio in London. She has had a number of relationships with men and with women but does not see why she should define her sexuality

**3.** She is the daughter of a single-parent mother who conceived and bore her as an act of defiance aimed at her straight-laced, right-minded parents, strict Catholics with French connections on her father's side. She went to a comprehensive school. She does not know who her father was/is. She has a tendency to fall for stronger or older men (the two are not necessarily identical). She has been a model. Has had bit parts in a couple of art films. What she has learned of life has made her a determined feminist. She had a Palestinian boyfriend who two years ago disappeared without trial into an Israeli concentration camp deep in the Negev: Ansar 3 (Ansar 1 and 2 being already full). Through him she has entered the world of couriers, of secret rendezvous, of dangerous enterprises, the world of the resistance

It is not easy to decide which life-story to choose. All three are commonplace in our society – or at least in certain parts of it. You may also like to ask yourselves why it was that she did not tell Peter a detail which she suppressed either deliberately or unconsciously.

It was this: when Grizelle rose from the table that evening she had said goodnight in a voice which was slightly high-pitched and like a child's. At the door she had lingered silently for a moment, looked fixedly at Lucy/Lucinda and shaken her head, laying her finger on her lips in a gesture Lucy/Lucinda remembered from years before. The Major had looked round suddenly in her direction but the door had closed behind her and she disappeared.

Did Lucy suppress this detail because she felt it to be merely another redundant manifestation of Grizelle's oddness, because she did not know how to read it or because she could now read it for what it was: a fleeting reference to that urgent whispered message under the stairs years before – a conspiratorial exchange between two women from which men were excluded, a warning of danger?

★

It was Sunday, so Peter imagined Lucy – which was how he now thought of her – might wish to lie long. They had in any case sat up till very late. So he lay and had thoughts about age and death which he tried to banish by reading about the lady with the deep cleavage, who had progressed to Hollywood where she was about to be bedded by a young stud; as he read his hand strayed to the spot on his chest where there was an itch that could, he told himself, be mere hypochondria, auto-suggestion. From next door there was no sound. Even if she had left as secretly as she had come he would still have heard the scrape of metal on the wall as she took the bike and the rustle of the gravel beneath the tyres. When his watch showed eleven he decided to get up and make coffee. She was standing at the window wrapped in a towel and looking out at the loch which was barely ruffled by a breeze from the north. They exchanged greetings like a couple of established friends, arranged that he should shower first and then make breakfast.

Later, on the loch, she took over the boat confidently and skilfully and he crewed as they sailed before the wind far up past island of the burial ground with its ruined chapel and slanting gravestones. On one side a road busy with Sunday traffic skirted the regimented conifers of the Forestry Commission; here and there on parking places above the loch middle-aged couples sat in their cars, read the papers, opened thermos flasks and munched sandwiches. On the other side the trees gave way to moorland where sheep moved haphazardly over the face of the hillside and broke from time to time into undulating flurries that settled again when the danger real or imaginary had passed. Lucy handed Peter the helm and took her camera, an old 35mm SLR Nikon, out of its case. Handling it with remarkable dexterity, she took shots of the blackfaced sheep and the Sunday motorists, of Peter screwing his eyes against the sun and wind. Behind him a rainbow leapt across the hills. He handed back the tiller and she laughed with pleasure.

'I haven't sailed like this,' she said, 'since I was at school in Switzerland; there was a lake and we had a sailing instructor. It's the next best thing to riding a bike. That was when my old man was in the big money. Lighting cameraman on all the big commercials. Features. His mother was French. From a very grand family with some sort of title but not much cash. And he wanted me to learn French properly.'

Hence Aunt Clotilde, thought Peter, and wondered how much more he might learn. But on their way back from the top of the loch they had to beat their way against the wind and were too busy to talk. When they were making fast Peter glanced up at the Big House and believed he could make out the Major on the top of the steps watching them through his field-glasses. He nudged Lucy's arm.

She followed his glance and smiled. 'I wonder what he'll say when he sees that I'm back in the bothie. But it was his idea in the first place to ask you to put me up – not yours or mine. So he can like it or lump it. I bet he's wondering where the bike is.' So it had been with some mischief in mind, some malice afore-thought, that she had wheeled it in to where it stood inside the bothie.

Peter lit the fire, blowing on the sticks till they caught. As the flames flickered up through the dry wood and cones Lucy held her hands to the warmth. The smoke, said Peter, would bring the Major strolling down with his dog to see what was afoot. But he did not come, nor did Garlinski, who was, said Lucy, not a bad old stick and had been nice to her when she used to come to visit her aunt – taking her out in the boat, letting her fish from the jetty.

But what was Peter doing here, she wanted to know. He prevaricated. It was quite complicated: on one level it was perhaps a return to the country of his origins to see what it felt like; whether he could ever live there; on another, quite simply a chance of peace and quiet. To do what? To write. Originally to write a boring academic book. Now, he was afraid, he had got into SF. Science Fiction. She was surprised at this for he didn't, in her opinion, look like an SF freak. She had had a boyfriend who was one once. At art school. Into UFO's and those funny circular patches in the middle of cornfields – and ley lines of course. Microbiotics and photographs of ectoplasm, whatever that was. Maybe it was her father's French background but she hadn't been able to live with all that shit.

What had she studied at art school? Photography. Followed by a number of jobs: modelling for art classes in – surprise surprise – Peter's college, for instance, until she was asked whether she'd like to be assistant in a Hampstead photographic studio run by a nice but not very business-like gay who had known her father for ages. Photographing weddings was the bread-and-butter of the place. And portraits, of course. Flattering pictures of children, icons of women for the exchange and mart of marriage, portraits of vain old men. But at least he wasn't continually wanting her to strip off and do glamour photography. Not like that colleague of Peter's – could he guess who it was? – who had propositioned her at a party and wanted her to pose for what sounded like a centrefold – split beaver, the lot – and then went off in a huff when she refused.

'Then I got married to an upper-class twit and gave it up. I was fed up with the whole business of manufacturing suitable images.' When her marriage broke up she had gone abroad for a bit. Met someone she had been very close to and travelled with him. 'Where? Oh, all over the place. The Middle East – here and there. Cyprus, for instance. When I came back I took photography up again. I had to live. But more on my own terms this time. Helping to run a photo gallery down in Cornwall.'

She stopped and looked out at the window where the sky was dark and overcast. From time to time the moon showed palely through a rift in the cloud. The lights had gone out in the Big House.

'We're not together any longer,' she said. 'Haven't been for more than two years.' She shivered a little and folded her arms across her breast as if to retain her body heat. He had come to stand behind her to look over her head at the night. He put an arm round her waist. She did not turn round nor did she seek to loosen his grasp. 'I'm cold all of a sudden,' she said. 'Will you cuddle me?' He got into bed beside her and found she was still wearing her pants. He accepted the signal and drew her back into his lap. She fell asleep quickly giving little deep breaths. Early in the morning she slipped out of bed. When she returned and came close to him for warmth he discovered that she was naked.

Electro-chemical energy passes between human bodies during sexual union. The male genitals are electrical on the exterior and magnetic within; the females are magnetic on the exterior and electric within.

So runs a commentary on Tantric Asana, which sees in sex – 'the bodily knot formed by man and woman in physical union' – a form of yoga. You may not feel you can accept it literally. But do you know a better description?

That day they spent in explorations. Explorations of each other's bodies, in the course of which he found on the inside of her thigh a little patch of rough skin and on her right arm, just below the shoulder, a delicate little pattern tattoed in indigo that reminded him of something, but of what he could not think. Her fingers and lips ran over his own black spot unheedingly. Later came explorations of parts, at least, of each other's pasts, each other's thoughts, feelings, tastes. Listening to her Peter became conscious of a deep sadness in her, of an area of silence she guarded carefully. He told her about Orna. An Israeli? she asked and he was aware of a perceptible distancing, a kind of withdrawal. Yes, he said, but not a Zionist. Ah, she said, and seemed to relax.

For his part Peter spoke about age and the increasing sense he had of time – its shortness – and its effects as he perceived them in his body and face. 'Sometimes,' he said, 'I see myself in a shop window or in a mirror when I'm not expecting it and wonder who this battered face belongs to and whose this ageing body is.'

At least, she said, he wasn't a woman and didn't have to confront the loss of youth on quite the same terms. 'Put it this way,' she said. 'Nobody would raise an eyebrow at seeing us together and knowing we are lovers. But if I were – what is it, sixty? All right sixty-four – and you were my age, imagine what they would say. You'd be my toy-boy. My stud. Fucking me for money or your keep or because of some extraordinary hang-up.' A mother-fixation, he suggested. 'I think the Oedipus complex and all that penis-envy stuff is a load of codswallop. Never mind. The point is that when I as a woman look in the mirror and see the little lines under my eyes and by the side of my mouth or see my breasts in a mirror and how they've changed I can't help imagining what I'll look like in twenty years. Post-menopausal. Dried out.' She was silent for a time then burst out laughing. 'What do you think the Major would say if he found us in bed together?' Peter surmised that the Major wouldn't really be so naïve as to think they had been shut up all day reading good books. But the chances were he'd be unable to resist the urge to try and find out.

In the event the Major first sent Garlinski as his emissary. He came in the early afternoon, knocking at the door and calling Peter's name, coming up to the kitchen window and peering in. The bedroom window was closely curtained. They lay under the duvet and giggled as the crunch of his feet retreated up the drive. In the evening it was the Major's turn to carry out a personal reconnaissance, knocking, calling, tapping on the window panes, rattling the door and then – to judge by the slight crinkling sound – pushing a note of some kind under the door. Lucy got out of bed and fetched it, unself-consciously naked. The note was written with a stubby pencil in characters rendered uneven by the grain of the wood of the door against which the Major had held the paper. 'Major Campbell's compliments and would Mr Sinclair be so good as to look in at the Big House at his earliest convenience to discuss a matter of some urgency concerning his tenancy of the bothie.'

'That', said Peter, 'is what one might call an ultimatum. But it can wait.' As she sat up in bed to read the note Peter laid a finger gently on her tattooed arm. 'I know,' he exclaimed, 'some Arab women have them. Tattoos like that,' and at once regretted it, for she slid down under the bedclothes as if to conceal the mark and turned her back to him. He felt her separateness and something else that might have been grief. It was some time before she turned to him again saying, 'I'm sorry. I can't explain. It's not your fault. I'm not cross. Just sad.' Then she drew him to her.

Early in the morning Lucy quietly wheeled the bike out on to the gravel. She was in her gear, booted and helmeted. She had produced a spare helmet and told Peter to put it on. The motor woke at the first kick; Peter mounted behind her with an arm round her waist and felt the tug and power of the machine as she accelerated up to the gatehouse, where Garlinski looked out sleepily too late to prevent their escape.

It was with some alarm that Peter felt the bike gather speed and lean into the curves on the road above the loch; gradually there came a feeling of security as he surrendered to her skill, learned to adjust to the tug of gravity and the sinuous movement of the bike past scree-covered hillsides, over humped bridges that made a little void in his stomach, along roads where the white markings unreeled for miles beneath them until they came to a stop and looked out to the dark outlines of islands scattered over the sea.

They ate tea and cream scones in a little restaurant which had once been a crofter's house. When they came in there was a moment of silence as the families on a day's outing to the West Coast, the ladies in brown and blue hats, the men in blazers and sports jackets, tried to locate, to identify the newcomers: Lucy/Lucinda in her leather suit, helmet in hand; Peter in an anorak, his face red from the wind and sun of their journey. Then the conversation started up again; old enough to be her father, said the looks and – had they been able to hear them – the whispered remarks.

'Have you ever ridden pillion before?' asked Lucy.

'Yes,' he said. 'In Italy once. On the back of a military policeman's bike. The road was being dive-bombed. I was very frightened and very annoyed because my new regimental cap blew away. I'd got it when I was on leave. And it had cost a lot of money.'

'I think that's an extraordinary thing to say,' she remarked and turned away to order more tea. He wondered why? Because, she said, presumably people were getting killed – he could have got killed – and it just seemed crazy to worry about a cap.

'A nice new one,' he said, 'very smart.' He laughed. 'You see, one of the ways to endure war or anything as terrible as war – if there can be such a thing – is to disregard it. Or see it for the bloody farce it is. Not let it get you down.'

'Suppose you can't?'

'Can't what?'

'Disregard it – at least not in that stupid British prep school sort of way. I know people – ' She broke off and turned her head away. In her silence Peter wondered whether to persist but he feared to come up against the same withdrawal as he had experienced in bed. Said instead that war stories could be dreadfully boring. But it was difficult to get them out of one's mind. The great thing was not to sentimentalise or romanticise them.

'For years after the war there were people, you met them all over the place, living in the good old days. Using the old slang – to prang, to swan, to go for a Burton, and in some cases genuinely thinking of them as the best days of their lives.'

'That's what my father thought. And you?'

'Sometimes I have nightmares. Which means, I suppose, that I haven't been able to deal with some experiences. But that's no reason to bore other people with them.'

'What about the Major with that shrine of his? I bet he goes on and on.'

'Actually he's quite reticent. Merely says he was chewed up a bit at the Rhine crossing. Which I take to mean that he was wounded very badly. Hence the limp.'

'Yes, I've seen the limp. But it's still boys' stories. A way of still being boys. Not getting old, I suppose,' she said and called for the bill.

Sometimes the cruellest wounds, the most accurate thrusts are delivered unconsciously.

Garlinski was quick to intercept them at the gate. 'The Major would like to have a word with Mr Sinclair,' he said and, letting them through, watched how the bike accelerated away down the drive. At the Big House Lucy/Lucinda brought it to a stylish stop with a little skid in the gravel, just as she had when she first arrived. Together they went up the steps and rang the bell. Mrs

Garlinski opened the front door and the Major emerged from his office to meet them. He was clearly taken aback by Lucy/Lucinda's presence. He had wanted, he said sharply, to have a word with Mr Sinclair himself. Mr Sinclair would know what it was about; the terms of his tenancy. Peter agreed that the terms said no other tenants but he had been happy to take Lucy in – the use of the name was a provocation – at the Major's request and because she was after all a member of the Major's family. Since she seemed to like being there he had no problems about extending his hospitality for as long as she might wish to accept it.

The Major snorted. 'You know what I am on about – both of you. Don't you think it is all over the village. Goings-on at the bothie.'

'Le Petit Trianon, Aunt Clotilde used to call it,' said Lucy. 'Because that was where you put your *petites amies*, when they came to visit you. It goes with *les menus plaisirs*.'

For a moment it looked as if the Major might strike her; but she stood her ground and merely said; 'For your peace of mind and good name, let me tell you that I'm leaving in any case. Tomorrow morning. At first light, I think they say in the army.'

Peter heard the words with a sense of loss and surprise but said only; 'I am going to take it that my lease is still contractually in order and shall stay on until it has run out.'

In bed that night he asked; 'When did you decide to leave?'

'During the ride – this afternoon.'

'You sound as if you had something on your mind,' said Peter as neutrally as possible.

'Don't we all? Don't you?' she countered and went on, 'Nothing against you. Something about me. Do you understand? I don't suppose so. You're not to take it to heart. I have things to think about. Things to do. But if you're really thinking of going down to Italy give me an address. You never know.'

Imitating the animal world the gurus adopted postures from the unchanging actions of the animals such as monkeys (bandara).

Tantric Asana on sexual behaviour.

They say Hippocrates called orgasm a little epilepsy.
Someone (but who?) called it *la petite mort*.

La Volpaia
San Vito
Provincia di Siena
1 August 1987

Dear Peter

This is by way of being an interim communication to say
that I'm fascinated by your prognostications which are, if I
may say so, unexpectedly pessimistic coming from a person
whom I suspect of being somewhere on the Left. Someone
who believes in the millenium, in human happiness under a
benign government. A millenarist, in short. And I have to
say that I am a little disappointed by your account of the
settlement on Andromeda. Am I to take it that they do
nothing but a little market gardening? Where is their
material base? Come on – convince me!

I thought you might like to see a photograph of my
'foxes' den'. Do you recognise it by any chance? Let me
know if you are coming down later on. At present I have
rather a full house; my partner's adolescent children plus
their friends and lovers. Difficult to know which are which.
But in September there will be some interesting people you
might like to meet – not all wargames freaks!
All good wishes

Urizen

The Fisherman's Bothie
Lochmore
August 1987

Dear Urizen

The point is well taken! I had on the one hand too readily
accepted your wargame at a sand-table level and on the
other – for reasons which are partly clear to me, partly
veiled (repressed?) – been too involved in the human interest
story (as they say) of David and Catriona and the fate of
Isabel Dufy to think through the situation on

Andromeda. Of course the inhabitants of the colony are not just engaged in hydroponics. They have a more concrete economic infrastructure which is as follows:

The first space probes to explore Andromeda did so at the beginning of the new century. What the cameras and sensors revealed was that beneath the greyish-white covering of the surface, which rose from time to time in seasonal dust-storms (this had long been known from astronomical observations), there were important deposits of metals: copper, for instance, in great nodes and probably (beneath the surface) blackish masses of pitch-blende – uranite. By the 2030s these discoveries were confirmed by the mechanical probes landed from the new generation of load-carrying space-ships.

By the time the Founding Fathers made their first landing they did so in the knowledge that if they could maintain their foothold they were masters of an extraordinary source of mineral wealth at a moment when experts were already predicting that, even taking into account the mineral lodes in the deep ravines of the ocean beds, the resources of Tellus were severly depleted. As soon as the colony was set up and a human ecology established, prospectors went out in two-seater capsules like those later modified to serve as military scouting vehicles. The casualty rate in these early days had been high. (It was on such a prospecting expedition that David's parents were lost.) The actual mining was carried out partly by very small groups of settlers working in their life-support suits and partly by mechanical diggers and articulated vehicles remotely controlled from the colony.

About ten times a year – sometimes oftener if atmospheric conditions were good and the solar storms not too intense and if there was a window – a cargo ship from Tellus would land, be loaded and take off with the ores. You will remember that one of the reasons why the Founding Fathers ventured out to set up a colony on Andromeda was their rejection, on conservative religious grounds, of the way society had developed on Earth; there were cynics among the deviants in the clans, however, who argued that the real reasons lay elsewhere. The clan had felt its position and wealth challenged by the great drug merchants, against whom they had led a crusade on the grounds – said these same cynics – that there was some moral distinction between their own rapacity and that of the cocaine barons. This moral smoke-screen masked the shrewd calculation that on Andromeda they would found a strong alternative economic base: one which they would defend against all comers.

Clearly the colony had not severed all links with Tellus; they required agents on Earth. The whole business of shipping and of unloading the cargoes of ore at the sites in Arizona and the Gobi Desert were controlled by the same clan as had provided the crew for the Mayflower. It was they who recruited from the *favelas* the armed guards to ensure the security of the landing and launching sites; they who negotiated the sale of the precious metals and financed the building of the colony on Andromeda. All of which brings us back to our wargame and makes it clear why the news of another landing on Andromeda was received with alarm. It could only mean that control of the launching pads on Tellus had somehow been lost. It presaged a challenge to the colony's power and a threat to its economic security.

Many thanks for the photograph of La Volpaia. It looks terribly familiar – but then these medieval Tuscan peasant houses have a great family resemblance and the name isn't that uncommon. There must have been a lot of foxes' dens in Tuscany once upon a time. I think I'd need to see it on the ground before I could say with confidence that I remember it. What of the weather down your way? I recall the downpours that accompanied the great thunderstorms of August after which the vineyards were washed clean of dust and the red earth steamed in the sun. I am more and more tempted to come down in September when the grapes are ripe and so sweet that to eat them warm plucked from the vine is like an injection of energy.

I expect your letter setting out my opponent's next move should arrive any minute now. Incidentally, I have been meaning to ask – can one know who one's adversary is? Or is that something to which only you are privy? The question intrigues me.

Yours sincerely
Peter Sinclair

You may think it strange that, having posted his letter to Urizen, Peter Sinclair should have spent the rest of the day following Lucy/Lucinda's departure concocting his Andromeda story. You might have expected his thoughts and feelings to be

occupied by a sexual experience which was unexpected, probably disturbing, one which (we may conjecture) led him to
ponder on the nature of sexuality, its practices and its
ambiguities; for in some recesses of his mind he had already
begun to give Lucy/Lucinda a new name: Ariel, one that
encompassed her hatred of restraint of any kind, her sexual
ambivalences and her passion for speed. What, I think, one has
to bear in mind is that the writing of fiction can be less a direct
expression of feelings and experiences than a filter that
transmutes them, and, if necessary, blocks them off: a way of
coping.

You may also think it a manifestation of sexism that at a deep
level his thoughts centred on her sexuality and not on the
possible reasons for her reticences; that if he did wonder what
these things were that she had to think about, had to do, it was in
terms of sexual jealousy that involved this friend with whom she
was no longer together, whose travels with her he so envied.

You may legitimately wonder, too, what this says about my
own daydreaming. You will probably conclude that the old
Adam is even longer-lived than Methusalem.


Ever since the founding of the colony it had been the custom of
the Control Commission to limit moots – meetings of all the
inhabitants – to certain ritual moments: the anniversary of the
landing of the Founding Fathers, the choosing of the scapegoat
and an annual assembly, the proceedings of which were tightly
controlled, the debate stage-managed and the outcome the
unopposed ratification of decisions taken beforehand by the
Council. There were, it is true, religious festivals, but these were
conducted in a great bare chapel whereas the moots took place in
the open; that is to say, under the huge arch of the geodesic dome
that enclosed the colony. The services at these festivals were
highly formalised, conducted in archaic and largely unintelli-
gible language and attended by most of the two hundred odd
colonists because only illness or duties were accepted as excuses
for absence.

When, a couple of weeks after the extrusion of the young woman, a moot was announced at half-hourly intervals on the monitors sited in workshops and living-spaces throughout the colony, everyone knew some major announcement was imminent. The colonists mulled over the news quietly in the refectories, in the workshops, in living spaces and communal dormitories. But people were guarded in their comments, limiting themselves to harmless speculation about an out-of-season freight-ship with fresh supplies of plants and materials – clothes, for instance, and mail – or venturing at most to suggest the possibility that the colony's human resources were to be increased and a satellite colony established.

What few among the crowd that stood in the moot hall and watched the huge high definition monitors had expected was the announcement (made with all the formal trappings of religion, the pomp of military uniforms and a tone of voice reserved for exceptional moments in the colony's history) that Andromeda was threatened with invasion; that should the invaders land it was the firm intention of the Control Commission to defend the gains of the Founding Fathers. The invaders would be challenged and forced either to submit or accept the consequences. The announcement was made by an elderly white-haired man in a light-blue general's uniform – a figure seldom seen in the flesh or indeed on their monitor screens by the majority of the colonists. Not a cruel-looking man, indeed rather avuncular in his manner, although it was rumoured (and significantly there was no official contradiction of the rumour) that he stood for the application of the moral codes of the Founding Fathers in all their severity; which included extrusion.

The announcement ended with the singing of a tune that went to words in the archaic ritual language – words everyone knew by heart although they did not comprehend them. That most people could manage the first line but could only pretend to mouth what followed was something that older members of the colony like Peter Sinclair, the wargames instructor, deplored; they saw in it a sign that the old standards had been allowed to slip dangerously. So David merely moved his lips as he stood (it

102

was obligatory to stand to attention with one's hand on one's heart when the tune was played) and listened to the familiar sound. He had heard the announcement with a mixture of excitement and fear. As a scout he would be among the first to make contact with the invaders. How would he confront that moment? What would it be like to face the fire of the enemy's laser guns? What would it feel like to fire back? To kill and perhaps be killed?

He had a need to feel safe, to find a moment's escape in the floating oblivion of sex. But when he returned to the living-space where Catriona was already lying on their bunk she was distant, wished not closeness but discussion – after all, she was his co-pilot and would be asked to risk herself with him.

'You know the saying; when it comes to dying we're all equal,' she commented with a laugh. So she felt the need, indeed a duty to herself to analyse the situation, to canvass probabilities, to raise difficult questions.

Such as? he asked.

Such as: suppose these were not really invaders but friendly newcomers who wanted to share the wealth of Andromeda? Why should they believe the voice from the monitor screen? There were some people who had a different theory.

Like who? David asked.

Never mind. The question was: how did they know that man was telling the truth?

Why should he tell lies? asked David. Why should they doubt one of the oldest, most respected of the Founding Fathers?

She told him sharply to stop being naive and to use his intelligence.

It was one of their most bitter exchanges since they had been together. When Catriona lay down and, with an accustomed gesture denoting her imperative need to be alone, drew the bed-cover over her head, David walked out of the sleeping quarters and into the communal hall.

A girl was sitting there. He knew her from the hydroponics lab. They talked: she was excited, asked how he felt about going on a scouting mission – he was a scout, wasn't he? – then suggested that they see if they could book in at the recreational facilities. The excitement of mapping the unfamiliar contours of her body, the surprise at the unpredictability of her reactions to touch and the sudden violence of her desire, terminated in the brief shock of his orgasm, a convulsive therapy that would, he knew, be of limited duration.


In the days that followed Lucy's departure Peter kept to the bothie. If he had to go shopping then he was up early and back before the Major was stirring on the steps, surveying his domains, letting his dogs loose over the long grassy slope to the edge of the loch. Garlinski watched his comings and goings but made no attempt to stop him or to enter into conversation and limited himself to a greeting that was half-military and might have been half-mocking. The weather had turned wet with low clouds over the hills and sudden downpours that shattered the reflections in the waters of the loch. One morning, after a night of thunder, the little river that ran past the village suddenly rose and came roaring down in a bore. It was weather for sitting at the word-processor.

As he watched the screen light up he wondered whether he ought not to employ his (limited?) time with something more serious than wargames and SF but merely found himself wondering how bold Bert Brecht could ever have hoped with his dramatic technique of alienation (which was after all an appeal to reason) to stem the flood of irrationality, prejudice, false consciousness, utopian hopes and false expectations on which Fascism traded? Might he not have been better employed writing in the Aristotelean mode he scorned, appealing to people's emotions, to their ability to identify with the unreal but powerful characters of the stage and so perhaps to (tabu word) feel politically.

It was with perverse satisfaction and a certain irony that Peter proceeded to translate a piece by BB himself, in which he actually admitted the occasional efficacy of Aristotelean drama which purges (whatever that might mean) men and women by pity and fear. But as he worked at the German he could not entirely banish the doubt that had for some time been growing: that he was discussing questions that had been perhaps once revolutionary, but ones which were no longer interesting (in the sense of being obviously relevant); that there was a danger of being trapped in the thought patterns of another time. Of celebrating the assumptions that had evolved in the political and military struggle against Fascism and had seemed unproblematic and universally, eternally applicable.

It was a measure of his isolation that he could not easily think of anyone in his circle of acquaintance – was Lucy an acquaintance or did she belong in some other more intimate category? And in any case where did she stand politically? Was she indeed a political person? – with whom he could discuss his problem. Except Duncan, of course, who was himself a prey to simplistic arguments and conspiratorial theories. It was perhaps a function of age, this sense of loneliness, of the impossibility of sharing certain concerns, ideas, remembered experiences. If so, he decided, there was not much one could do but thole it. As one tholed a shrinking expectation of life itself.

> Thole: v. Now n. dial. or arch. (OE tholian = O. Fris
> tholia. OS tholon, OHG dolon, ON thola, Goth
> thulan, from IE \*tol–\*tel–\*tul as in L. tuli = I bore.)
> To bear, to submit with patience to, to bear or put up
> with, 'abide' or tolerate.
> > *Shorter Oxford English Dictionary*.

Dear Peter
Thanks for the postcard. This is the most boring one I could find. Isn't it amazing? Love Ariel. PS. I have doubts abut my new name. Have just read *The Tempest*. Prospero is a terrible old patriarch, don't you think?

Garlinski brought Lucy's postcard down from the lodge one dull, rainy day. No doubt it had been read, puzzled over, interpreted by Mrs Garlinski, perhaps reported by her with exaggerated casualness ('by the way, Major') as she brought the mail and the daily paper into the laird's office by the front door where he ate his solitary breakfast. Undated, monochrome, it showed a knoll with a flagstaff and a couple of park benches. The memorial flagstaff, St Keverne's, said the text. Peter laughed and stuck it up above the fireplace.

Over the next few days, as he laboured at his word-processor he would look up at the curious icon and reflect on its text. Was Ariel right? What had made him assume the role of Prospero? And who then was Caliban? Duncan? What rich veins the woman who once used to unravel his thoughts and dreams and fears in the talking cure would have found there, what intricate working and reworking of Shakespeare's text, what displacements, condensations and revisions, wish-fulfilments, elaborations, overdeterminations! And would have been shrewdly right in her analysis. But here by the lochside there was no one with whom he could pick over the ravelled skein and tease out the truths he hid from himself.

Apart from the postcard no other mail came: nothing from Urizen who must be waiting for the next move from Israel or Venezuela or wherever, nothing from Anna, not even the usual card from some Aegean island with a non-committal formula, a joke about her fellow holidaymakers.

Dear Ariel
    I accept your reservations about the role I have cast you in. But you must admit there are certain quite obvious resemblances on your side to that most swift and mercurial spirit and in me to the old magician, who is – as I am ready to admit – an unreconstructed colonist and patriarch (which I hope I may not be although in these matters men can be great deceivers of themselves and others). At all events, a role in which I hope you would not cast me irrevocably. What I keep asking myself are questions about Ariel's sexuality. Is Ariel male or female or both and does it matter? I have decided that it doesn't, but the question disturbs me, raises doubts about myself and my own

sexual responses that are uncomfortable and hard to accept.
When will you be this way again? When shall I see you? When
Prospero asked Ariel that same question he/she said: 'I drink
the air before me and return/ or ere your pulse beats twice.'
Sometimes I look out of the window and half-expect to see
you materialise there in your gear. No doubt to vanish just as
suddenly. But Prospero, to do him justice, has another good
line, which is: 'I shall miss thee/ But yet thou shalt have
freedom.' Send me another postcard. When I leave I'll let you
know my new address. Remembering.

P

To break the monotony he was diligent in transferring to his
word-processor the daydreams that came on these wet autumn
days when it was comfortable to walk and chancey to sail, for
the rain was driven across the water to spatter on his windows
by sudden gusts of wind that came down from the corries in the
hills across the water. Yet even here he was confronted with
problems for he was beginning to see that there was an
increasing divergence between his daydreams about Andromeda and the more limited requirements of Urizen's wargaming fantasies – one which might soon become irrecon-
cilable. But his dreams were too insistent to ignore. He could
only follow them, wherever they might lead.

When David returned to the living-space, Catriona had gone. It
was too early for her shift – unless there had been some change in
her roster that she had not told him about. He was not unduly
worried for she was a person who required a certain autonomy,
a freedom which he understood although he found it hard to
accept in practice. His own autonomous act in going to the
recreation facilities with the girl from the hydroponics lab was
one of a very few occasions when he had exercised the same
freedom. Perhaps she, too, had gone out to find a partner; if so
she would tell him later – for she was resolutely, relentlessly
honest in such matters – without revealing who it had been, on
the grounds that it was none of David's business. If he really

wanted to know, she had said in the past, he could always ask to see the records kept at the facilities; but David had preferred to remain ignorant.

What concerned him more at present was the fact that she appeared to have been in some way intimate with the young woman who had suffered extrusion. Now there were many innocent ways in which people could share their activities and interests, he, for instance, was on good terms with his fellow wargamers, but friendship did not go beyond the gaming sessions and a few drinks over which to discuss the results. But in Catriona's case there seemed to have been intimacy (sexual perhaps, which in this context was less important) that was potentially dangerous if it had led to the sharing of inadmissible doubts and the formulation of dangerous hypotheses.

The more he reflected on their last conversation the more anxious he became; for even within a partnership like theirs such thoughts were perilous and should be reported so that they might be eradicated by a course of well-tried therapies (with drugs if necessary) in the colony's hospital, which had long experience in dealing with the mental illnesses that inevitably arose from a way of life that was necessarily controlled and circumscribed. To report them was in the interest of everyone for, to take Catriona's case, if she expressed them publicly (which could mean in the hearing of one of the Commission's agents) she would lay herself open to the most serious penalties.

If it came to that, he reflected, he would himself be in danger for having deliberately failed to report her to the authorities as was, he could not deny it, his duty. How could he persuade any tribunal that he had not been aware of the way Catriona's mind had been working? He would have to confess that he had; but he could not bear the thought of denouncing her. There was too much between them of closeness, comfort, joy – shot through, admittedly, with moments of anger and disagreement, of pique and resentment and (on his part) of jealousy; but so far they had always overcome these moments so that there was, or had been, a certain trust between them not only in day to day life on Andromeda but on those occasions when, in their twin scout capsule, they went out over the ash-grey face of the planet, totally reliant on each other. So he must try to talk to her; persuade her to keep her thoughts to herself, although she would not be easily persuaded.

But what if she and the condemned woman had not been alone? Suppose there had been a network of such sceptics and doubters, questioning the wisdom of the Control Commission, undermining the security of the colony? It was not a side of life in the Colony that had interested him much in the past but he was aware from casual references, hints, suggestions from his fellow-workers in the hydroponics lab that the Commission had a highly efficient internal security system which was credited with sophisticated methods of surveillance, human and electronic, that allowed it to track down and locate any centres of disaffection, to intervene at an early stage and take prompt action.


Peter worked undisturbed. The Major he saw occasionally, standing at the top of the steps going up to the Big House, surveying the loch, but he kept himself to himself; Garlinski was about the place as usual, silent, greeting Peter with his half-military salute, unsmilingly remarking that it was 'grand weather for the ducks'. Peter began to hope that some sort of truce might have been declared between the Big House and the bothie and that the present calm might continue for the remaining weeks of his tenancy. On a couple of occasions he was surprised to see Grizelle come down to the edge of the loch and walk gingerly out on to the jetty. He had never before seen her outside the immediate precincts of the Big House. Once she merely stood on the shore and looked out over the water. Another time she sought out flat stones and sent them slithering over the surface of the loch with what looked like an old and practised skill. On each occasion either Garlinski or the Major himself soon came down after her and gently but firmly led her away.

On the fourth occasion a darkening of his window made Peter

turn to find her peering in with her hands on either side of her face, shielding her eyes. When he rose and went to the door she was already standing there. He did not need to invite her in for she slipped past him with a slight smile and slowly explored the space. Would she like a cup of tea? Of coffee? he asked. A drink? Whisky perhaps? She looked at him smilingly. There was a slight dusting of powder on her cheeks. Lipstick was awkwardly and approximately applied to her lips. For the first time he saw, through her faded looks, what she might have been like when she was a young girl running down to the water's edge to send flat stones skimming across the surface. There was something tentative, hesitant, as if she were afraid of breaching some rule of behaviour, of risking some punishment, about the way she inclined her neck; the motion with which she raised the curtain briefly to look into the back of the house; the gesture with which she picked up the glass of whisky he had poured for her and raised it to her lips.

'Cheers,' she said in a clear childish voice. They drank in silence. Peter invited her mutely to sit down but she shook her head. 'Lucinda?' she suddenly asked and looked round questioningly.

'Gone,' said Peter.

'Good,' said Grizelle. 'Such a nice girl.' She spoke no more but finished her whisky. As she set the glass down there was a knock at the door that made her look nervously round. It was the Major.

'Ah, there you are, Grizelle,' he said, 'we were wondering where you had got to.' He took her firmly by the arm and raised her from her chair. 'So sorry to interrupt,' he went on as if noticing Peter for the first time, 'but I think – if you don't mind – I'll take her back with me.'

All that day and the next Peter waited for some explanation on the Major's part – or perhaps some fresh interdiction on the lines of: 'You will kindly not entertain my sister and give her whisky in the middle of the morning.' But none came.

Instead as he walked up towards the village one afternoon, he was surprised to hear a car slow up behind him and the familiar braying voice say: 'Care for a lift?' At the road end the Major said, 'Well, this is where I take the Glasgow road. I expect you'll want the village.' Peter thanked him and got out. Before he drove off the Major leant over and said through the half-open door, 'I hope you didn't take it the wrong way – my coming in like that. Nice of you to look after her. It's just that I worry if she strays. It's not very easy sometimes. Anyway, enjoy your stay. Another three weeks, isn't it? You never know, the weather might change. Good day to you.'

Peter watched the car drive off and raised his hand in a ritual gesture, acknowledging that the olive branch had been extended, confirming that he accepted it.

When, the last weeks over, he packed, loaded his car and went up to the Big House to make his farewells there was a brief chat and a glass – a *deoch an dorris* – for the road. Yes, he said, he might very well come again. Would the Major remember him to his sister, at which the Major finished his glass and laid it down as if to say that they had taken long enough over their farewells. At the gate Garlinski waited, accepted a five pound tip and thanked him with a formal bow.


Now, says Propp, a new character enters the tale: this personage might be termed the donor, or more precisely the provider. It is through him that a magical agent comes into the hero's hands. Question: what will that magical agent be in these modern times when magic is devalued into mere trickery, the sleight-of-hand of the video editor, the illusions of the advertisers, the peddlers of the enchantments of consumerism? Perhaps the agent – whoever it may be – will also help the author out of an impasse; which is that he has come perilously near to effecting a closure – might, had he developed his fantasy about the Major's sister much further, have been led to insert here a death by drowning which he has stored in his word-processor and labelled 'Finis'.


The motorway was full of holiday cars, packed with children,

**111**

luggage, mattresses, dogs, toys. At a service station Peter collected a coffee and a sticky pastry; as he consumed them he pondered his route. He was in no special hurry. Could if he wanted veer west, skirt the Welsh marches until he struck a road to Cornwall; but he dismissed the idea, did not feel that he had the right to intrude on Ariel's untrammelled freedoms, was in any case fearful of presenting himself unannounced in her territory, where all sorts of surprises in the shape of boy or girlfriends might await him, like that friend she had met on those vague travels of hers in the Middle East and Cyprus. And what if Sycorax should prove to be there, completing the cast – the witch who had held Ariel prisoner for so many years? Did she exist as an aged aunt, a tyrannical mother, the mother superior of some neighbouring convent, a retired headmistress, a jealous nanny long retired but still tenacious in her attempts to supervise the details of her charge's life, or whoever owned and ran the photographer's gallery?

He decided not to risk the encounter, made his way resolutely out of the haze of muzak, smoke and petrol fumes, and drove south to that flat of his on the top floor of the block (grade II listed building, said the estate agents, mentioned by Pevsner) that leant towards the park like a toy liner made with a child's building bricks. At the porter's lodge he was greeted with the blend of subservience and insolence which the chief porter had cultivated over years of service in big houses and now, at the end of his working life, deployed in this caravanserai for widowers and widows, bachelors of both sexes, producers of television serials, writers of romantic novels, the occasional academic, a beautiful young man with no obvious livelihood and an equally good-looking young woman who was, said the porter with the suggestion of a leer, a model.

There was the usual pile of mail – gaudy trash mostly inviting him to indulge his greed, to win immense sums, to borrow money, to insure against old age, to buy a variety of useless, ugly knick-knacks, but no magical cures for fear or the black spot that inspired it. As he walked down the long impersonal corridor off which the little two-roomed flats opened, he was

112

already winnowing the rubbish from the genuine letters. Some bills. A tiresome letter from the Inland Revenue. From the College, notification of meeting of the Council, that cross-section of the Establishment. A letter from Italy. Typed. From the office of the mayor in a small town in Tuscany. He turned it to and fro in his hand and wondered where they had got his address. The text with all the formality of official Italian invited him to be present at the celebrations to mark the liberation of the town of San Vito to which he had in no small measure contributed. If he accepted he should get in touch with the London office of Alitalia, which would issue him with a return ticket. Naturally the Comune would provide him with suitable accommodation. They would be grateful if, in the event of his accepting, he would indicate whether he required a double or a single room.

A postcard: the image a piper on the ramparts of Edinburgh Castle; the text:

> Dear Peter
>    Thought you might like to do a semiotic analysis of this. Seriously though, how are you, you old reprobate? How is your sex/intellectual/cultural life? Have applied for a job with some phoney liberal Trust. Not a bad salary which I shall accept as a tiny redistribution of wealth. Gave your name as a reference. I don't care if you do mind.
>
> >                                 Fraternally,
> >                                 Duncan

The first time he saw San Vito sitting on its absurd hill was early one June morning. The plane had dropped him and his four companions accurately through the cold night air to land in a deep, secluded valley. By now it would be back at its base in Bari, where he had spent the last months learning the techniques of the saboteur, and working at his Italian, which was the rusty tool of a graduate in the history of art; but mention of it in an application for a transfer to more active service had been

**113**

sufficient – together with assiduous lobbying of acquaintances involved in special ops – to pluck him from the photographic interpretation unit where the army had stuck him on the basis, presumably, of his knowledge of the Italian painters of the Quattrocento.

What prompted his effort to break out of the no doubt important but often unexciting business of reading the black and white images, the verticals, the obliques, which the fliers' work had brought back from far behind the riverlines where the armies fought and bled, had been a feeling that although perfectly fit he was contributing in a very indirect way to the war against Fascism: a war in which he had enlisted out of deep political conviction. Added to that was the puritanical desire to escape from Naples, the Sodom and Gomorrah of the south, where the hospitals had more cases of VD than of wounds and the opera house with a fine sense of irony performed *Madame Butterfly* to audiences composed largely of US sailors. Beyond that again a trembling need, an obsessive urge, to learn how he would face combat and the possibility of death.

Four Italians had dropped with him for motives ranging from political commitment to the desire for revenge and the urge to kill. Now all five of them were at their immediate goal. In the chill mist that lay waist-deep in the valley bottom where they had dropped they had collected their parachutes and moved into the woods above. Having buried the parachutes they now sat in the undergrowth at the edge of the trees and looked across a landscape of vineyards, olive-trees and cornfields. Peter could see through his field-glasses the peasants yoking their steamy oxen beside the squarely built farmouses, and the girls, distaffs in hand, driving their sheep out to graze on the terraces under the vines. To the south a haze hung between them and San Vito.

It was strange and exciting to see a landscape, so familiar from aerial photos and from the large-scale maps in Bari, become concrete, in some ways familiar, in others oddly different; for what he had not been able to imagine in the stifling heat of the hut where the briefings were held over a mosaic of blown-up black and white photographs was the deep lush greenery of the little valleys, the thickness of the undergrowth, the way the vineyards rose in terraces of red soil on the hills that undulated towards San Vito. One by one he identified his landmarks: the church at San Gusme, the road junction at the hamlet called Le Tavernelle, the farmhouse of La Volpaia.

### La Volpaia
Beautiful and characteristic restored farmhouse transformed into a villa on a property rich in woods in the hills of Chianti between Siena (35 kms) and San Vito (10 kms), 2.5 km Le Tavernelle with foodshops. Wide view of the countryside. Perfect peace and quiet. Garden area. Swimming pool (14×4). Parking.

*Country Life* 1974

As he scanned the hills, focussing for a moment on a woman with a pail walking up the path to her well, he knew he was about to draw this rich and gentle landscape, these houses and their inhabitants, into a wargame plotted hundreds of miles away with chinagraph pencils on maps that were impersonal, uninhabited. Here, real blood would flow; for as he lifted his glasses to the summit of the hill in the distance beyond La Volpaia he could see, rising above a clump of trees, the aerial assembly of the radio station and signals centre it was his mission to destroy. As they sat they broke open their ration packs and breakfasted. On a road that ran dustily towards San Vito there was an occasional cloud as German trucks drove south towards the front.

Aldo, the stocky boy from the valley of the Po – expert in explosives, eager to avenge a partisan brother hanged by the Germans on a length of telephone wire – had gone off to scout. He reported that there were no Germans about, that the peasant girl he had spoken to had asked no questions, shown no surprise. But the whole neighbourhood would by nightfall know through its own networks, as the news passed from farm to farm, that there were strangers about. Which was nothing new. There was, said Aldo, no need to worry about the peasants. They were used to strangers, escaped prisoners-of-war, ex-soldiers heading back to their homes in the south, people who did not say their business and were not asked.

All day long they sat and watched the movements in the fields, the German traffic on the road, the allied planes high up trailing white threads of condensation through the sky, flying unchallenged, shaking the landscape with the drumming of their engines, bound for the cities and communication centres of the North. The long-range fighters swooped and danced on the flanks of the great formations. '*Dai*', said Aldo, '*dai* – give it to them!'

At dusk they moved back into the heart of the wood and under a rock made a bivouac and a cache for their supplies: the ammunition, the explosives, their Stens and one light machine-gun, their grenades. Then in the gathering dark, spangled with fireflies, Peter, with Aldo as bodyguard, walked through the fields past the farm at La Volpaia to the small villa – the summer home of a businessman from San Vito? – set at the end of an avenue of pines where there should be someone called Dario, who opened to them, warily, demanding passwords; then in the big bare room with high-back chairs ranged against the wall said he had begun to think they were never coming although there had been the coded message the night before on *La Voce di Londra*. He was middle-aged, thin, perhaps a lawyer or teacher, whose Italian was liquid, clear and intelligible after the dialect of Naples.

Peter thought he could hear someone moving about in the back of the house. Once, a child cried briefly and the man went to the door and called in a low voice, 'Maria!' There was the soft sound of feet on the tiled floor and a woman's voice stilling the child. The man shrugged impatiently, came back to the table on which Peter had spread out his maps and gave an appreciation of the situation; which was hardly as it had been described to him in Bari.

First of all there were at most twenty men on whom Dario

could count. Between them they could muster some shotguns and a few cartridges, a First World War rifle without ammunition, two revolvers and some explosive stolen from a lignite mine over towards San Vito. Some of them had been in the army in this war or that other one in 1914. As he understood it, said Dario with an ironical smile, their task was to harass the German lines of communication. Ambushes, sabotage of bridges, that sort of thing. He had even heard a whisper that they were to seize and hold the clump of houses at Le Tavernelle until such time as the allies dropped parachutists; which sounded like a suicide mission to him.

Peter listened and wondered who this man was, what had made him commit himself to this dangerous undertaking. Was he – the question could not be put or at least not now – a comrade, member of the same Party to which Peter owed his allegiance? How reliable were the rest of the outfit? Dario answered his unspoken question. The band was not like the big formations – the Garibaldi divisions – people said were active in the high Appennines, but they were all people – peasants, ex-soldiers, a couple of students, some youngsters, dodging conscription into Mussolini's tinpot army – who felt that something must be done if they were to look each other in the eye when they were free men once more. That was the important thing. The allies would get there in any case. There would be something called 'the Liberation', but a gesture – if nothing else – had to be made by people like himself who had political convictions and loyalties that had shown them the inside of the regime's prisons: some contribution to their own liberation.

'Right,' said Peter. 'the proposal is not that we hold the houses down here at Le Tavernelle but that we (a) destroy the radio station beyond La Volpaia as soon as possible and that we (b) harass German convoys moving along this road here.' He pointed to a defile far across country where, in a gorge, the hills crowded together a road and a stream that ran on down to the undulating country round San Vito.

Dario considered. 'If you attack the radar station there will be

**117**

reprisals. Ten Italians for every German killed. Houses burnt. Women and children slaughtered. You are sure it is worth it?'

Peter looked at his tired strained face. 'I have my orders,' he said.

'Right,' said the man. 'The main thing is to take as many Germans with one as possible.' Then he turned to the map and coolly, quietly, began to plan the attack.

Four weeks later when San Vito was liberated only Peter was still alive of the trio that had sat by the light of the acetylene lamp.

Dear Ariel
    I am off to Italy. You'll find me at this address if by any chance you are down that way in the next few weeks: La Volpaia, San Vito, Tuscany. The grapes will be ripe by then.

Ciao,
Prospero

## PART TWO
## Another Part of the Forest

From the white cloud-cover small irregular darker formations rose like stepping stones in a flood of foam. Peter sat in the Alitalia plane, watched the gentle shifting motion of the mists and felt safe, suspended apparently without movement in time and space, cut off from earth. His thoughts drifted into daydreaming in which the white floor of the clouds became one with the dust-covered face of Andromeda over which – if he chose one line of narrative – his hero and heroine would soon be flying in their scout-capsule, pushing forward to pinpoint, identify and perhaps challenge the strangers who had arrived on the planet. But he was undecided.

It was true that in his wargame he had described the two characters as responding without question to their orders. However he was no longer interested in the sand-table exercises of Urizen's wargaming but in a narrative with a logic of its own. Now the question that obsessed him was this: was it certain that Catriona would obey orders and take her place in the two-seater craft with its laser guns and heat-seeking missiles? If she was indeed one of a group of dissidents might they not try to force the Control Commission at least to review its tactics – for instance to parley with the intruders instead of seeking to eliminate them? What if they seized the communications centre and began to call on their fellow colonists for support against the Commission?

The hostesses assiduously trundled food, drink and duty-free goods up the aisle but he preferred not to eat, dozed instead and let the story develop in his mind like a film he could run and re-run on the editing table of his imagination. What was crucial was David's reaction to the stress his partner's thoughts and actions placed on his loyalties; the extent to which his conformism, his readiness to subject himself to discipline and authority, would assert themselves and condition his behaviour. What began to form in Peter's mind was something like this.

It was almost twenty-four hours before the couple met again. Both had been on duty but it was also clear that Catriona had slept elsewhere. In the meantime there had been more announcements on the intercomm, more official faces on the monitors, more people alerted to stand-by for the special duties to which they had long ago been allocated. Above all the scouts were to be ready to man their capsules at an hour's notice. This last piece of information David saw flashed up on the screen a few minutes before Catriona returned to their living-space.

'Well,' he said.

'Well,' she replied.

'Are you going to put on your gear?' he asked, 'I expect you know we're on stand-by.'

She sat down on the couch and looked at him coolly. 'Yes,' she said at last, 'the answer is yes. I've talked to friends of mine. Never mind who. I will follow orders unless I'm asked to open fire on the so-called intruders. Why? Because I think they are a group that wants to establish a colony and to exploit the planet in peace along with us. But under different conditions.'

How did she know? David wanted to know.

Catriona did not hesitate. 'We have contacts in the communications centre. They see all the traffic with Tellus and they believe these newcomers are not dangerous. They put a virus into the computers of the missile batteries round the launching pads, immobilised them, and took off. But they are no danger – unless you think it is dangerous to want to found a colony based on equal rights for all its members, on full consultation, on the rule that all property must be held in common.'

122

'Old stuff,' said David, 'Peter Sinclair calls it twentieth-century socialism. So they're Communists.'

'If that's what they are I'm one too,' replied Catriona. 'So now do your duty and denounce me.'

David looked down on a face that he had seen express love, desire, amusement, anger; now it was very calm and serious.

'If you don't denounce me I shall come with you in the capsule. But I reserve the right to take what action I feel is right.'

'Then you will kill us both. If we disobey orders Commission Control will destruct the craft.'

She nodded. 'That's a risk I'm prepared to take. But if you are afraid you know what you have to do.'


The voice of the pilot announcing that they were passing over the Alps and in half-an-hour would begin the descent to Pisa broke into his daydreaming and turned his thoughts to the question that for a couple of weeks had been intermittently in his mind and now imposed itself more urgently: what sort of reception awaited him in the town hall of San Vito and what had prompted him to accept the invitation? It had been a few days before he had determined to do so. Fear of falling a prey to sentimentality, to the political exploitation of what had been grim and frequently messy operations, of being involved in necrologies illustrated by blurred, faded photographs of the dead: all this had made him hesitate. But in the end he had accepted both the invitation and the ticket as a means of escape from tedium, from the sense that his writing had run into the sands, from loneliness, from his fears. Possibly also, though this he hardly admitted to himself, in an attempt once again to outface death which he had once succesfully avoided in the hills around San Vito.

At the airport a driver held a placard with his name on it. The viaducts of the autostrada lifted them south till at last, to the left, on its hill he saw the dome of the cathedral with its shrine to St Vitus, the dancing saint, and the slender tower marking the Palazzo del Comune where he was drawn into the rhetoric of

**123**

celebration, embraced, fêted, and inserted into a chronology and a history he did not recognise – a history in which certain events on the margin of the war had become legendary battles. So a couple of days later in the hall of the Comune on a platform where the banners of the partisans mingled with the heraldic emblems of the ancient town, he found himself listening to a long speech from a Communist senator – a small self-important man with a ruddy face and white hair, in his day a heroic figure of the Resistance – and then acknowledging in his unpractised Italian the plaudits of an audience of ageing men and women who claimed him as one of themselves but whom he did not know, did not remember.

He was being, he felt, inserted in a legend which he could not decently disavow for it was charged with too much emotion, too much genuine feeling, too much political nostalgia. He could merely take pleasure in the fiesta, the generosity of spirit that had inspired his invitation and the exuberance of the occasion. 'There aren't many of us left,' his neighbour at table reminded him, reinforcing his sense of mortality, as the long, Tuscan offical banquet began. On his left was a man of his own age, tall with a sharp nose, who walked with a crutch because one day in July 1944 a bullet had shattered his thigh bone. They had embraced and clapped each other on the shoulder claiming old acquaintance; but Peter in truth did not remember him – could only presume that he was the boy who had lain on the grass calling on his mother when the affray above La Volpaia came to an end with the sharp crack of exploding grenades


What Peter remembered most clearly of the early morning attack on the radio station was the scent of the crushed thyme together with his own mixed sense of excitement and fear as the attackers – his own group and ten of Dario's men – broke from the cover of the wood and began to cross the bald summit of the hill where a little clump of army huts were clustered round the aerial masts. The garrison were sleepy, off-guard, half-dressed; but they fought. In the confusion Peter was aware of one of his

124

group running ahead across the grass; of someone falling with blood masking his face; of the sudden screech of a ricochet as the German machine-gun opened up; of firing a burst with his Sten and perhaps hitting a soldier at the window of a hut; of throwing a grenade in at the door; of the silence that quite suddenly fell.

In the huts there was a dying officer, a couple of dead boys and two pale, frightened middle-aged men with their hands above their heads. Aldo, the youngest of his group, raised his Sten and fired half a magazine. As the men heeled over, twisted and fell, he said: 'For my brother.'

Then there was the sound of an engine starting up beyond the huts. Peter ran out and fired at the driver of the motorcycle combination which was lurching and swaying down the path through the trees to the road below; but it was too far away and going too fast to be stopped. Aldo got out his gear and laid cutting charges to the aerial assembly; the fuse hissed briefly, the explosion toppled the mast. Quickly Peter went through the huts looking for documents, picking up what might be code books, unpinning what looked like battalion orders from a notice board; 741 Signals Troop, he read. A solid identification and useful, no doubt, to someone back in Bari. Bending over a dead boy he took from under the bloodied shirt the metal identification disc that bore on each half his name and field-post number, snapped it in two and put one piece in his pocket. There was a little group of men standing in the midst of the grass where Dario lay shot through the head. A little farther away a young man with a bullet wound in the thigh groaned and called on his mother.

Some of the local fighters had been lingering at the edge of the wood. Now they came forward and looked with satisfaction at the dead in the hut. One of them fired a shot at a body. There was a jerry-can of petrol in a corner of the hut. Peter poured the petrol over the floor and over the bodies and set it alight. The smoke of the fire rose high into the morning sunlight as they made their way across country to lie up in the safety of the woods and plan their next action; but when the punitive column arrived about midday few of the peasants in the hillside farms

125

had time to flee. They died with their wives and children and their white oxen in the burning ruins of their homes.

His hotel bedroom gave on to the square where a fountain splashed quietly in the dark. In the morning he would go out and look at the bronze panels round its base that told the cycle of the year and of peasant life: the pig slaughtered in January, the vines pruned at Easter, the vendemmia in August. He had first seen it forty-five years before when the square had been a confusion of French colonial troops, of armoured cars, of partisans (real and not so real), of men in medieval costume with banners celebrating the Liberation. From the balcony of the Comune a man was orating and waving his arms. The bell in the slim medieval tower gave out long heavy booming notes through which, far away, he could hear the sound of the guns. He had stooped to drink from the fountain and then run his finger over the bronze as successive generations had done seeking luck and good harvests, polishing the bronze here and there to a gleaming yellow. Now it was a gathering point for backpacking youngsters, British, French, German, for whom the moment he remembered was hidden by the deep amnesia of history.

He took breakfast along with a coachload of German tourists – men and women of his own age. What memories, he wondered, did he bring to San Vito and its countryside, this man, thin, brown, white-haired, who came over with his youngish blonde wife and asked to share his table. Perhaps they had last seen each other fleetingly in the confusion of an ambushed convoy. Their guide summoned them and the couple left with a little formal gesture of thanks. He sat in the quiet of the empty restaurant and decided he had to make a decision.

It concerned La Volpaia, the fox's den. He could no longer pretend to himself that he did not know the farm, could admit that the uncertainties he had expressed in his letters to Urizen had been shifts to avoid confronting certain memories. The choice was simple. Either he took his courage in both hands and went there or else he took evasive action; hired a car and drove off through the scorched hills of Umbria and south to the beehived Etruscan necropolises, for instance, where the young women and the young men painted on the walls of the tombs prefigured with their long noses, dark eyes and black curling hair, those one could see any day in the streets of San Vito. If he did decide go to La Volpaia should he call first or should he simply – as it were – take the place by storm? Who would he find there? What might his welcome be? A moped ripped the quiet of the dark, then surrendered the square once more to the pulsing rhythms of the fountain. As he fell asleep he thought it would be nice one day perhaps to share these sounds, this kind of one warm night with Lucy/Lucinda/Ariel.

The hero, says Propp, is transferred, delivered or led to the whereabouts of an object or search which is generally located in another kingdom. He can fly through the air (on a bird); travel on the ground (on the back of a horse or wolf); is led (a ball of thread shows the way); makes use of stationary means of communication (climbs a stairway, finds an underground passage; follows bloody tracks; defeats the inhabitant of a forest hut). On the other hand, says Propp, with engaging frankness, sometimes the hero simply walks to the place itself. We have had flight through the air; how does our hero proceed to the fox's den? And is the creature that lives there as trickily dangerous as Foxy Loxy who, you will remember, met Henny Penny, Cocky Locky, Ducky Lucky and Goosey Loosey as they walked along and walked along to tell the king the sky was a-falling, lured them into his cave and bit their heads off with one snap of his big white teeth?

The Comune insisted on giving him a car to take him to La Volpaia. Some sort of mental reservation, some hint of in-decision had made him leave his luggage behind him in his hotel, consigned with many recommendations to the proprietress; black-costumed, opulent, tyrannical, but impressed by the official car. So he had seen suitcase and lap-top word-processor brought down and stowed away in her inner sanctum, but not before he had extracted the field-glasses he had foresightedly brought with him. Now as they came out of the town's massive Etruscan gateway and began the serpentine descent to the valley he looked towards the hills where old keeps marked medieval frontiers.

On either side of the road he saw dying olive trees, victims no doubt of some vagary in the EEC's agricultural policy. Where there were still vineyards the concrete posts marched over the hills on which terraces had once followed the gentle contours and beneath their vines had provided grazing for the sheep which the peasant girls herded with well-aimed clods, stones and shrill cries that carried far along the valley. No, said the driver, there were no more peasants; all gone to the cities. There was more money there and a less sacrificed life. There were a few Sardinians here and there though. Making cheese and ricotta for the foreigners who had taken over the old farmhouses. You had to watch out for Sardinians. A bad lot, some of them, with nasty habits. Such as? Such as kidnapping. Such as holding up motorists at night and taking their money.

Peter looked about him. The landscape was partly as he remembered it – the red soil, the little river below the road; but time had blurred it. The woods seemed thinner. An asphalt road had replaced the dusty metalled one on which he and his group had placed little anti-tyre mines that looked like horse-shit. It was a struggle to persuade the driver to let him dismount a couple of kilometres short of La Volpaia and make his way onward on foot; this the driver took as a reflection on his capacities, a suggestion of shortcomings which would have to be explained away when he got back to town. Peter was reduced to pleading guilty to the notorious madness of foreigners who insisted on walking when there was a perfectly good car, offered a tip and promised to explain to the authorities that the blame was entirely his.

Climbing up the hillside over abandoned terraces he reached the edge of a wood and, looking down, caught glimpses of the car as it took the winding road through the valley to San Vito. He was, he imagined, more or less on the edge of the wood where they had sat on the morning of their drop. If that were so, then the clump of houses at Le Tavernelle should be down on his left and the hill behind La Volpaia, where the radio station had once stood, to his right at about 30 degrees north. There was a clump of houses all right and that hill with the bare top might be the one he sought; in which case the square block of buildings in a re-entrant halfway to the crest was La Volpaia, the *fattoria* where once 'the factor' – as they said in Scotland – had lived and extracted from the sharecropping peasants on behalf of the ancient family of the Ubaldinis half of all they produced.

He looked at it through his glasses; built in the days when this was debatable land on the border between Florence and Pisa, it was a like a Border peel with an external staircase to a long balcony and a door on the first floor. It looked as if it had been carefully restored. There were a couple of cars parked under an awning at the side of what had once been the threshing floor. Some people were moving down over a grassy slope towards a swimming pool. On the balcony that ran from the top of the stairs there were bright patches of colour; towels and bathing costumes laid out to dry. In the shade beneath the stairs he thought he saw – he refocussed his glasses to check – the gleam of metal that might be a motorcycle. There was no reason why he should jump to conclusions but the sight of it spurred him to begin the walk down one side of the valley and up the other, which was longer and harder than he had remembered it.

The path led up between the abandoned terraces to the edge of the wood. Somewhere near here there had been – might still be? – a curious pool in which pale crayfish used to swim. Aldo had pointed it out to him in the course of a reconnaissance the day before the attack was mounted; but he could not recall exactly where. Each with a *pennato* – the machete-like bill-hook that was the peasant's tool for a multitude of tasks – they had gone up through the wood till they emerged on the edge of a clearing near the radio station and began to work, talking quietly; estimating distances, lines of attack, the siting of the garrison's

**129**

defences. A couple of German soldiers lay sunbathing; they raised their heads to watch a couple of peasants cut the undergrowth and tie it in bundles. Since that day the undergrowth had flourished, for it was no longer tamed by sheep, so that he had to push through deep and tangled bushes. A couple of times he heard a snake rustle in the dried leaves. Then the trees thinned and he could see the clearing. Of the hut there was no sign. A few blocks of cement, half-overgrown, showed where it had once stood beside the radio mast.

A little to one side of them a kind of cairn, a pile of stones with a plaque set in it, recalled that here Dario (Corsini Luigi), awarded the gold medal for military valour, had given his life for the cause of liberty in July 1944. There was a withered wreath at its base tied with a red, white and green tricolour ribbon and another with a red one. It was exceedingly still, the air pungent with the smell of herbs. Peter turned back over the short turf. He could recall details of that day but it was as if they referred to someone else with whom he could no longer identify. He thought uneasily of the peasants murdered in their steadings and of other killings; like that of a German straggler, looking for eggs or milk maybe, whom they had surprised sitting beside a path through the vines. When he made a move to get his rifle Aldo had slashed his throat with his pennato. The body was there somewhere among the high broom on the slope beyond La Volpaia.

Turning back through the wood Peter walked to the very limit of the trees and from the cover of the bushes looked again at the farm, which now lay slightly below him. Through his glasses he could see five or six people in or around the pool. A woman, brown and bare-breasted; A couple of teenage girls sunbathing; some boys of the same age, playing like puppies, pushing each other into the water; two older men, brown and oiled, who sat in wicker chairs, talking and drinking. Was one of them Urizen? A woman appeared on the balcony and removed a towel, dark-haired, plumpish. Her movements reminded him of Anna. He could no longer see the motorcycle which was no doubt hidden behind the external staircase; but in the land of the Guzzi what was surprising about its presence?

As on that morning when they had dropped into the valley he felt himself an alien intruder, whose presence could only disturb the calm of this well-heeled Arcadia. But, as then, there was no escape. To get back to San Vito he must at the very least cadge a lift, phone for a car, hire a taxi from the nearest village – if such a thing were possible. Pass himself off as an eccentric, a mad dog walking in the midday sun, an amateur historian collecting medieval farmhouses. A likely story. He got up and began to walk towards the sound of the laughter from the pool.

There was a gate at the entrance to the courtyard with a tile set in the wall; on it, a couple of foxes and the name – La Volpaia. Beside the plaque a bell which he rang. Eventually a middle-aged Italian woman appeared, mustered him and asked sharply what he wanted. He wanted, said Peter, to see the master of the house, whom he believed to be a friend of his. '*Momento,*' said the woman and disappeared. There was a long pause. Then at the top of the stairs a round head with a tonsure of black hair appeared and an English voice said querulously; 'Yes?'

'I am looking for Christopher Williams,' Peter shouted. The head vanished and reappeared as its owner began to come slowly down the stairs and into the courtyard. It belonged to a man in his sixties with a round face in which the eyes were sharp, blue and quick-glancing. His chest, above a prominent brown belly, was thick with dark hair. He wore a long towel like a toga.

'Yes?' he said again advancing towards the gate, challenging and suspicious.

'You are Urizen,' said Peter, 'and I claim my prize of one hundred pounds.'

The man threw his head back and gave a burst of laughter which was like a comic performance long rehearsed – part of a repertory. 'My dear man,' said Urizen, 'do come in! You must be Peter Sinclair. You can't be anyone else because, of the other two players, one is here and the other lives in Venezuela. What brings you this way? How come? On foot? My dear man, you'll have a stroke. Or heat exhaustion. Come along and have a drink. You will stay for lunch, won't you? Do you recognise the place?'

Urizen did not wait for an answer but led the way through a long cool room – once the peasant kitchen – and out on to the terrace above the pool. The topless woman looked up at the new arrival and then slid into the water and began a steady crawl that suggested she had a quota to fulfill. Two young girls on their mats turned over on their fronts as if the presence of a stranger called for a gesture of modesty. One of the boys stood on the edge of the pool, looked at the new arrival then teetered and fell backwards into the water.

'This,' said Urizen as they approached the wicker chairs where a man sat and smoked a Russian cigarette, 'is Peter Sinclair, Peter, meet your opposite number, Itzak Peled.' The two men shook hands. Peled was slim, in his sixties; a thin sharp sensitive face that might equally have been Arab or Israeli. 'Itzak is a writer. As well as a wargamer. You'll get on well. There's only one rule – no reference to you know what. Remember I am still Urizen and there is a security ban. Otherwise what shall we all do in the winter months?'

'Ultra top secret,' said Peled and laughed. On his right shoulder there was a mark, a slight hollowing of the flesh, that might have been mistaken for the scar of a carbuncle but which Peter guessed was an old bullet wound.

'But I know you,' said Peled. 'You married Orna Safran. She brought you to the kibbutz.'

'Kiryat Zvi,' said Peter, 'Twenty years. It's a long time. A lot has happened.'

'Such as?'

'Such as that Orna and I are divorced. She's back in Israel.'

'I know,' said Peled. 'A generous and quixotic lady. She's mixed up with a group – part of what I believe you in Britain call the loony Left – that want to show solidarity with the Arab women of the West Bank. I have the greatest respect for them. But they fail to understand the iron necessity of politics. Her son now – Yoram – it can't be easy for him. After all he'll be doing his military service, won't he?'

'And you?' said Peter quickly, refusing the gambit – was it a conscious gambit? – that must lead to argument and revive the pain he endured each time, on the TV screen, he saw Israeli soldiers firing in response to the taunts of Palestinian women, children and youths in the streets of Gaza or the West Bank towns and asked himself: 'Is that Yoram? Is my son, too, so ruthless in his fear and impotence when face by the *intifada*?'

'Me?' said Peled taking a little time to light a cigarette – was it a conscious ploy – before replying: 'Still living on the kibbutz at Kiryat Zvi. Coping with the ageing process. Aren't we all? Writing a little. And wargaming of course.'

Urizen, having changed from his toga into shorts and a vivid shirt from which his brown belly protruded, came up with a tray of drinks. 'Pimm's No 1,' he announced. 'One of the better British inventions. Tell me,' he said turning to Peter, 'is this the place you thought it might be?' Peter nodded. 'A couple of those kids down by the pool,' Urizen went on, 'were exploring in the thick broom up there the other day and they came back with this they had dug up. Just under the turf, they said.' He fished in his shorts and produced a piece of metal with a jagged edge as if it had been bent and split along its middle. Whole it would have been oval. Peter took the metal and turned it over. Just legible: the name and the field-post number of a German boy who had died forty years before and lay up in the broom where he and Aldo had buried him, not very deep, for there was a little time, but well hidden away.

'He was about their age,' he said.

Peled put down his glass where the moisture pearled and mint and cucumber floated coolly. 'Do we have a mystery?' he asked. 'Can we try to solve it?'

'No – no mystery,' said Peter. 'Just the savagery of war. The Germans put people like us against the nearest wall. But I still don't feel good about that morning's work.'

'My worst moment,' said Peled, 'was a raid on an Arab village. We had laid the charges against the wall of a house ready to blow it. Then inside I heard a baby crying.'

'But you blew it just the same?' said their host with detached curiosity.

'What else could we do?' said Peled.

Peter got up and walked to the edge of the terrace. It was on the tip of his tongue to ask whether it had been iron necessity that had sent the bombs screaming down on the Chatila where the Palestinians were packed in the refugee camps in anger, defiance and squalor. But he decided to let it pass: a moment of what Orna would have called 'liberalism' – a failure to speak up because of phoney rules of behaviour, conventions, etiquette, that showed more respect for the comfortable man who was his host than for the victims of state terrorism. He could imagine her anger, which in the end had invested and destroyed their relationship, recall her voice, her bearing, and the warmth and passion that had still bound them on the visit to Kiryat Zvi.

High-walled, the kibbutz of Kiryat Zvi lay on a hillside that looked across to the Jordan valley and the low brown heights beyond: tidy houses set in an expanse of grass where the sprinklers threw little rainbows; the administrative block with the communal kitchen and laundry; the dining room where on Saturday nights the affairs of the community were debated. The guest room was bare – a couple of camp-beds, a couple of chairs, a wash-hand basin.

Said Orna: 'This is to show that the comrades – the *haverim* – still believe in the old simple life. But there's a resident poet. Itzak Peled. He'll want to meet you.'

'Why?'

'To give you the once over. Check your intellectual credentials. Suss out who this goy is that has an Israeli girlfriend. Some people think Itzak is actually a high-ranking officer in Mossad. Intelligence.'

'Is he?'

Orna shrugged. 'How should I know? He's from an old family – here long before the state of Israel. Speaks Arabic. Was in the Palmach. A kind of commando. Operating in the Arab villages. My father told me. But that's all I know.'

The one-room study of the poet, Itzak Peled, was shaded and cool. There was the sound of water trickling down through a layer of moss held between metal gauze that filled the window-frame instead of glass. The books were polyglot – unexpectedly French and Spanish rather than German or Czech or Polish. His family, the poet explained, were Sephardim, refugees from the Spanish Inquisition, who had lived in Jerusalem since the sixteenth century, under the Ottoman Empire and then under British colonial rule until the foundation of the State of Israel. So he had been naturally drawn to Spanish literature. Machado, for instance, with his stoicism and irony. *'Mi infancia – son recuerdos de un patio de Sevilla – mi historia – algunos casos que recordar no quiero*. My childhood – memories of a patio in Seville – my history – some events I don't want to remember. I see from your reaction that you understand some Spanish,' said the Poet.

'I know Italian,' Peter replied.

'Spanish,' said the other, 'is Italian crossed with Arabic – not just in its vocabulary but in its harshness, its bite.' He had grown up in Old Jerusalem speaking Arabic, one of the great languages of the world. Playing with the Arab children. Shopping with his mother in the narrow streets of the old town where the lanes were crowded, odorous of leather, coffee, spices, mint, the shelves of the booths piled with lukum; had his visitor ever eaten lukum with pistachios? It had been one of his great regrets that the founding of the State of Israel had meant war with a people whose language and culture he had always respected. When the kibbutz was first settled, there had still been Arab shepherds on the hills outside the perimeter. As they watched their flocks they played on their flutes. All gone now. It was a great sadness.

'He is,' said Orna as they lay awake in the warm night and talked over the day, 'a great seducer – of women and men. Watch out for him.'


Looking over to the woods where his group had bivouacked that first night after the drop he found the whole landscape subtly changed. Never wild, it had in those days been enclosed, almost claustrophobic, which was why the dropping zone had been chosen there, with dusty metalled roads, passable only by

**135**

carts, that became tracks when they turned off into valleys where the heat set off a fusillade of bursting broom pods. At night the mist lay waist-deep in the little valleys. Now the sun flared on the windscreen of a bus and cars came and went along the new asphalt roads. Everyone had vanished from the poolside. From within the house came the thudding rhythm to which today's young people danced obsessively – as it seemed to him – inwardly concentrated, abstracted, like dervishes. He felt the stone of the parapet warm under his hand and thought of the boy Heinz Muller, who would by now have been in his fifties, citizen of the Federal German Republic, and might have come, too, on a coach tour of Toskana with his youngish wife and shown her where he had first drunk the red peasant wine.

Behind him he heard more and different voices. Turning he discovered Anna who greeted him with an ironical inclination of the head. With her was a thin man with greying hair and a slightly distant look, which might have been due merely to short-sightedness. 'This is extraordinary,' said Urizen. 'Everybody knows everybody it seems. Like the dénouement of a bad thriller.'

'Peter,' said Anna, 'you haven't met my husband. Alan, this is Peter Sinclair, who used to be at the college. You've heard me talk about him.' Alan assented politely.

Peter enquired whether they were staying long.

'Only passing through,' said Anna with a slight smile that was meant, he knew, as a reassurance – and he wondered what she and her husband had found to say about him in bed, over the breakfast table, in the bath, as they walked in Richmond or some other park. Conversation was broken by the sound of a gong at which signal Urizen ordered them all indoors. Peled made to rise from his deckchair, turned to stub out his cigarette and pressed it on the back of Peter's hand. Peter waved aside apologies. As he walked into the room where the guests were arranging themselves at table in groups governed by fields of force that were obscure to him, he paused for a moment and attempted to assuage the pain by pressing the long glass that had held his drink to the red spot on his skin. Then Urizen, seeing him hesitate, beckoned imperiously and bade him take a place between himself and Peled.

It is common, Propp points out, for the Hero to be branded just as it is quite usual for him to be set the difficult task of guessing the distinctive marks of a tsar's daughter – some birthmarks presumably not normally revealed (until such time, that is, as she finds herself in bed with the frog prince) except perhaps to a faithful old nurse or waiting woman. As for the villain he normally appears twice in the tale.

At the far end of the table sat the woman who had swum so obsessively in the pool. Above the square neck of her yellow linen dress her skin was a brown glow.

'My companion,' said Urizen catching the direction of Peter's glance. 'Geraldine and her brood. At least some of them are. She's Irish-Catholic. Which is a bit of a problem for both of us. Since we cohabit. You must meet her properly later. By the by, everything you see on the table is organic: the bread, the salad, the grapes. I have this wonderful little man, Nello, a genuine *contadino* who took to organic farming like a duck to water. I always think that one has to have a well organised life-support system, don't you? So we have Nello and his daughter, Graziella – she's the one you spoke to at the gate – and then *her* daughter, Assunta, who you'll see any minute now. Then there's a jack-of-all-trades in Le Tavernelle who can fix anything from a shower to a loose tile. He deals with the septic tank – but not when we're actually in residence.' Urizen threw back his head and laughed loudly to signal that he recognised the pomposity of the expression. 'But they are really all sterling people. Including the mayor of San Vito – a Communist, of course, but as I always say the CP here is really like the Labour Party at home. He invited us as usual to the annual do the other day – for the

Liberation – but I really felt that it was all a bit old hat by now and thought he wouldn't mind if we gave it a miss. I do think it's a mistake to keep looking back. There is so much to be done for the future –in the ecology, in the moves towards an international order, in furthering mutual understanding. Between Arabs and Jews, for instance. Which is why Itzak is here. I run a sort of trust built on my father's not altogether ill-gotten gains; anyway the trust aims at bringing different sides on a question together. In seminars. With scholarships. Because I am persuaded that if only one can get the most obdurate men – and women; we mustn't forget the women – together miracles can sometimes happen.'

Urizen paused as Assunta handed round the coffee, 'As I was saying, if you can get people into the same surroundings and then into the same room it's amazing what will sometimes spring from small beginnings. I ran a very successful meeting here between some women from Derry and Belfast at Easter. Catholics and Prods talking, arguing, getting to know each other away from the ghettoes of the Shanklin Road and the Bogside. It will take months, maybe years, before we see any fruit. But fruit there will be. And so with Itzak I am aiming to set up a get-together between Jews and Palestinians; an *agape*, a love feast, if you like, because I believe that is what we must build on – the love of one human being for another. You know: young men from the Gaza Strip and others from the Jewish settlements on the West Bank actually *talking*. Because talk they will and talk they must if peace is ever going to come to the Middle East.' Itzak nodded and twisted the cardboard holder of his cigarette. 'I've got a remarkable and very energetic young man to help me – gave you as a reference, which was good enough for me.'

'Duncan Hogg,' said Peter with a mixed sense of amusement and alarm.

'That's right – the very best kind of Scot. I am most impressed. The Scots,' Urizen went on, turning to Peled, 'have an amazing amount in common with you Jews: a strong work ethic, great respect for learning and education and for the Sabbath – '

'Not so much any more,' Peter interrupted.

'Well at least a desire to get on in the world,' Urizen went on, 'along with a certain seriousness which I find attractive. But you'll see for yourself. He'll be arriving tomorrow or the day after.'

At the far end of the table the young people rose, chattering like a flock of birds, and left the room. Anna and her husband had gone already with a brief word to the woman who sat alone at the end of the table and played with a piece of bread. Then she rose in her turn, turning at the door to look back at Urizen.

'Siesta time,' said Urizen. 'You will stay, won't you, Peter? I'll get Graziella to show you your room in the *dependance*.'

The room was shuttered cool, whitewashed. Once it had been the bedroom of this peasant house just down the hill from the *fattoria*. Here, generations of men and women had been conceived, born and died. Now there was a low, hard, healthy bed, a table with a scattering of books celebrating the splendours of the Quattrocento or evoking in black and white the vanished culture of ox-carts, threshing floors; shepherds in black cloaks driving their flocks along the white roads to summer pastures in the high Appenines; peasant girls, distaffs under their arms, spinning the woollen yarn through their fingers, and watching how their few sheep grazed among the vines. A piece of pottery that might have been Etruscan with dried flowers. Peter lay down and wondered, before drifting into sleep, where Anna was lodged, what Duncan was up to, whether to stay and find out or leave after supper.

When he woke it was still early, just after three. The house was silent. There was no noise from the pool or from the gardening except the sawing of the cicadas which came and went in waves. A lizard flickered on the wall by the window. From down the corridor there was the soft fall of naked feet. Whose? Stalking in whose chamber? He focussed on a line of light that slanted down from a chink in the shutter and, closing his eyes, allowed the afterimages – purple, blue, red – to swim across the darkness. A childhood pleasure retrieved. Opening his eyes he let thoughts of David Balfour and Catriona drift through his mind like the afterimages that still swam in his vision, forming

**139**

and reforming, waxing and waning, perhaps fixable if he had the determination to hold them. But for what purpose? To prove a thesis to Urizen? Or to give substance to fantasies in which Lucinda/Lucy/Ariel was now one and the same as the young woman on Andromeda who now slept in the living space in a posture he could not imagine, with one hand on the pillow and the other caught between her thighs just above the knee where there was (as he knew) a tiny patch of rough skin – a little enduring spot of eczema – on which her fingers rested.

David was sitting by the bed when from the intercom on the wall there came a message prefaced by his number and by Catriona's. They were to report at once to their unit to receive orders. He bent over and shook Catriona's shoulder and she turned in her sleep. Her face at such moments was clear and smooth without the lines that increasingly had begun to mark her features. 'We have to report,' he said. 'Be quick.' As they ran down past the installations they passed other colonists moving through the streets to take up their positions on the perimeter defences and listening posts as they had often done in defence exercises; but now there was feeling of tension in their swift, purposeful scurrying and the way they handled their weapons.

David and Catriona had to rendezvous at the low hangars near the Commission Headquarters where the ground-crews were already checking over their capsule, testing the communications systems, removing the guards that were normally secured over the firing mechanisms of the laser guns, scrutinising the space suits with their highly reflective surface that would repel the dangerous rays beyond the shelter of the colony's domed structure. A couple of ground-crew came forward to equip David and Catriona. David looked across at Catriona who was quickly, deftly securing her suit. Then, as the ground crew prepared to slip the helmets over their heads, he said; 'Good luck, Catriona.' She smiled at him before the silver casque hid her face.

David took a deep breath as his was fitted in turn. From now on there would be no direct contact with her, no way of seeing her face; there would be her commands in his ears and her voice as she responded to the instructions of Control, for she was commander of the craft. When they had settled in their places, one behind the other, the lid of their capsule was lowered and secured. The intercom crackled and Catriona's voice came over instructing him to check all instruments and weapons. Then the ground-crew began to move their craft on its light trolley towards the ejection port. They sat in the lock with the door behind them already closed till the controller's voice came through. They were to carry out a recce to the west, proceeding as far as Herringbone Ridge. They were to report back any movements by the invaders but not to engage them unless specifically ordered to do so.

The outer door of the lock swung slowly open. When Catriona pressed the button for ejection there was a barely perceptible moment of what felt like hesitation, then the motor flared and they were off, wheeling to find their bearing and course. The whitish surface of Andromeda, scarred by workings where today the remotely controlled diggers lay idle, began to slip past beneath them. Glancing upwards David saw with a moment's vertigo planet Tellus glowing deep in space. At Herringbone Ridge Catriona brought the capsule down in a white plume of dust, checked with Control and then ordered David to unship the snow-cats. This was the hardest part – to leave the relative shelter of the scout-car and momentarily set foot on the surface where the deep dust was pierced here and there by reefs and outcrops of rock; pink, grey, black. There was a practised moment – but still a moment of risk and uncertainty –as he turned off the oxygen in the capsule and, holding his breath, connected his supply line to the cylinder in the snow-cat. Catriona's voice came over clearly: 'We are to deploy and set up our laser guns on the ridge to cover the flanks of the alien forces and wait for further orders.'

Which was all very well, thought Peter as he showered in the corner of his room, but where was the tingling sensation of fear and excitement he had experienced as he sat in his hut with the light turned off and watched the pale hands of his watch – he had left it in the sun all morning to bring up the luminosity – move towards his zero hour. It was late, almost one in the morning. He would be over the dropping zone at about half-past-two for the plane would go out to sea and then stooge up north before turning in over the coast of Tuscany to reach its target. He had eaten without much appetite in the mess and drunk a few brandies with a couple of friends. There were no toasts and no rhetoric; the uncertainty of the operation imposed a devious tactfulness which meant that they discussed the latest round of organisational infighting and whether the new batch of WAAF officers would add anything to the gaiety of nations or prove to be safely engaged to gentlemen from the Brigade of Guards or some other posh outfit. It was not until he went off to his hut that they wished him good luck, told him to keep off the Chianti, and said they would no doubt meet up in Florence or some other delectable city where he could put them wise about art. And, for Jesus' sake, to remember that enemy identifications were crucial.

In the hut he strapped on his revolver and looked once more at his map: La Volpaia; Le Tavernelle; San Vito. Names. Tiny clusters of houses on photographs taken as the fast, unarmed photo-recce planes swooped, levelled out, then in a second run tilted to get an oblique shot. In his anxiety he had left himself with ten minutes at least in hand. They seemed to be taking an inordinate time to pass. His gear was packed in his bedding-roll on the stripped bed; when he was gone it would go into stores. To wait for him. Or to be auctioned and only personal effects (if any) sent home to his next of kin – to be precise to his father, Mr Alastair Sinclair, The Bungalow, Links Road etc, etc. He knew the drill, for he had inherited the hut and the camp-bed from a Captain Smith, J., who had gone for a Burton just off Elba, leaving – to judge from the photographs in his kit – a young blonde wife in a striped cotton dress and a blond child (boy?) of a year or so.

142

When he stepped out it was into a tepid night. In the hangar his companions were talking quietly together. He went over and asked, were they OK? OK, they said. The youngest, Aldo, the boy from the Po valley added, '*Siamo stati a donne.*' So they had found in the brothel down the road from the camp a transient affirmation of life. Their plane taxied up and out of the dark. When it entered the patch of light by the hangar its propellers were blurred like the soft wings of the death's-head moths probing the pale flowers that climbed the walls of the mess. The sergeant instructor helped them on with their parachutes and checked the harnesses. Then with a 'Good luck, sir' saw them into the place.

Peter was aware as he climbed up into its belly that he was doing something irreversible, that there was no turning back. He felt a spasm of fear – an overwhelming panic at the thought of death and a wish to be somewhere else. He had a momentary giddiness as if he might faint, mastered it and took his place with his back to the fuselage along with the others. The corporal in charge of the drop clambered in and the door closed. The plane taxied bumpily to the end of the tarmac. Turned into the wind. Sat for a moment as if summoning up resolve and then moved forward, gathering pace until Peter felt it lurch and lift into the air. The others were quiet. He could feel the wall of the fuselage grow cold as they climbed. Then the engine settled into a reassuring pulsing rhythm. He breathed regularly and lightly and let time flow through him, neither anticipating the moment that must come nor trying to arrest its arrival. Did condemned men, he wondered, try to hold on to time in this way in their last hours?

When the moment came for the corporal to say 'This is it, then' he was amazed to feel how calm he was. After the stomach-turning drop into the cold night air and the moment of uncertainty before the parachute cracked open overhead he was detached and in control of himself, peering down to where the landscape was dappled with the shadows of clouds, with woods and scrub and fields. When it began to rise up to meet him he was ready for it, rolled over as the sergeant had taught him, caught at his harness and, pulling in the chute, began to gather it up. Above him the others drifted down like immense dandelion tufts. The containers floated a little way off. The engine of the plane changed its note as it turned and made for the coast again. In the dark they checked their gear and made for the cover of the woods.

When in the early evening he emerged from his room he passed doors behind which others – but who? – were stirring. As he made his way across the threshing floor and up the stony path to the *fattoria*, from under his feet grasshoppers rose to describe erratic parabolas and land with a flash of pink and blue among brown grass crushed by the burden of summer. On the terrace Urizen was seated by a low table with a pile of mail. 'There really is no escape these days – all this faxed stuff. Have you ever thought of getting one. A fax, I mean. Great for wargaming. So much quicker. By the way I took the liberty of ringing your hotel and telling them to send your stuff up this evening. I hope you don't mind – but it would be crazy for you not to be here for a few days. I do like Anna. Such a nice down-to-earth lady. You'd have thought she could have done better than that boring treasury solicitor. We were up at Oxford together. He was old at twenty. But there's no accounting for tastes. And Itzak. They tell me he's a very good poet. Not that I can judge, of course, but a thoroughly civilised person. Fascinating, his blend of the Orient and the West. Very modest too, because I understood he was quite a high-ranking officer. I've often thought – haven't you? – that there is something interesting to be written, sociologically, that is, about the kibbutzim. Harbouring these poets and artists. String quartets and communal living. That sort of thing. Culture and work on the land. And producing all these young officers to fight in Israel's wars. It's almost medieval. Work and pray and fight – that sort of thing, don't you think?'

'I think you'd find a lot of the work is done by Palestinian labour these days,' said Peter. 'On the cheap.'

144

Urizen looked up sharply. 'A pity you won't be here for the Arab-Jewish symposium. But I had better deal with this bumf. Why don't you go with Geraldine? She's got some sort of trip organised for this afternoon.' Twisting in his chair he called her name and brought her coolly out of the house, taller than Peter expected; wide-hipped, early forties, reddish hair piled high on her head, freckled skin. She came and stood behind Urizen's chair. As they talked he stroked her thigh possessively. She mustered Peter with polite indifference and said with a touch of an Irish accent that she was going to a kind of open day on an estate up the valley – that they bred oxen and that Peter was welcome to come. So that was settled, said Urizen, and with a pat on her bottom dismissed her.

At first no one spoke much in the car as it climbed the road towards the head of the valley where Peter remembered silver fighters twisting and stooping over German convoys. Not Geraldine who as she drove hummed tunelessly to herself, absorbed in some train of thought she could not or did not wish to share. Not Anna nor her husband nor Peled who sat between them. At last, near the top of the pass, a castle appeared, grey and machicolated, on the other side of the valley.

'Guelph,' said Anna's husband.

How did he know, asked Peled.

'You can tell,' said the precise voice, 'because of the crenellations. Square-topped in the case of the Guelphs. An indented triangle in the case of the Ghibellines. Just as they were distinguished by the cut of their beards and doublets. Even the way they wore the feathers in their caps.' Peled suggested that there might be a good wargame there somewhere. In the thirteenth century, Anna's husband went on – it was all well-documented – there were times when no peasant hereabouts could plant vines or gather grapes or live in peace on a farm and the roads were haunted by highwaymen, thieves and robbers. 'That reminds me,' said Geraldine suddenly but with great matter-of-factness, 'we mustn't be too late. There's been an epidemic of hold-ups on the roads. People losing their valuables. The locals say it's the Sardinians.'

The cypresses lining the avenue were dark index fingers tracing the slow motion of the sun on the dusty road. Just behind the villa, cars – the registration plates spoke of owners from all over Northern Europe – were parked in spots of shade. In the courtyard under an awning there was a table with crostini, salami, prosciutto and the unsalted bread of Tuscany. Round it men and women, careless in the assurance of their dress, of their bodies, the colour of their tan, the fall of lock over an eye, the half-intentional revelation of a breast, greeted and eyed each other, exchanged gossip, passing from partner to partner in a dance that was unstructured and yet purposeful. Servants in striped jackets and white gloves handed round cold white wine and iced tomato juice: 'Real juice,' said an English voice, 'but what else? Tarragon? Oregano? So simple! Beautiful!'

Peter found himself on the edge of the crowd next to Anna who said; 'Well, how are you?'

'Not bad,' said Peter, 'trying to write that book. But not getting on. Being distracted. And you?'

Anna shrugged. 'As you see,' she said. 'I can't grumble. The college? It's all about the new realism these days – you know, sponsorship, backing by industry, education for the sons and daughters of the well-heeled.'

'I was thinking,' said Peter. 'There used to be a marvellous spring on the slope above La Volpaia. Very deep. With little freshwater crabs in the bottom. Beautiful cool water. Have a look for it.'

She said she would look then added; 'It must make you sad.'

'What?' he asked.

'All this,' she said. Then she was separated from him as a man climbed on to a chair; seventy-ish, a slightly blotched complexion, clipped moustache, clipped vowels; introduced himself to those who might not know him as Major Sempill-Gordon and announced that they were about to see the only remaining centre breeding the white oxen which had once been the work-

146

animals of the whole region. His wife, the Contessa Aldina degli Ubaldini, who was on vacation, had asked him to welcome them all to this estate which had been in her family since the twelfth century and to give them a glimpse of *la vita contadinesca* – that peasant way of life whose passing he was sure his guests all lamented.

A young Italian led out a great gentle slavering beast with a nose-ring, which snorted and looked placidly round. Timorously at first and, then more daringly, the guests approached and, encouraged by the boy, ran their hands over the greyish stubble on the ox's warm back and thighs. It shifted a little on its fore-hooves and they scattered with little cries of fear that were only half-simulated. Then in groups of six the guests were led down to the stalls where the other oxen lay and ruminated, their bellies shaken by commotions and eructations. The air was pungent with ammonia. As Peter's group filed towards the doors an ox rose, lifted its tail and spattered a woman and her escort. She gave a cry and ran out.

'All that methane,' said someone. 'Thins the ozone layer. A good job there aren't too many of them left.'

Back in the courtyard there were sorbets and espressos, liqueurs, pan di Spagna. Peter found himself beside Geraldine.

'Cheer up,' she said. 'It could be worse.'

'I was asking myself whether it was really worth it.'

'What?' asked Geraldine.

'Life, I suppose,' said Peter.

Geraldine shrugged. 'How should I know? Are you a Catholic?' she asked. Peter shook his head. 'A pity,' she said. 'It can be a great comfort, the confessional. Just as good as a shrink and much cheaper.'

'But suppose you're not a believer?'

'Tough shit,' she said and took another brandy.

'I was recommending Holy Mother Church and the confessional to your friend Peter here,' said Geraldine's voice in the warm dark.

'You mean he's an *anima naturaliter christiana*?' asked Urizen.

'How the fuck should I know,' she replied, 'I just think he needs to cheer up a bit. A good father confessor might help.' Urizen gave one of his great false laughs.

'No way,' said Peter. 'I'd rather try to manage without props.'

'But,' objected Peled from the other side of the balcony, 'you are – unless I've misunderstood Urizen – some sort of Marxist. A socialist, shall we say. Now we've all been socialists in our time. But mostly we grew out of it.'

'I remember,' Urizen chipped in, 'selling some inflammatory paper outside my college. My father threatened to stop my allowance unless I desisted.'

'So you stopped – naturally,' said Geraldine and poured herself another glass of Martini.

'Go easy on the booze,' said Urizen with a jokiness that barely masked anxiety.

'I simply feel,' said Peter, 'that there must be a better way of regulating our lives and those millions of others who can only live the hunger and squalor of the third world – of the *favelas* –the way we live and work and share wealth, or organising the society into which we are born, which Marx said is not of our own choosing, than either capitalism or actually existing socialism has been able to come up with.'

'Ah,' said Peled, 'do I get a whiff of heresy – the sulphur of Trotskyism? We had kibbutizim – would you believe it? – that were torn apart by the treason trials in Czechoslovakia. Remember? Old Communists standing there, holding up their trousers and listening to the death sentence. Thank God I am not a European Jew. I do not bear that legacy. Of course I was on the Left when I was at the Sorbonne, before the war. But that was natural. One had to be a socialist or a Thomist. As a Jew I found Thomism difficult. All right – so you feel there must be an alternative. How do you know?'

'If I didn't believe there was an alternative I think I would have given up long ago. As it is, it keeps me going.'

'I like that,' said Peled, 'pure Pascal. The wager: either there is a possibility that God – or the good society, justice, the

148

brotherhood of man or whatever – exists or there isn't. So you toss. Heads or tails.'

From the shadow where Geraldine sat there was a sound of a glass falling and breaking which brought Urizen to his feet to help her rise and walk like a blind woman into the house. Peter rose and looked out at the valley where the mist was gathering in long pale swathes. 'I think I'll take a turn,' he said and walked round the end of the house and on up the hill to where the well should lie at the foot of a cherry tree. It was further than he remembered but at last he could hear the faint pulse of the water.

A figure came down towards him: Anna, who stopped to say, 'I found your well. I'm leaving tomorrow early. You look sad; don't be. When it comes to it the most one can hope for is to have been happy now and then. To have been close to another human being.' She took his arm and they walked slowly down the path where the peasant women had carried their copper pitchers to and from the well. 'Take me: you've seen Alan. A nice man. A bit boring, not very interested in sex; but he's good to me. We'll both take early retirement and go and live in a cottage. Sussex, I expect. Deepest Toryland. I'll give talks in village halls about cloutie wells. Maybe write a book – if Alan and the garden will let me. But we had our time together, didn't we? Your trouble is you always want something else – something more. Something beyond. I bet you're in love again. Yes? You were in love with me too, remember?' She kissed him on the cheek. 'I have good memories of us,' she said and went quickly off downhill.


Various characters, says Propp – who else? – place themselves at the disposal of the hero, teaching him a formula, a magic incantion, that will stand him in good stead. So why not Blaise Pascal, master of conic sections, mathematical prestidigitator, inventor of the calculating machine; long-nosed, a thin line of black moustache above lips that are full and curved and slightly cleft, slightly pouting, in the drawing for which his father noted he 'used this body as of right'; a mouth that is unchanged in that other portrait in middle-age (although the hair has receded off

**149**

his forehead) and only pursed in the death-mask where the nose is long and pinched and the eyelashes thick with plaster. Thirty-nine years old on the day of his death in August 1662.

So why relevant to Peter Sinclair or to that train of thought which I pursue behind the masquerade of plot and narrative? Not because of those other sayings of his – about man as a thinking reed or how terrifying he found the silence of infinite space – but because he proposed that in order to live in a world which he found intolerable he had, as a believer, to decide the existence of God by a toss of the coin. There was nothing to lose and all to gain. So heads or tails? Socialism or barbarism, as Engels – was it Engels? – said. So Peter Sinclair bets on the possibility of a realm of justice on earth and would no doubt argue that good men and women had staked their lives on that wager, that he had actually known some of them (as indeed did I) and recognised them to be brave, generous spirits.


In his room, where the tiles were cool to his bare feet Peter found his luggage, including his word-processor, piled in a corner. When he switched it on the tell-tale light glowed; so the batteries were charged. Sitting on the edge of the bed he began to recall and set down how David and Catriona had been summoned and, in their snow-cats, now lay on Herringbone Ridge, looking over to where the intruders were raising little flurries of dust.


It was difficult to make out what precisely they were about; setting up bivouacs perhaps, contriving a shelter against the gamma-rays, planning their next move. David listened to the exchanges on the intercom as Catriona reported back to Control. The strangers were not advancing. Not many – fifty perhaps. No, there was no definite sign of offensive weapons. She requested permission to advance closer and to gain more precise information. They reply was a sharp negative and the comment 'advise you not strangers but intruders'. There was a long silence broken only by occasional crackles and then there came a new voice, difficult to follow at first so that it forced David to fiddle with his headset in an attempt to read it more clearly. 'Brothers and sisters,' it was saying, 'we have come to Andromeda –' then a burst of interference drowned it. David switched to an alternative frequency on which the voice of the Controller came over loud and clear: 'Capsule to withdraw and report to Control.' David switched on the ignition of his snowcat and turned its nose towards where the scout-car lay a couple of kilometres back on the reverse slope.

What interrupted his writing was the noise of a car coming up the road to La Volpaia. After a long interval there were voices, the sound of the car reversing, turning and running down into the valley back to San Vito. The note of the engine faded into the warm night as the hills closed round it. Steps came down and into the farmhouse. Someone was shown into a room. There was a silence into which the song of a nightingale broke fitfully. Peter lay down on the bed and attempted sleep. But sleep slipped from him in the dark, fleeing before him down the corridors of time at the end of which was the black hole that would suck him into oblivion. To override his anxieties and fears, the appalling thought of the void, of loss of identity, he clung to his longing. He would wait a week, he resolved. If she had not come by then he would go.

'Nice place he has here,' said Duncan next morning when Peter found him on the terrace looking remarkably spruce in open necked-shirt and shorts that showed the glint of reddish hair on his thighs. 'For an old-fashioned Lefty you've some queer friends. Do you know who he is – Mr Christopher Williams? No? Not interested? Don't want to know where he got his loot? Man, you're remarkably incurious. I boned up on him and his trust when I applied for the job. Hey, listen – I did a great interview. You'd have been proud of me. I'll tell you what clinched it. I just happened to mention Paolo Freire – Brazilian,

**151**

isn't he? – educating the people. All that reformist shit. I knew then it was in the bag.'

Peter went to the edge of the balcony and looked down towards the pool where Geraldine was doing the crawl, to and fro, to and fro. But Duncan was not to be shaken off. 'Don't tell me you've never heard of Williams' faggots? Not what you're thinking either – you with your dirty mind – real meatballs with all that lovely gravy, just like old Mr Williams used to make them in his wee cooked-meat shop. Try them on the kids – they'll love them. Actually they're made in a factory up near Liverpool. I had a job there once, after all I'm only an ordinary working chap, in the summer holidays – what your friend would call the long vac – fetching the carcasses from the refrigerators. Jesus, it was cold. You hang them on hooks and strip the meat. With knives, of course. Fine sharp knives. About half-an-hour to strip a carcass. Piecework. There's a couple of women with clippers that go over the bones to see how much waste there is. You'll not believe this; they actually weigh it. If there's too much left on the bone you lost points. Very instructive. Taught me a lot about surplus value and nearly put me off meat for life. But I couldna afford to be a vegetarian. So, like I said, I'm getting a wee bit of the loot. And helping to channel it to deserving causes. Why don't you put in an application? You never know your luck.'

All morning Peter watched him as, like a suspicious animal, he sniffed the place out, coming back from time to time with little pieces of intelligence. Such as that the dame in the swimming pool and Williams had separate bedrooms. Did that mean they didn't have sex? That the two girls who were the woman's – the two kids were just their boyfriends – didn't even have the decency to cover up their tits when he walked down to look at the pool. No doubt Peter liked that kind of decadent behaviour. That there was a great office with telephone, fax machine, word-processor, the lot. He had rung his Mum in Dundee just to tell her he was all right. He was going to enjoy it here. But Peled was a funny guy – he couldn't figure him out. What did Peter think?

Peter said Peled was a poet and a wargamer.

Duncan burst out laughing. 'You're not serious! When I was a kid in school we used to play battleships – on squared paper. I have two cruisers and a submarine to your four detroyers and frigate. We played a lot in the last term of the sixth form – after Highers were over. But grown men! What the fuck do you see in it?'

'It's a game like any other. Chess. Poker. Bridge. Patience. Pontoon. A pastime. An excuse for not doing other things.'

'Maybe you should have toy soldiers as well. Have wee battles. It's fucking pathetic. You and your generation refighting your bloody stupid battles. You'd think you'd have got over it by now.'

'I'm not sure,' said Peter, 'that it's something one can ever get over. But if it's any consolation this wargame is set in the future.'

'Sci-Fi – kids' stuff,' said Duncan. 'Maybe you'll be able to sell the film rights. Make a killing. But you'd better be quick before some idiot in the Pentagon pushes that little button.'

'Duncan,' said Peter, 'why don't you just lay off for a while. Till the end of the week. Then I'll be going back and you can get on with setting up that Arab-Jewish seminar or whatever.'

'Waiting for a visitor, are we then? She said she might be passing through. Didn't she tell you? Saw her in London. It's all right I didn't go to bed with her. But you're right – I should be getting on with my work. The protestant work ethic and all that shit. By the by, she won't be too happy about meeting Peled.'

'I shouldn't have thought she'd mind one way or the other.'

'That's where you're wrong – don't say she didn't tell you – about her boyfriend? The Palestinian. He's in a camp away in the desert. In the Negev. Ansar 3, it's called. No word of him for a couple of years.'

That afternoon Peter remembered the tattoo on her arm; indigo, like the tattoo seen on the shoulder of an Arab girl in a wartime Cairo brothel. He had, he told himself, no right to feel jealousy, disappointment. Why tell Duncan and not him? But he

**153**

pulled his coverlet over his head and was miserable at the lack of trust.

Over the next few days a routine developed around the swimming pool, the long meals and the talk on the balcony in the warm evenings. Peled was urbane in his military-looking shorts and his bush shirt with its carefully ironed collar, expounding the importance of archaeology as one powerful weapon to determine the inalienable right of his people to occupy Palestine. It was no accident, he admitted with a smile, that some of the best soldiers had also done some of the most successful digs or that archaeology was an Israeli national hobby. He had a way, which Peter found difficult, of turning to him and attempting to co-opt him, appealing to him flatteringly as an outsider with a certain special knowledge and experience of Israel, tempting; seducing him, Orna would have said, raising memories to which he reacted edgily. Of Kiryat Zvi and walks with Orna on the walls of the Old Town in Jerusalem in the days when they did so in a state of complicity that was physical, emotional, political. Touching too accurately for it to be entirely innocent on vulnerable points, wishing to be reminded how old Orna's (Peter's) son would be now. Old enough, no doubt, to be doing his military service in the Gaza Strip or the West Bank. Not an easy job – in fact a messy one, but no doubt he would bring to his task the humanity and liberal principles he had learned from his mother; the Israeli army was after all in a true sense a citizens' army without what used to be called bullshit, but imbued with a democratic spirit.

Peter said he hoped his son might not have been as ruthless as these boys you could see on television firing at the women and children of the *intifada*. A cowardly front for terrorism, said Peled, the real gunmen stay well hidden. When their interchanges became too sharp, Urizen would intervene, emollient and reasonable, and turn the conversation to the projects and good causes he conceived and funded.

His days were spent in drafting long memoranda, projects,

prospectuses, in international phone calls, in anxious super-
vision of Geraldine's drinking and attempts to separate her from
the large jug of dry Martini she carried with her from chair to
chair and from chair to table, setting it in the shade by the pool,
retiring with it at siesta time or at night. Peter watched Duncan,
attentive but unobtrusive, putting two and two together,
deferential without being subservient, a good listener, busy in
the inner office, winning golden opinions.

It was late one evening. The group had been sitting discussing
Green scenarios. From inside the house there came the deep thud
of rock. Urizen had risen to fetch from his study a paper he was
working on; a proposal to be put to the EEC for subsidising
organic farming. Geraldine was – as she seemed to prefer –
sitting in the shadow with her arm stretched on the back of the
wicker settee which was her place, her undisputed favourite
seat, her throne from which she observed and listened and
occasionaly interjected an opinion, a comment, caustic and
shrewdly aimed. Duncan stood behind her. Peter was suddenly
aware that Duncan was running his finger along her arm from
the wrist to the elbow and on to her shoulder. She made no
attempt to move away. The skin, thought Peter, will be cool and
there will be a gentle down on it.

Urizen came back and settled into his chair in a pool of light
from the lamp overhead to read the opening paragraph of his
paper which, he said, encapsulated the whole argument: at once
environmental and economic, making sense in both domains.
As he read the rest were silent. Again Duncan ran his finger over
Geraldine's skin. Peter looked across at Peled and saw that he too
was following the tactile high risk game.

Suddenly Geraldine got up and said she was sleepy. 'Night
all,' she said. Urizen broke off for a moment and then resumed
his reading.

It seems unlikely that it is only in the male that there is a high erotic charge to moments of exploration and discovery, the tracing of the line of a muscle, the palping (if it is not too technical a term) of flesh, the discovery of folds, the trembling perception of patches of smooth hidden skin? How do we disentangle our memories and trace them to their roots; how do we, for instance, separate tactile ones that spring from experience from those drawn from texts: an image from a film, a passage from a book? If I describe Duncan's tracing of an erotic track up Geraldine's arm how much is my own memory of first contacts with a body that would perhaps become known and familiar? How much is it reinforced by the memories of that passage in Stendhal where he describes the cat-and-mouse courtship played out on just such a summer evening by Julien Sorel, the peasant boy, ambitious and thwarted in his ambitions, who as a gratuitous act sets out to seduce his employer's wife, making his first erotic, physical contact one evening in the garden where the husband is angrily berating the Jacobin tradition.

Julien, says Stendhal, was irritated. 'He drew his chair up to that of Madame de Renal. The darkness hid all his movements. He dared to place his hand very close to the pretty arm which the dress left uncovered. He was agitated – he was no longer master of his thoughts. He approached his cheek to the pretty arm and dared to place his lips on it.' And from what source, I wonder, did that image, that concatenation of impulse and action, come in its turn into Stendhal's mind? From what erotic moment in his life? How much does my Duncan Hogg, for that matter, owe to Julien Sorel, ruthless seducer, ambitious arriviste, who ends up on the scaffold and was himself derived by Stendhal from a working-class boy tried and condemned in sad reality for attempted murder?

'A novel,' Stendhal says somewhere, 'is a mirror travelling along a highroad.' What it captures are figures, incidents, feelings, which we may think we have left far behind us on the journey but which endure in the depths of the mirror.

★

When Duncan came to his room early next morning before breakfast Peter half-expected that it might be out of bravado – the hope of some hint, some passing reference to the erotic play of the previous evening which could not have gone unobserved. But Duncan's thoughts seemed to be running in another direction – on Peled. What, he demanded, did Peter know about the man?

That he was a kibbutznik, he replied, an Arabist, a Sephardi.

'Don't give me that shit,' said Duncan. 'I mean what's he up to. What's his organisations?'

Did everyone have to have an organisation, Peter asked.

'You should know,' said Duncan. Peter shrugged. 'Because,' said Duncan, 'I think he's CIA.'

Peter remembered across the years Orna's warning about Peled and his links to Mossad; but a stubborn reticence that cloaked enduring sadness and sense of loss made him hold back the words.

'I know what you're thinking,' said Duncan, 'You're thinking I'm daft. Not right in the head. Because that's what you do think but haven't the guts to tell me to my face. But one day I'll remind you about this wee talk of ours. It'll be a moment to savour, as they say.' He took up a book from the table. 'How can you go around looking at this stuff and getting pleasure out of it,' he said after a while. 'Paid for in sweat and blood. How many people died building that cathedral in Florence? Tell me. And what were they paid? I feel sick when I put foot inside any one of them. Which marks me down as a Philistine and a barbarian, don't tell me. If I had my way I'd put a bomb under the lot.' He rose to go. 'By the way there's a wee message came over the fax. For Peter Sinclair, no less. And guess who sent it. She's due the day after tomorrow.'

Andromeda would help to fill the interval. Since first he began to allow them to form, Peter had been in any case insistently conscious of images, situations, reflections, speculations and hypotheses of which Andromeda was the centre. They came to him at odd moments, unexpectedly, unsummoned – or so it emed. Once they had emerged into consciousness he would consider them, run and re-run them as one might a videotape of a piece of film, accepting or rejecting them according to a logic which was in part that of the narrative (which might allow of certain developments and not of others), in part that of his characters (which might preclude certain courses of action on the part of the women and men with which he peopled his fantasies).

Urizen had said (not altogether ironically) that he would be able to dispense with the expense of the postal services and deliver Itzak Peled's next move in the Andromeda game by hand. As indeed he did with a great play of secrecy – in an envelope marked ULTRA TOP SECRET, which Peter stuck in a pocket unopened. The truth was that he had lost interest in the wargame and was now obsessively concerned with the fate of his characters out there on Herringbone Ridge where the declination of Andromeda's poles made the sun's rays strike at an acute angle, casting pockets of dark shadow in valleys and hollows that might conceal movements, concentrations of space-craft, forces gathering for an attack. Now he was at a turning point in his fabrication of the narrative and must make a choice which, while conscious, would be determined – indeed overdetermined – at other deeper levels to which he had no easy access.


Overdetermination: the fact that the formations of the un-conscious – symptoms, dreams (to which I would add the kind of daydreaming we call novel-writing) can be attributed to a plurality of determining factors. This can be understood in two different ways.

  a  the formation in question is the result of several
      causes
  b  the formation is related to a multiplicity of
      unconscious elements which may be organised in
      different meaningful sequences, each having its own

      specific coherence at a particular level of
      interpretation

The second reading is the most generally accepted one.


With none of which Peter would have disagreed. The problem he confronted as he felt his way forward among the images and verbal patterns that presented themselves, emerging and concretising in a dance of signifiers, was that he must decide what action Catriona (Lucy/Lucinda) would take at this juncture. Would she obey orders and return to the capsule and so to base? Or would she disobey and propel her snow-cat across the couple of kilometres that separated her from the strangers to test their intentions? In which case what would be David's reaction; if, for example, Control ordered him to take her under fire with his laser gun for disobeying orders? Alternatively what would lie in wait for Catriona if they returned together? Would she not be under suspicion? Might her friendship with the young woman who had been extruded not be known to the authorities? In which case what would happen to her and to David, who would presumably be guilty by association?

It was a problem Peter carried around with him, constantly feeling it niggle away on the threshold of consciousness. It was with him when he was falling asleep; it returned when he woke. It would present itself in the middle of a conversation so that he became abstracted, in some sense not present – rapt, like Macbeth at the banquet – until someone (Duncan as like as not) called him back. He took it with him when he walked up the hill from La Volpaia and pushed into the thick broom.

It was about ten in the morning and the air was warm among the bushes. There was a crackling of ripe bursting pods like the sound of distant musketry. The grasshoppers broke from the cover of their camouflage under his feet and leapt before him. Over breakfast he had contrived to get out of one of the boys who horsed about round the pool some vague indications of where they had found the piece of metal he now carried

**159**

constantly in his pocket. The boy had told him little – and little that he did not already know – as he struck up the hillside which was more bewildering than it had been on the day when they had brought the body up on a peasant cart and he and Aldo had laid it in its shallow grave. Some scruple made them lay a piece of sacking over the face before they began to shovel in the loose, sandy soil.

There was no determining now where the spot had been; the boy's indications had been too vague, the broom too thick, one clump indistinguishable from the next. A patch of broken turf and scattered sand raised his hopes so that he squatted down and began to dig with his fingers, wondering how much sand he must scoop away before he found a death's head. He was ill-equipped. His nails broke on the roots of the broom. Even using his Swiss army knife it was slow work which he abandoned, asking himself what his aim was. To confront the dead man? To pinpoint the grave so that someone – the Red Cross perhaps –might come and exhume the bones and lay them in the German war cemetery on the other side of San Vito with a cross and a name and a date – 15 June 1944; a site of pilgrimage for ageing men and women like those German tourists who had filled the breakfast room in his hotel and among whom he had moved unrecognised, the killer of their son, husband, lover, the man who was guilty of that necessary, wasteful death?

He shut up his knife and rose to walk further up the hill, looking down on the serpentine road along which in twenty-four hours Ariel would perhaps come on her motorcycle. The curtain of the broom suddenly thinned and he found himself on the edge of an enclosed patch of turf in which Duncan lay palely between Geraldine's brown, annointed and receptive thighs. They were neither conscious of the sun nor the insects that played on their flesh nor the grass on which they grappled together, only of the fuse that linked them and burned towards orgasm. Certainly not of Peter as he turned away. A twig snapped under his foot as he set off down hill. They would not hear it.

★

As he turned the nose of his snow-cat towards the ridge where the capsule lay, David looked over towards Catriona. He seemed to detect a slight hesitation before she switched on her jets and began to converge on the same course. There was still a slight crackle on his headset but no traffic between her and Control; what messages, he wondered, were coming from the intruders over the wavelength he had abandoned earlier? But he knew he must not monitor it; nor had he any desire to do so when, their weapons and equipment stowed away in the scout-car, they locked themselves down in their cockpits and after a tiny moment of suspense that lasted no longer than a deep breath, took off, flying low towards the colony which they could see as a blip on their monitors and then as a silvery dome in whose side, using thrust and counter-thrust, they found the entry-port and docked. When they stepped out of their craft the ground crew were there, swift and practised, to remove their gear before they walked over to the Control Centre for separate debriefings.

David's interrogator was that Peter Sinclair who normally ran the wargames. Now his tone was much the same, ironical and sharp, sceptical. His questions were at first routine: the flight – how had the capsule functioned? The laser-weapons? – how easy to handle and set up? Then what could he tell him about the intruders: numbers, equipment, movements, possible intentions? To all of them David found quick, precise answers which his interrogator noted on his electronic pad.

Now the examination took a turn David had feared: had he heard any transmission from the intruders? Had the voices been friendly or hostile? In what language? It was difficult to know, said David, the frequency had at once been jammed. In any case, in accordance with standard signal procedures he had immediately switched to an alternative frequency so as to hear what instructions might come from Control. He was aware that the soles of his feet were sweating slightly; but perhaps his anxiety did not show on his face.

Sinclair considered for a moment before asking why David's co-pilot had wished to move closer to the intruders? Presumably to try to see their weaponry and movements more clearly, David suggested; visibility had been poor because of deep shadows in the hollows. Yes, said Sinclair, but what about the word she used in her request to move closer – 'strangers'? What would David think if he came across it, in a wargame for example? Was it not a curiously neutral word that might conceivably point to some confusion or doubts in the user's mind? By the way, what would David himself call them? David had no hesitation: intruders, aliens.

Sinclair considered a moment. How long, he asked, had he and his co-pilot been together? As pilots almost two years. 'You know what I mean,' said Sinclair with a touch of impatience, 'you share a living-space.'

'Eighteen months,' said David.

Sinclair nodded. Then he must have a pretty fair idea of her attitudes. Was she, for instance, critical of conditions on Andromeda or of the way in which the colony was run? Had she been under any sort of strain?

David was aware of the sweat breaking out on his back. Catriona, he said, was a very conscientious worker. Sinclair interrupted to say that the managers of the electronics plant were best fitted to provide a record of her work and made a sign for David to continue.

Like everyone else, David went on, she complained from time to time about some of the inevitable restrictions imposed by conditions on Andromeda. In his view it didn't mean anything.

Isabel Dufy – Sinclair spoke the name calmly – how well had David known her?

Not well.

But he had used the leisure facilities with her – how often?

Three times, said David, when he first arrived on Andromeda.

Sinclair looked down at his notes. 'That's what the records say. I am going to assume they are correct.' But what of Catriona's relationship with this same woman who had, after all, been found guilty of conduct which endangered the colony and sentenced to extrusion?

162

David thought they had got to know each other during the last solar storm when the women went into the deep shelter.

'Yes,' said Sinclair, 'there can be problems – particular friendships, they used to be called in some religious establishments long ago. But go on.'

He wanted to add, said David, only that from his point of view – as a scout – Catriona was totally reliable as a co-pilot and he would be happy to carry out any mission with her to which Control assigned them in future.

That, said Peter Sinclair, was a very generous thing to say – entirely what he would expect of David. But it was also perhaps just slightly naïve – as generous people often are.

There was silence between them for a few minutes as Sinclair ran over his notes, made a final entry and said David should have a good rest and hold himself ready for further debriefing if necessary. Somewhere, David knew, there must have been a microphone to record their session. Now his debriefing would be compared with Catriona's. He felt fear rise in his throat.

Back in the living-space he lay and watched the monitor. There was a newscast with pictures of their capsule taking off towards the intruders, who – said the announcer – had been kept under surveillance by brave pilots chosen for their skill and trustworthiness. There were some rather vague shots from the video camera in the nose of their capsule of distant movement among clouds of white dust, raised 'according to the reports of the scouts by a strong party of intruders, who appeared to be consolidating an operational base.' Then came shots of the scout-car returning and Catriona and himself walking over to be debriefed.

'The Control Commission,' said the report 'is proud of the excellent work carried out by the scouts, who discharged their duties in an exemplary fashion.' That must presumably mean that Catriona's account had tallied with his own. David felt his fears fall away. He lay down, drew up the coverlet on the bunk that folded down above the table, and relaxed into sleep.

★

Peter Sinclair was sitting in his bedroom, which the closed shutters shielded from the noonday heat. As he wrote he stopped from time to reflect, running back over the text to find those spots where a word repeated itself like a note struck too often and too insistently. The dépendance was quiet and empty. Duncan had gone off to drive Peled down to the coast to meet friends whose yacht had put in at Porto Santo Stefano. They would not be back till late.

In the heavy silence Peter listened for the noise of a motorcycle mounting the hill and coming to rest with a crunch of pebbles in the courtyard. He was torn between excitement and a certain nervousness. He had not warned Urizen that a young woman might come looking for him; had not done so partly out of a kind of shyness, partly out of fear of looking ridiculous should she not appear. Once he put aside his word-processor and walked quietly, stealthily to the end of the corridor where there was an empty room. If she came it would no doubt be allotted to her for neither Urizen nor Geraldine – nor for that matter Peter himself – could assume that she would wish to do otherwise than sleep alone. He wondered for a moment whether he should look for flowers to put by her bedside, but dismissed the thought – as he did that of leaving a note of welcome on her pillow. Perhaps she would come to find him in the heat of the afternoon or the cool early morning when the mist still lay in the valley into which he had dropped and for the first time looked over to La Volpaia; he must not build any hopes, give rein to his desires and imaginings, but turn back to the keyboard and that other woman who, as he was beginning to realise, was the true Principal Character of his daydream.


Catriona too had watched the picture of their sortie on the monitor in the small bare room where she had been waiting now for at least an hour. The newscast had been as she expected – no doubts about the identity or intentions of the 'intruders', a communiqué couched in the language Isabel Dufy had first taught her to decipher and interpret, paying attention to the words used over the closed-circuit television or in the weekly bulletins displayed in the communal halls and dormitories to describe those women and men in the colony picked out for mention; observing the shades of approval or disapproval that ran from industrious, reliable, brave to unsatisfactory, unreliable, uncooperative, anti-social, the latter being the term used when a colonist was sentenced to extrusion – and therefore, when her time came, to Isabel Dufy herself, whom Catriona knew as brave, questioning, determined, unafraid.

Sitting at the small bare table she wondered whether she herself would have it in her to be equally steadfast; for instance if they confronted her with the evidence of her attempt to get closer to the 'strangers' of which Control must certainly be aware, just as they must be aware – the monitoring service where Isabel had once worked would by now have submitted a transcript – of the content of the message she had heard coming over her head set: 'Sisters and brothers, we . . .' and had been drawn by these words to move forwards, to disregard the command to withdraw that crackled over her headset from Control, drawn by the need to ask what had brought them to Andromeda from Tellus where – if Isabel had been right – wealth, power and violence were the instruments of politics and government.

From what she had seen on the screen she could conclude that in his debriefing David had not been critical of her moment of hesitation; but there remained, she knew, the question of language. 'Strangers' was what she had said, and even at a moment of crisis the voice from Control had corrected her.

When the door behind her opened she did not look round but waited for her interrogator to occupy the chair that sat ready on the other side of the table. It was a man – fifty-ish, fair thinning hair, a sharp face, who introduced himself as Peter Sinclair and added that perhaps David might have mentioned his name – because of wargames.

Catriona said yes, she had heard the name and waited.

The man asked whether she would like anything – something to drink, to eat – but she shook her head and wondered where he would begin. To her surprise it was not with a question but with a congratulation on a mission successfully accomplished – a joint effort naturally, with her partner, David, who had paid tribute to her skills as a scout and had said he would be happy to make more sorties with her. A nice man, David, and a good reliable member of the colony but not, she would no doubt agree, very sophisticated in his thinking, not what one might call an enquiring mind; which did not for a moment mean he was stupid – his record at wargames was impressive – but then wargaming was a special and rather curious form of mental activity rather like traditional chess or its refined three-dimensional versions in which the bright young people of today pitted their intelligence against that of the computers in the communal halls.

So not someone to be bothered by questions of language whereas she, Catriona, unless he was much mistaken was interested in language and its codes. 'Code' naturally described a complicated system of signs evolved by a particular society – the colony on Andromeda, for instance – and it was only rarely that individuals disregarded the codes, consciously or unconsciously used words in an unusual way. In either case the reason why people broke the rules was always interesting. It could be something which surprised the speaker herself – but she no doubt knew that even our unconscious acts had their deep reasons – or it could be an act of defiance, a gesture of bravado to register some important difference of opinion or of perception with society.

To deliberately defy a code constructed by a society could be dangerous; it was liable to make people feel insecure, as if their grip on reality and in particular social reality had been loosened; which was one of the reasons, incidentally, why certain forms of writing were rightly regarded with suspicion, both on Planet Earth and here on Andromeda, as the product of neuroses (not to say psychoses) that were socially dangerous.

But no doubt these were matters she had discussed with her friend, Isabel Dufy, a highly intelligent young woman, who had most unfortunately broken the regulations on which the whole

166

colony depended for its safety and security. The Commission had therefore had no alternative but to punish her by extrusion. A great pity. A great loss to Andromeda. Such human resources were difficult to replace. What was particularly sad was that – he was being indiscreet in revealing this but he believed he could rely on Catriona not to break a confidence – she had been nominated for impregnation by sperm from the bank laid down by the Founding Fathers.

But she must be asking herself when he was going to come to the point – well, he would come to it soon. But first she should know that – as was normal practice – there was a tape-recording of all traffic to and from the capsule and snow-cats including a message from – what should he call them? – the 'intruders, aliens, strangers'? He would like to play the tape back to her.

The machine he laid on the table between them was small and compact, at its heart she could see the tiny spools begin to move and hear through the static her own voice reporting back – routine messages of speed and course, brief responses to instructions to land, to unship the snow cats and push forward to the ridge. Suddenly the intrusion of that other voice – a woman's – speaking across the grey powdery waste to sisters and brothers but quickly drowned by jamming and then her own voice again; 'Am advancing a kilometre to discover intentions of strangers.'

Her interrogator stopped the tape. 'There is of course a recording of the whole message from that woman. Some day we may get around to listening to it and analysing its content. It repays study. But what interests me for the moment is not the message itself nor that you wanted to advance a kilometre, although that was strictly speaking going beyond your orders, but why you used the word "strangers". Perhaps we might discuss this point.'

Beware of men with power when they are most polite and reasonable, Isabel had said; that is when they are most dangerous. They are reasonable because they know how great is the power invested in them and their courtesy is a weapon they use to entrap women in particular.

'Strangers is a neutral word,' said Catriona at last, 'to describe people one does not know.'

'But we – that is to say Control already knew who and what they were.'

'But I did not know. I still don't.'

Peter Sinclair looked at her with a slight smile. 'But your knowledge or lack of it was unimportant. The fact is that they had officially, on the grounds of reliable intelligence, been defined as "intruders", "aliens". We may not know their exact intentions, their objectives on Andromeda, but there must be a strong presumption that they constitute a threat to the colony. I see you do not accept my logic. One would have expected someone like you – after all, you are a child of the state, aren't you? – to adopt the official term. But perhaps you had some grounds for your doubts.'

'Intruders and aliens are strangers too,' said Catriona, 'I wanted to be sure. I was going to have to fire on them perhaps. It isn't easy to fire on a sister.'

'I understand that,' her interrogator rejoined, 'but perhaps you didn't recognise in these few words the language of a faith long discredited. One that exists in distorted and perverted forms in the *favelas*. It is the faith in us – in humankind – as a brotherhood or sisterhood who might somehow live together in harmony and well-being. It is a very old dream of both men and women: a millenarian faith. You know the word?' Catriona shook her head. 'It is the dream that from time to time throughout the centuries has haunted the minds of men and women – or women and men as your friend will have taught you to put it – who believed with passion that it might be realised on earth and who have been tortured, burned, hanged, beheaded, shot for it. They were undoubtedly brave people but their dream has remained a dream.

'If you knew some history – or did Isabel Dufy teach you some? – I could demonstrate to you how this dream has possessed whole sections of society and led them to claim to have inaugurated a new age. But while power may have changed from one set of hands to another, fundamentally nothing changed. Power remained power, rank remained rank, privilege privilege. For such, I am afraid, is the nature of human society and always will be. It is a sad truth with which we have to come to terms for everyone's good. The dream is, of course, a generous and seductive one and those of us who have the honour and responsibility of directing this colony understand your moment of hesitation – however mistaken – which you fortunately overcame and turned away from the siren voice of sisterhood and brotherhood. So I do not intend to interrogate you further.

'But I am going to lay one task on you: as you leave you will be given at the security control a package. It contains a manuscript of which you will take great care. For two reasons. It is an historical document which casts light on events a century ago from which we may still hope to learn valuable lessons. The second reason? It is that the document was written by my grandfather whose name I bear – so it is, in a real sense, an heirloom. You will take it back with you to your living-space and read it carefully. I shall examine you again to see what you have learned from it. Then the matter will either be considered closed or we shall have to take further steps towards your re-education. One way or another the treatment must succeed. Failure would mean that your case was very grave indeed. But at least you must concede that we who must concern ourselves with cases like yours can be both patient and understanding.'

He rose and signalled to her to follow him down the long muted corridor she had traversed on her arrival. Behind them she was aware of doors closing quietly in the long padded alleyways until they reached the security check-point where invisible beams scanned them before the door swung open on to the space beneath the great plastic dome. As it did so a woman in the dark uniform of the security services stepped forward and handed Catriona a bulky envelope. Then she was alone on the empty assembly place.

It was late at night. The lights under the dome were very low –presumably for security reasons; it was with difficulty that she could read the label on the package. RESTRICTED, it said.

Then her number and name. Underneath someone had written: 'For eyes of recipient *only*.'

As she walked through the silent colony towards her living-space her thoughts were full of Isabel Dufy; memories of her passionate mind and uncompromising spirit. How often she had talked of her great hope that somewhere there might be women (and men) like herself to whom she could talk openly and without fear: sisters and brothers. Looking up into the dark Catriona could see the disk of Planet Earth, the shadow of its night and the brightness where the sun revealed great patches of ocean and the dim outlines of continents from one of which the sisters and brothers had ventured through space to Andromeda.

Suddenly she was seized by fear. What, she wondered, if she were wrong? If these were indeed invaders who threatened the whole colony? If Isabel had been mistaken, deluded? As she walked along the empty passageways between the living-quarters she revolved her doubts anxiously in her mind. By the time she reached her block, however, she had found her way to the certainty that Isabel could not have been a mere dupe. But in that case how should she herself face the next days or hours? Did she have the courage?

In the living-space she found David asleep on the bunk above their table. The monitor on the wall was on as always but the sound was turned down. She watched what she guessd must be one of the many replays of tape showing the capsule returning and herself and David being escorted off for de-briefing. She could imagine the terms of the commentary. There would be no doubt about the name the announcer gave to the men and women, who, out there, were establishing their encampment among the dusty valleys of Andromeda and considering their next move, sending out their messages to their sisters and brothers, scanning the radio frequencies for some answering signal. She switched on the reading lamp, opened the packet carefully – it was elaborately sealed – and took out a sheaf of greying duplicated typewritten pages. The title on the first page puzzled her: *An Apology for My Life and Beliefs by Peter Sinclair: 1987*. The note that followed gave some help.

**170**

Note: *I am using the word apology in the orginal Greek sense of an account, a history. I do not intend to apologise for my life, merely to try to explain it to myself and to some of those who will come later.*

Catriona took out her electronic note-pad and began to read, a task made difficult by her unfamiliarity with an extended text; her reading was confined to instructions on the pale-blue screen of her VDU at her work-place. There were, besides, references to wars and civil wars, to parties and regimes of which she had not heard, to political struggles never mentioned by anyone except Isabel Dufy. But some passages caught her attention; made her pause and try to tease out their sense.

'I belong to that generation which grew up in the aftermath of one great war. We were convinced that another must come soon and that it would involve us. From this it followed that one strong impetus – not the only one but a determining one – behind our political commitment was a desire to fight for peace, against war, against the merchants of death and their clients, the Fascist states.

'It was our determination to fight Fascism, together with our perception of the social injustices of capitalism – poverty alongside wealth, scarcity alongside profusion, the oppression of the colonial peoples, the exploitation of men and women for profit – that made us give our allegiance to the Party which seemed to make our causes its own: *the* Party. It was the Party which, as the Bolsheviks, had engineered the revolution in Russia. All over Europe the men and women who were its cadres had given examples of courage, intelligence, constancy in their dangerous and illegal work. They were what one of their number on trial for his life had called "dead people on leave".'

Reading this passage Catriona recalled what Isabel had told her of the movements in the *favelas*, the plots, the insurrections that over the years had flared round the palace-fortresses of the clans; of the women and men who planned them in secrecy and hardship, who without thought for self or fame or reward suffered prison and persecution and met cruel deaths. She scanned the pages looking for a clue to the aims of this Party and its members.

**171**

'What the Party proclaimed was an international brother-hood, a society without exploitation, a vision of freedom and peace. These were not ignoble aims. The Party said they had, to a great extent, been achieved in the Soviet Union by the Russian Bolsheviks. It is true that the bourgeois press maintained the contrary: that the Soviet Union suffered under its leader, Joseph Stalin, from an oppressive and dictatorial regime; but that same press lied about many things both at home and abroad of which we had certain knowledge. This was a powerful reason for our refusal to accept the evidence of Stalin's terror. We read the press of our enemies as if it were a photographic negative: what was black must be white, what was white, black. Searching for a parallel I can think only of those dissident Russian intellectuals who in the Seventies called for the USA to use the atom bomb on Vietnam and cheered the fall of Allende's socialist govern-ment in Chile.'

From this passage she picked out the definition of the aims of 'the Party': international brotherhood (What about the sisters? Isabel would have said), an end to exploitation, a vision of freedom and peace.

Perhaps this was what her interrogator had been talking about when he spoke of impossible dreams. Much that followed was obscure to her. What she did understand was that the author had taken part in a war to defeat Fascism (whatever that might have been) and had hoped for a new and better society to result from it. But his hopes appeared to have been disappointed.

'What came of it was not a new socialist Europe but a Europe in which the old social and political force reasserted themselves. Europe was split down the middle by a so called Iron Curtain; the world was the site of power struggles between the Americans and their allies and the Soviet Union and theirs. To some of us who had been members of the Party it was a time for painful reflection, for the nature of Stalin's tyranny could no longer be denied; the evidence of the great prison camps, the record of mass-murder, were too circumstantial, too terribly documented.'

She had difficulty in following the writer's account of his

172

mental and moral struggles to come to terms with these truths and to decide what he could honestly retain of his old hopes and beliefs in the face of the evidence. Yet throughout the years of doubt and despair in which the author appeared to have been active in various political sects with which he was then disenchanted, he still clung to the hope in what he kept calling 'the dream of something'. What that dream appeared to be was a just society in which the great wealth of the earth was distributed equitably among its inhabitants and the exploitation of men and women by others, of one race by another, of one sex by another, would at last – at some perhaps distant date – be banished from the earth. As she wrote down the words she recognised that Isabel Dufy had been a dreamer of the same dream.

As she read she was suddenly aware that David had wakened and was watching her.

'What's that?' he asked suspiciously.

'Something I have to read.'

'Who says so?'

'The man who debriefed me.'

'Oh – but it went all right?' said David, and added re-assuringly. 'The communiqué said we had done well. Brave and resourceful scouts, they called us.'

'I expect so,' said Catriona.

David rolled over on the bunk and flicked the remote control to turn up the sound on the monitor. To the resonance of a long trumpet-like note the badge of the colony came up on the screen: the cone-shaped nose of a space-ship on which the word Mayflower was emblazoned. Then, just as when the threat of invasion was first announced to the assembled colonists in the moot-hall, an elderly white-haired man spoke from the screen in a voice that was reedy at first but grew in strength as he announced that the Control Commission had decided to place the colony on the highest state of emergency.

It was, he said, the duty of each man and woman to be on the alert against the enemy who had established a base on Andromeda but also against those who might spread rumours and undermine the colonists' will to resist. Colonists must without fail at once report to the security services or public order officers any sign of weakness, any defeatist talk, any spreading of rumours. Those found guilty of such behaviour would be dealt with without pity, for it was clearly treasonable. It was a time for each man or woman to display their loyalty to the principles of the Founding Fathers. The future of Andromeda lay in their hands. The Control Commission was confident that by discipline and watchfulness they could ensure the future of the Colony, its prosperity and what was more important its way of life, the moral values for which the Founding Fathers had stood.

He was succeeded by announcer who, as an indication of the seriousness of the times, wore his defence corps uniform. His voice was grave. The intruders were establishing their base and preparing for offensive action. Fresh teams of scouts were standing by to make further reconnaissances and to report back on the dispositions and movements of the alien forces. Meantime security on the colony had been tightened and the first arrests of persons responsible for undermining morale had taken place. The screen showed a man and a woman, their faces pale with fear, escorted by a group of public service officers with laser-guns. 'Their fate,' the announcer's voice continued, 'will be decided by a special tribunal. We have a statement from that tribunal's President.'

With a start Catriona recognised in the sharp features of the President her interrogator. She looked up at David but he was intent on the screen and hushed her when she made to speak. The voice of the President was harsher than she remembered it from her debriefing as he declared:

'As all colonists know by now the Control Commission had decided to resist the threat to the wellbeing and security of Andromeda by alien forces. They are, our intelligence sources tell us, adherents of a dangerous sect with its roots in the *favelas*. But we must overcome these backward and anarchic forces, by whatever means are necessary, up to and including the use of our laser batteries.

'We are determined to preserve our community and its way of

life based on hard work, respect for authority and just recognition of the individual's contribution to the colony's well-being. Let me ask you to keep in your memories the two traitors you have seen on your screens. Some of you will have recognised them. Perhaps they worked beside you in the hydroponics lab or in the electronic workshops. I have to tell you that they have since been tried by the special tribunal, found guilty and executed. As President of that tribunal I shall have no hesitation in passing judgment on any others brought to us.'

The monitor reverted to the transmission of abstract patterns, the heartbeat of the great mother sounded out again, soothing and comforting. There was a long silence between the couple.

'I hope we are going to be sent out again,' said David, 'I want to see them run when I get them in my sights.' Catriona did not react. 'Or do you think the Commission is upset. That there is a bad mark against us?'

'Why upset?'

'Because like an idiot you used the wrong word.'

Catriona shrugged. 'I have to finish my reading. We'll soon see.'

David turned off the light in the bunk and drew the coverlet up to cover his head. The circle of light from the lamp fell on a line written a century before by a man of whom Catriona knew nothing and whose thoughts were entangled in a web of language that was strange and difficult.

When David rose just before midnight to go to his shift she was still reading. She would be expected, she knew, to report as usual in the early morning but she was determined to stay in the living-space, to take notes and attempt to make sense of the document. What struck her as she read on, skipping passages in which the references were too obscure, the connotations of the language too veiled, was the writer's pessimism as he analysed the corruption that had overtaken men and women who in their youth and middle-age had willingly, freely, risked their lives for the oppressed of Planet Earth. Now, as he wrote, they sat in the seats of power, protected by their secret police who hunted down their adversaries, and displaying all the arrogance and love of privilege that had marked the old ruling classes.

'Today, in 1987,' ran the faded typescript, 'their rule has produced a generation to whom the word "socialism", instead of speaking of hope, equality, freedom from exploitation, has come to mean oppression, exploitation, the stifling of joy. In their despair many have understandably turned to old mysticisms, to the comforts of religion – that old opiate by which the people down the ages have drowned their sufferings and despairs – to superstition, to the zealotry of nationalism and the evil legends of antisemitism, venting their anger on men, women and children of other races or other beliefs, marked as different by dress, skin pigment, language or culture. Meantime the heads of the great international enterprises, the politicians who represent their interests and the media people who are their mouthpieces celebrate the death of socialism. It will be another generation at least before it will be possible to discuss seriously and hopefully humanity's dream of something.'

The document ended suddenly. As she gathered the leaves, set them evenly in a pile and replaced them in their envelope Catriona wondered whether the final pages were missing – or withheld. Then she gave in to fatigue and fear, laid her head on her arms and slept.

The bleep of her pager wakened her. When she answered, a voice told her to report for further debriefing. To bring her reading matter with her. As she walked towards the Control Commission building, it was almost dawn but Tellus still stood brightly overhead. There were patrols in the streets and open places, stopping people on their way to their shifts, checking identities. Why was she not at her work-place? they asked, then after a quick exchange over their intercoms they waved her on. There were no problems about entering the Control Commission Building and only the briefest of waits in the entrance hall where her details were again checked on the computer and the package with 'the reading matter' taken from her.

Then a middle-aged and not unfriendly woman accompanied her down the muffled corridors to what was perhaps the same room as before. A table; two chairs; a door in the wall opposite her that suddenly opened to admit her interrogator, who nodded to her as he sat down and laid before him on the table what she assumed must be her personal file and on it the packet that contained Peter Sinclair's *Apology*. He began by apologising for calling her at such short notice – had she got any sleep at all? He hoped so, but the situation was serious. She was one of the colony's best space-scouts – they had of course, meantime, sent out another crew – but she might be called on again.

First, however, the authorities and he as their representative had to be satisfied that they could rely on her judgment – or to put it more strongly, on her loyalty. There had been further discussion at a very high level of her 'mistake' – he would call it that for the time being – in using the term 'strangers'. He had been asked in what he hoped she would recognise as a generous move to explain to her the dangers that lay hidden behind what some people might dismiss as a mere slip of the tongue. But slips of the tongue, as a famous twentieth-century psychologist wrote, had their reasons.

Did Catriona, he asked, have any idea why – in line with instructions from such high quarters – he was taking so much trouble over her case? Catriona looked at his sharp features but could read no answer there and shook her head.

'You are called a daughter of Andromeda. Why?'

'Because I am an orphan.'

'And you have never wondered who your parents might have been?'

'In the home we were told not to wonder. We were lucky; the whole colony was our father and mother.'

'But I expect you still did.'

'Yes,' said Catriona, 'sometimes.'

'Well, we'll come back to this again perhaps. But meantime I would like you to tell me why the Founding Fathers came to Andromeda?'

'The Founding Fathers came to Andromeda to escape from the decline of morality on Tellus, on Planet Earth.' Catriona had no need to think as she recalled words that she had repeated hundreds of times in the home, in the colony's schools and later in the cadre classes when she was training as a space-scout.

He nodded as she spoke. His next question was also easy – too easy – perhaps a trap. 'And what type of society did they plan to set up on Andromeda.'

'A society in which work has priority over heedless pleasure, in which wealth is centrally and wisely distributed for the benefit of all – a just society.'

'What might some think were its drawbacks?'

The answer to his catechism came readily to her tongue. 'That life is difficult and restricted in many ways. The reasons are . . .'

'We know the reasons. Go on . . . But?'

'But it is not only just; it is also a moral society in which we learn the importance of discipline, respect for authority, that the good of the community is more important than the good of any individual in it.'

'And on what does the colony depend for its existence?'

How many more of these routine questions could there be – questions asked and answered a hundred times in classes all through her childhood and youth?

'The Colony depends for its existence on the shipment of precious ores back to Tellus. The profits from that trade make the existence of the colony economically possible. But the Founding Fathers did not approve of the amassing of wealth by individuals. The wealth of the Colony is employed in scientific research and on the development of the settlement on Andromeda as a base from which one day pioneers will take off to other planets in our system. These new settlements will embody the social and moral teachings of our founders.'

'Good. You know your catechism. But of course it is possible to repeat things by rote and deny them in one's heart.' He looked sharply at her. 'What was Isabel Dufy's dream precisely?'

Catriona was silent.

'I must warn you that failure to collaborate at this point would have the most serious consequences.'

As if she did not know that her fate was hinged on some word,

178

some phrase she might unwittingly utter in this conversation which was charged with threats, littered with traps.

'She thought,' she said, 'that there could be a society somewhere – some time – where we, women and men, could live free and equal, free to regulate their own lives, equal in sharing the great wealth of Tellus, of Andromeda. Of other planets out there.'

'And do you share her dream?'

Catriona's mouth was dry. 'It would be very beautiful,' she said at last and waited for him to speak: to utter the words that could decide her fate, which might be that of the two frightened figures she had seen on the monitor. There was a moment's silence during which the interrogator fiddled a little with the file and the packet, aligning one on top of the other and both with the edge of the table, as if considering what the next question should be. At length he opened the file and drew from it a piece of paper.

'I want you,' he said, 'to read something for me.' He opened the packet, consulted a note on a slip of paper, and found a page which he held out to her. 'From the top of the page', he ordered.

Catriona did not remember the page. It was one she had skimmed over, for she had been unable to fit it into any framework that her education and training provided.

'Well, go on,' he said.

'Tragically, after the war that saw the destruction of German Fascism,' she began, 'the socialist lands of Eastern Europe were ruled by men who lived in luxury at the expense of the class they claimed to have liberated. They had at their disposal villas, imperial palaces and hunting lodges where they tracked and killed the deer and the bears and the lynxes and the wild boar and after the hunt feasted and drank among their courtiers, their mistresses and whores. Meanwhile their wives and daughters, their sons and their dependents amassed gold, jewels, furs. In their special shops they could buy clothes, dresses, underwear, scents, along with video recorders, jeans, Walkmans and thigh-high boots imported from the capitalist West.

'Meanwhile the workers over whom they ruled in the name of socialism searched in bare-shelved shops for indifferent, botched shoes and clothes, for poor meat and vegetables, queued sullenly for the liquor with which they sought the joy denied them in their drab lives. In the private dining rooms of the great hotels the high functionaries of the socialist states entertained politicians from abroad, fraternal delegations of trades unionists, foreign businessmen, engineers, consultants. In the bars and lobbies young women who had bought their licence to carry on their profession by collaborating with the police, reporting conversations, compromising designated clients, waited to sell themselves to guests of the state or tourists with hard currency.'

Catriona paused a moment. She had found the passage difficult and had stumbled from time to time, faltering with incomprehension and fear.

'That's enough,' said the interrogator. 'Do you understand what you have read?'

'Some of it,' said Catriona. Her own voice sounded unreal to her. Far away. Detached.

'It is a description, by a man who lived for the dream your friend dreamt, of the evils to which it led. What he and people like Isabel Dufy have never understood is that their dream is based on a fundamentally mistaken view of human nature.'

As he spoke his face became animated, almost flushed; his voice lost it cool restrained tone. 'What they refuse to admit is that human nature is flawed beyond redemption by greed, desire for power, selfishness, envy, self-indulgence, unbridled sensuality, laziness, anger. Centuries ago wise men identified certain of these traits, catalogued them and describe them as the seven deadly sins: pride, envy, anger, lust, laziness, gluttony, sloth. But siren voices arise from time to time and proclaim another view of human nature. Time and again they assert its nobility, its potential for good, its generosity and – incredible as it may seem – maintain that by trusting human nature we can realise the dreamers' utopia. Recently they have been heard on Tellus calling from the *favelas* and seducing the impressionable members of the clans. They did it once before, not long after you were born. Have you heard of Alita? Did your friend, Isabel, never mention the name to you?'

Catriona nodded silently.

'She was a powerful and dangerous sorceress. She and her followers gathered together twenty-one years ago in the name of justice, freedom, equality. But what did the movement lead to? To banditry, sabotage, terrorism, acts of murder, kidnappings. I will not speak of the sexual licence that accompanied these other crimes. What I would assert is a law of nature is that the dreamers of such utopias end up as fanatics, killing and oppressing others in the name of justice, peace and love.'

He stopped and there was a long pause. Catriona felt a sweat break out on the soles of her feet, at the base of her spine, on her hands – the same sweat of fear as she experienced when she knew she must press the button that expelled the space-car and sent it cruising over the white-powdered deserts of Andromeda. She had learned to control her fear, to slow her breathing, to hold panic in check. She did so now as he opened her personal file and from it took out what appeared to be a couple of photographs which he laid face down on the table.

'I have here,' he said, looking at her intently, 'two identity card photographs. They are the photographs of your father and mother.' He laid a forefinger on each photograph and slid them apart on the surface of the table. 'They were doctors, both of them. Their chosen field was exobiology; the science without which we would never have been able to survive on Andromeda. The Founding Fathers had already begun to plan a settlement. There had already been reconnaissance flights to explore the surface of the planet and report on its resources. They funded your father and mother, gave them a laboratory, encouraged their researches. But your parents deceived their benefactors. They listened to corrupt voices, dreamt fanatical dreams and had to be dealt with. In the records of the colony you will read that they were sent on a two-man reconnaissance flight that unfortunately had to be aborted.' Like a conjurer he moved the photographs to and fro on the surface of the table. 'I have one last question for you. Do you want to know their names and do you want to see their faces? Yes or no?'

Catriona watched the movements of his hands. Her own she held caught between her thighs as she mastered her fear.

'No,' she said. 'I do not.'

She watched as he slid the photographs off the table and returned them to her file. Then he got up. He was smiling. 'I knew I was right,' he said. 'Some of my superiors did not believe me,' but I said you were a true daughter of Andromeda. I asked to be allowed to put you to the test. I hoped you would come through. I would have perhaps found it difficult to pass sentence on a young woman like you.' He rose, picked up the file and the package, and said: 'I shall report our conversation to the Commission. It will, I expect, be a formality. On the other hand, they might require me to examine you further. In either case you will not have long to wait.'

The door closed quietly behind him. But she knew she was only apparently alone. From some corner the surveillance cameras were recording her every movement, the play of her features, her posture as she sat and waited.


Peter wrote to pass the time, to fill the vacuum of Ariel's absence. She did not come that afternoon nor that evening which brought Duncan and Peled back late, excited, voluble, to recount an adventure: how as they negotiated a winding road in second gear people had appeared in front of their car waving an electric torch and signalling to them to stop. But Duncan had stood on the gas, as he put it, the car had responded and they had picked up enough speed to throw off the pursuit. Peled believed he had heard a shot as they pulled away.

'Sardinians,' said Geraldine, 'I warned you about them.'

And the talk turned to the strange way in which Italy was at last being united, one regional culture penetrating another, the Mafia establishing itself in the cities of the North with the drugs traffic and the Sardinians bringing to the mainland their ancient tradition of kidnapping and highway robbery. Peter could imagine the spot where the ambush had been laid. As the talk went on around him, with Urizen's deep voice providing the pedal notes, he remembered the road winding up from the coast plain past the signposts that warned of bandits and how the German trucks had climbed slowly towards San Vito with grinding gears, a rifleman on each running-board and another behind the cabin.

There were few houses near the pass, only grass and bare rock; which was why he had chosen it for the ambush with the light machine gun sited to enfilade the road and the others in the rocks above the road with hand grenades and rifles. As the three trucks came up through the cool morning shadows a landmine hidden in the dust of the road blew the tyre of the first machine which slewed and blocked the pass. The escorting troops jumped down and shook out along the roadside.

From the other side of the glen the machine-gun laid its cone of fire upon men and trucks; the hand-grenades cracked, setting off an explosion that threw debris and smoke high in the air. At the tail of the convoy the last truck began to back down the hill, contrived to turn. Some boys in field-grey ran after it and swung themselves up over the tailboard. The bullets from the light machine-gun threw up spurts from the road and ricochetted off boulders. A couple of bodies lay on the dust; a wounded German rose and began to crawl into cover by the roadside.

The boy from Lombardy ran down into the road, turned the bodies over, took a helmet as a trophy and then fired a shot at the wounded man who collapsed and spilled his life-blood on the ground. Two days later the front passed over in a confusion of grinding tank tracks, shell-fire and tracer bullets. It was an allied shell that caught the boy from Lombardy in the open and cut him in two.

A question from Urizen brought Peter back from his absence; but for a moment he was confused and did not know how to answer.

Duncan laughed and said, 'I wonder what he's got on his mind.' Peter excused himself, blamed the heat and the wine and said if they would excuse him he thought he had better turn in.

183

But he did not sleep. Instead he lay and waited and felt the slow passage of time. The night when they dropped him into the valley there had been moments of waiting when he faced the little panics that seized him. Now, as a mosquito drilled its way through the warm dark towards his face, he fought back a greater panic at the thought how the circling, gyrating earth bore him and everything on it inexorably to extinction, of how little time he might have left; imagined how he would pass it; thought too of how he would have to spend those minutes in a waiting room, discreet, muffled, upholstered, before being admitted to the consultant who would examine him, probe gently at his black spot, scrape it with a scalpel to detach a tiny sample of skin. Then there would be another time of waiting till sentence was pronounced. After that, how long would he have? How would he fill it? How would he combat time, with what weapons, what resources?

Yet in his days among the hills death had been his constant companion, when he slept or woke, at his side, ready to seize the moment of ill-luck when a bullet, a shell, a landmine, a knife, a noose of rope or wire might make him its prize. He had been conscious of the constant presence but had been able to discount it, to gamble on the odds of war and of battle, which carried some men through to safety. As in the end they carried him.

But now the terms of the game were different, the odds stacked inexorably against him. No embrace, no close fit of bodies, no exchange of humours and mucus and fluids could exorcise time and its powers. He turned his mind to Catriona, whom he had conjured up and given a life that extended far beyond the parameters of Urizen's wargames. (He must, incidentally, tell Urizen that he could no longer continue to take part in the ritual.) He wondered how she might have dealt with a waiting time that was limited, ominous, demanding an answer on which her life, as she realised, might depend.

As he stood next evening on the terrace, glass in hand, looking down into the valley where the shadows were gathering, he saw a metallic glint of sunlight on a motorcycle which, yes, did turn

184

off and climb up towards La Volpaia giving him just enough space to watch its progress and time his descent to the courtyard where, removing her casque, Ariel laughed and exchanged a friendly kiss with dusty lips. When they reached the terrace together Geraldine smiled but did not stir from her settee; Urizen received her with a gesture of welcome that was part of his practised role, although the surprise was genuine.

'My dear, welcome to La Volpaia. I'm so glad Peter told you to look in on us. Have you come far? From Bologna? From Lugano! You must be exhausted. Geraldine, my dear, where shall we put our new guest. Lucy is it? There's a room empty in the dépendance with a wonderful view over the valley where you can put your things and have a shower and so on. I expect you will want to sort your sleeping arrangements out yourselves.'

As she was being led off by the maid, Duncan appeared and greeted her with 'Hey, Lucy!'

Geraldine looked over at Peter, raised her glass, which Duncan had replenished in what to Peter seemed a distinctly proprietary way, and said: '*Complimenti.*'

Peter replied with a formal inclination of the head which Duncan observed with a slight smirk. Urizen, for his part, brushed aside Peter's apologies for lack of warning and was tactfully inquisitive, trying to establish the nature of the relationship, placing the young woman socially, wondering if she would be interested in a taking some photographs of La Volpaia – on a professional basis of course. He would, said Peter, have to ask her himself. He could not answer for her.

When Lucy came back she struck Peter as at once familiar and strange, for he had not seen her before wearing a long linen dress that left her arms bare and showed the tiny tattoo near her shoulder. Peled joined them, urbane and courteous in a slightly old-fashioned way, saying that one thing he had learned in the State of Israel was not to be surprised at what young women were capable of. Peter watched Lucy's face as Peled spoke but she had no obvious reaction unless there was a certain abruptness in the way she turned to ask Urizen whether he was a wargamer too.

So, in talk of everything and nothing, the evening passed and Peter found himself with Lucy walking down to the dependance where in the cool whitewashed corridor she kissed him gently and said, 'Goodnight, see you tomorrow.'


There should be a glossary of the kiss – the signal we give each other formally or informally within relationships that range from social and familial through the whole gamut of sexual pairings: men with men, women with women, men with women, women with men. It would accept and start from the OED's staid definition 'a touch or pressure of the lips' but would extend, detailing the coded messages a kiss can convey, exploring its whole range from the kiss of peace and the kiss affectionate to the goodbye kiss I gave my mother on her death-bed before I turned away from her frightened, uncomprehending glance.

It would necessarily discuss the difference between the varieties of touch or pressure of the lips (the fleshy folds at the orifice of the mouth, as the medical dictionaries call them) on a cheek or a brow; distinguish between the import of a kiss on the closed lips, its duration, the intensity of the charge it transmits through the tender skin. It would seek for and not find better words to describe the tingling anticipation of that contact than those Dante, six hundred years ago, put in the mouth of a woman relating how as she sat and read with her lover, 'he, who shall never be divided from me, kissed my mouth all trembling . . . that day we read no farther.'

It would discuss the soft yielding of the mouth which prefigures the opening of other more secret lips and point to how the mingling of breath, of saliva, of juices, the darting thrusting of tongues mime a different offering and different penetrations by finger, sexual toy, or organ: the play of yoni and lingam in which as lovers we seek out the most inviolate, most sensitive and closely guarded places of each others' bodies; hazarded and exposed, trustfully and without shame, to a partner's touch and pressure, to the warmth of a mouth, the snake-like explorations of a tongue, the sudden wildness of lips and teeth that make us cry out from expectation, pleasure and orgasm.

Within such a glossary, where would you place the kiss the Prince gave Sleeping Beauty or the Princess the Frog Prince? They are questions to which Propp does not seem to have an answer, although he does identify among the tasks proposed to the hero – such as to deliver a hair of the king of the sea, to obtain seventy-seven mares, to pose an unsolvable riddle – the (on the face of it) simpler one of kissing the princess in a window; which may of course be merely a prelude to that other harder task of finding out the distinctive marks of the tsar's daughter. More importantly, how would you interpret the gentle, affectionate kiss Ariel gave to Prospero at about midnight in the dimly lit, white-washed corridor?

It was a question Peter put to himself as he lay and thought of her proximity, remembered – though of such moments he knew our memories are fleeting and insubstantial – her body and its responses, its open acknowledgment of desire, its frank seeking of pleasure, its urgency and its imperious demands, its un-expected strength and ability to impose itself on him in a kind of affectionate combat, shot with sudden flashes of anger on her part, of barely suppressed violence, demands and commands that tested him to the point where the electric storm of consummation shook his body and exploded behind his eyes. What she had signalled by the kiss might be merely that she was tired from her long ride; it might mean that something had changed in their relationship – which was, perhaps, too strong a word for some more tenuous link which he, one-sidedly, attempted to reinforce by his literary charade of Prospero and Ariel; a fantasy (however real their physical encounters, how-ever intense the shared experience of desire) into which he had woven hopes and expectations he barely dared to formulate to himself, for they were perhaps merely weapons in a rearguard action – a forlorn hope rather – in the confrontation with age and death.

An imperious knock wakened him very early. Duncan. 'Didn't want to burst in on some primal scene,' he said with a grin, 'and catch you exchanging body fluids. Seriously though – I've been up since crack of dawn faxing stuff for Peled. That ambush last night, he thinks it was the PLO. He's persuaded our host, Christopher (Faggots) Williams, no less, who's in a great tizz about it and thinks it's all part of a conspiracy to fuck up his Arab-Jewish seminar. Talk about paranoia!'

'You should know,' said Peter through the insect-like buzz of his electric razor. Duncan went to the window and threw open the shutters. From below there came a splashing sound as someone dived into the pool. Duncan watched in sullen silence.

'Who is it?' asked Peter.

'Not your friend. Bad luck, old chap,' Duncan mocked.

'It's maybe none of my business,' Peter countered, 'but do you know what you are doing?'

Duncan closed the shutters as if to preclude an answer and walked up and down the room. 'Hey, you should have seen the boat Peled went to visit. An ocean-going yacht – aerials all over it. Crew of six. A couple of nice-looking birds. The captain's ex-Israeli navy. Peled disappeared below. I chatted the young women up but then I got pissed off and went and looked at the harbour. I think there might be great future for piracy on the high seas. Expropriating rich playboys and playgirls. Pity I get sea-sick – I'd sink the whole bloody lot.'

'*Le Capitaine Kydd de nos jours.*'

'You're a petty bourgeois intellectual snob. When you were doing your French verbs they were trying to turn me out as a plumber.'

The morning had taken a turn Peter had not envisaged. His thoughts and fantasies had been directed towards the cool room where Lucy was asleep or stirring. As he and Duncan walked together up towards the main building he was edgy and taciturn. On the terrace the young people came and went, oblivious of all others, teasing, laughing, squabbling, debating plans. Peter thought enviously how the day – and not the day only – must lie before them, unproblematic and spacious. No sign of Lucy. He drank a quick coffee and walked off up the hill behind the farmhouse followed by an incomprehensible shout from Duncan.

Skirting the edge of the wood he tried to tease out old paths among the undergrowth, and eventually struck up between the scrub oaks and the tall beeches beyond till suddenly he reached a pool in shade so deep that the grass was sparse, and the leaves from last year still drifted on the surface of the water. In the clear stillness he could see the ghostly white darting motion of crayfish and remembered how he had sat with Dino and drawn up their plan of attack on the radar station here in the safety of the trees.

When he re-emerged he chose a terrace where the vines had been allowed to deteriorate, rank and untended, and looked down at the farm and the valley. Even without his field-glasses he could follow the comings and goings at La Volpaia, believed he could distinguish Geraldine sunbathing by the pool while Peled and Urizen held a peripatetic conversation on the terrace. Suddenly Lucy and Duncan appeared in the courtyard. She was wheeling her bike. For a few minutes they stood and talked then she kicked the engine into life and with a gesture he recognised raised her hand as, casqued and doubletted, she accelerated into the first curves.

For the rest of the morning Peter remained in the woods as if they offered him a protective screen, as they had once before from the light German reconnaissance planes drifting noisily like enormous dragon-flies through the narrow valleys. Now they offered some slight haven, cover from the doubts, hesitancies and jealousies that assailed him. He did not return at midday but found his way through the terraces to a metalled road at the end of which there stood, close-shuttered, a two-storied house with a low wall and a metal railing.

By the gate a tarnished brass plate said: *Dott. Corsini Luigi. Avvocato.* He hesitated before pushing the gate which gave easily; evidence perhaps that in spite of its blind windows the place was inhabited. After a long pause his knock brought to the door a woman in her sixties, wearing the black dress of lifelong widowhood.

She mustered him from under her grey hair and said simply, interrogatively, '*Si?*'

For a moment he was tongue-tied, then said he was English and might he come in? She stood aside without a word and he found himself in a room where in the half-light the chairs were ranged along the walls as he remembered. On the end wall a photograph of young man. Fixed, formal: Dino. Beneath it in a glass case a gold medal. The woman indicated a chair, asked if he would like something – a liqueur, a coffee? When she had left the room there was no other sound in the house except her movements in the kitchen from which on that night there had come the whimper of a baby so that Dino had cried 'Maria,' and the noise had been hushed. She must have been quite young; nineteen or twenty. Newly married.

She set a tray on the table with a plate of small dry biscuits.

'I knew Dino,' said Peter after he had sipped his coffee and nibbled at a biscuit. She did not react. 'It is the first time I have been back,' he went on, 'to see – I just wanted to see . . .'

The woman sat with a hand on each knee. 'The widow of Dino, gold medal of the Resistance – that's what I am. All they have allowed me to be for forty years. His Party needed me that way so that I had to be seen on platforms, at anniversaries. They lay a wreath up there every year. But this year I would not go. I have had enough. There was someone who would have married me and taken me to Canada. A good man. With my son. But they persuaded me to stay. But this year I said no, and in December I am going to Australia. My son's a good boy. He's married out there. Has a business. I want to leave. I want to die as myself, not as Dino's wife. He lost his life and I have never had one.' She stopped, pushed the plate of biscuits towards him and was silent.

'He was a brave man,' Peter said, 'I'm sorry.' At the door he shook her hand and said: '*Buona fortuna* in Australia.'

She thanked him and watched him down the path then, before shutting the door, called after him, 'It's not your fault.'

190

He knew it was her knock and rose quickly to greet her as she entered. She allowed her hand to rest in his as they sat together on the edge of the bed. It was, he recognised, a gesture that admitted to what had passed between them but set a limit to what might pass here and now, or perhaps even in the future. Her first words were a formula he was familiar with; had heard it spoken – had spoken it himself – how many times? Always the marker of a cadence if not a caesura in a relationship.

'We have to talk,' she said, and rose to walk about the room. Peter waited, fearful of what might follow. 'Why did you ask me to come here? All right – not ask – kind of suggest it?'

'You mean Peled,' said Peter. She turned sharply, demanding to know how he had guessed. Because, he said, Duncan had told him about her friend – prisoner of the Israelis in the Negev.

'Sometimes Duncan can be a idiot,' she said.

Why, he asked, had she confided in Duncan and not in him?

She stopped by the bed and laid a hand on his shoulder: 'Because we got drunk together in Glasgow. Because there was nothing between him and me and there was between us. I'm sorry. What did you think?'

'I was hurt. But what was I supposed to think, unless that it must be very hard for you?'

There was a slight gentle pressure from her hand before she withdrew it, rose and walked to and fro in the room. 'In some ways I wasn't sure I could trust you. Not in that way at least. Still don't know. I'm sorry'.

Peter expostulated: she knew where he stood politically. His views on Zionism and the Palestinian struggle. She shrugged and said a lot of people had the right attitudes but they weren't for real. Sounded good at dinner parties and meetings. But not where politics meant doing something concrete. She rehearsed her suspicions: an Israeli wife – all right, ex-wife. All right, an anti-Zionist. But still an Israeli citizen with a son – if Duncan had got it right – old enough to be in the Israeli army, patrolling the Gaza strip maybe. And what about Peled, who had been high up

**191**

in Mossad? Hadn't he known him for years? Which was what Duncan said. It didn't look good.

How could one explain the twists and turns of life, thought Peter? And how they can suddenly confront us with memories, guilts, sorrows from our past which it is difficult enough for those who have lived through it to explain or understand – far less for someone from another generation sitting in judgment. He tried, not protesting his innocence, to explain the concatenation of events, some of them far in the past, which had brought both him and Peled to the same summer farmhouse in this precise corner of Tuscany. He had learned, he said, in life to accept the bizarre randomness of chance. Not to attempt explanations which could easily be paranoid, seeing connections where none existed. There was no way, for instance, to explain the chance that had allowed him to survive while his name might just as easily have been on the monument up on the hill along with those of the dead. Which was all a very long time ago but was some sort of proof that he believed in putting political convictions to the test of action.

She stood by the shutters looking out over a landscape over which there hung a veil of heat and light. When she closed the shutters the room became darker and it was difficult to distinguish her features as she turned to look towards him. 'I want you to do something for me. I won't explain. The less people know the better. The less you know the less you can give away. I bet you learned that when you were here before.'

Peter protested. 'Sometimes people give things away without even meaning to,' she went on. There was a pause while she considered. Did he have a camera? No – then she would lend him one.

'I want you to go to Santo Stefano and take a photograph of this yacht Peled visits. It's called the *Sharon*. I need to have the film by tomorrow night. Will you do it?'

He rose as she came towards him and they hugged. He did not see her again till dinner when she was at the other end of the table next to Geraldine, distancing herself from Peled perhaps, laughing and whispering conspiratorially, sharing some confidence. When he got back to his room the camera lay on his bed.

**192**

One of the tale's favourite elements, says Propp, is the proposal of a difficult task to the hero. The range of tasks is formidable. It includes ordeal by food or drink, eg: to drink a great deal of beer; ordeal by fire, eg: to bathe in a red–hot iron bathhouse; tests of strength, adroitness, fortitude, eg: to pick up the head of a decapitated dragon, to milk a herd of wild mares; tests of supply, eg: to deliver a hair of the king of the sea or to obtain a wedding dress, ring and shoes; ordeals of choice, eg: to select sought–after persons among twelve identical girls (boys); riddle-guessing, eg: to recount and interpret a dream; hide and seek – to hide oneself so that discovery is impossible.

When the task is resolved the hero is recognised, the false hero exposed, the hero given a new appearance, the villain punished. Finally and inevitably the hero is married and ascends the throne, is installed as ruler and patriarch; the tsar's daughter is his wife and subject. Under which heading would you place the task this hero has been set, and do you think the solution proposed by the logic of the fairytale, told and retold over the stove in the peasant huts of Eastern Europe, holds good in – as we say – this day and age?

The stones of the quay were hot underfoot. There was a smell of diesel oil. Along the mole where the yachts lay moored, young bronzed men moved surefootedly among the hawsers. On the boats they went about small tasks, deft, absorbed, and yet conscious of the muscled tautness of their bodies, the natural elegance of their movements. The harbour was half-empty. As he drove down from the hills to the coastal plain Peter had seen sails scattered over the water as the boats stood out to sea on the off-shore wind of morning. On those that remained the young crew-men went about their tasks watched by brown, tow-haired children while the owners and their guests chatted under awnings, read, drank, flirted, and gave themselves up to the heat that eroticised their gestures; the line of a thigh, the inclination of a neck, the tiny shadowed crater of a navel, the prominence of a pubic bone.

There was no one on deck on the big sea-going motor yacht flying the white and blue Israeli flag: the *Sharon*. With its long foredeck, its high bows, its feel of speed and manoeuvrability, it should, Peter felt, have been painted battle-ship grey like the motor-torpedo boats he had seen in this same harbour when he came down to embark on his way back to Naples, hobbling because of the superficial but painful wound where a shell-splinter had struck him just above the knee. It was, as Duncan had said, bristling with aerials, upright or set at acute angles, with tips that quivered in the slight breeze, long delicate antennae like the fine palpi of a crustacean.

Climbing up steps on to the wall of the mole he began to take photographs. Someone – but who? – would scan them closely using skills which had once been his. He ostentatiously aimed away from his target. Even so he noticed that one of the crew of the *Sharon*, a young woman in shorts, came up on deck and studied him through field-glasses. It was a moment that recalled other reconnaissances with Aldo, other deceptions, other sub-terfuges, other dangerous games which he thought he had put behind him but was now playing at the behest of a young woman whom he knew and did not know, whose realities were hidden from him, with whom he had been – in the terminology of the law-courts – 'intimate', but to whom he was still a stranger. As perhaps in the end we always all are to one another. Yet he felt himself bound to her by liking, by affection, by admiration, perhaps even by love.

It took him some time to shoot his roll of thirty-six exposures, which would include – as part of his subterfuge – shots of a seagull on a bollard, a view of the harbour and the old town rising behind it, looking much as it did on a fourteenth-century fresco in the chapel where the bones of San Vito had ended their dance.

He drove back along the coastal plain, skirting unfashionable beaches, then turned right through the Maremma – were there still wild boar, half-wild buffaloes, in what remained of its wild

194

and tangled thickets? – before pushing up into the foothills of the Appenines by the road where he had laid the ambush. But he could no longer identify the precise point where the hills squeezed road and stream together. The highway had been widened and asphalted; the scrub was thicker, his visual memory inaccurate. He lost speed as he tried to find his bearings, till, startled by the urgent hooting of a lorry and trailer hard behind him, he abandoned the attempt and accelerated away towards La Volpaia, over which there lay the drugged stillness of afternoon.

There was no sound in the dépendance where he walked quietly to Lucy's door which opened to his slight, hesitant tap. She had drawn a sheet round her and tucked it in like toga. He held out the roll of film. She put an arm round his neck and drew him to her. 'Come and lie down,' she said. Her skin was cool against his. They lay together trustingly and talked with low voices.

There had been a row at lunch – between Duncan and Peled – about the Holocaust. Urizen simply hadn't been able to calm them down. Duncan had been on some sort of a jag and there was no stopping him. Had said the deaths of eight million people were being exploited in a disgusting way to stop people crititising Zionism. That Auschwitz had been built into the ideology of the Israeli state. Said it was bullshit to believe that Palestine had been a land without people waiting for the Jews – a people without land. Peled had said anti-Zionism was the same as anti-Semitism. Geraldine had weighed in and said this was bollocks.

'Peled got really nasty. Turned to me, said he was surprised I hadn't anything to say. I said I had my own thoughts but didn't feel like sharing them. The long and the short of it is, Duncan has given in his resignation. Peled is packing. Geraldine is pissed out of her mind.'

'I sometimes think Duncan has missed his vocation,' said Peter.

'Which is?'

'To be a terrorist.'

Lucy/Lucinda/Ariel made no reply but lay for a little on her back looking up at the ceiling. Then said, 'Maybe you're right,' she added – inconsequentially as it seemed – 'I am off this evening.'

'Can I ask where?'

'You can but I can't tell you – because I don't know. I shall get my orders.'

'Take care at least.'

She laughed. 'You can be very sweet,' she said and drew his hand over her body.

'Write to me sometimes,' he said that evening as she raised her helmet to her head, started the bike and with her customary gesture of farewell drove through the gates of the courtyard.


*When, having read thus far, you asked me, in your direct, challenging way: When are you going to write about a woman who isn't a victim? Because, as a woman, I am tired of reading about suffering women in books and seeing them suffer in plays and films, being written off, killed off, eliminated. Why can't you think up a strong independent woman who isn't just a girlfriend – like this woman Lucy or Lucinda or whatever you call her?*

*I found it difficult to answer except to say weakly that in our society women have traditionally been victims, dominated, denied their freedom of action.*

*You shrugged and said it was my story I was writing and it was up to me.*

*I have to confess that as a writer I have followed the movements of my daydreams which are inevitably shaped and determined more than I might care to admit by the kind of society I have spent my life in and the ideology I have absorbed. Beyond that there is a problem, one we are familiar with in another context: the representation in fiction or film or drama of positive women or men who can be as unrealistic in their 'realism' as the rhetorical men and women of Stalinist iconography. But my thoughts about Lucy/Lucinda – inchoate as they were – were more positive than you perhaps imagined. I wonder if you will agree?*

★

196

The terrace was strangely deserted. Urizen had apparently driven Peled down to Santo Stefano and would not be back for supper. Of Geraldine there was no sign. The young people had taken off like a flock of birds to spend the night at a villa of some Contessa down towards San Vito. Graziella, the housekeeper, served the meal with the air of someone to whom such domestic crises were familiar. Standing by the table she began to question Peter with the directness of a peasant. How was it that he spoke Italian – not like some people who came who could only say please and thank you and do this and do that – but knowing all the words?

He had been in these parts a long time ago, during the war, he explained. Did she remember those days? Peter asked her. Yes, she said, she had only been a young girl of course, but she remembered those days. Such scares! Her father had been a partisan. All those soldiers. The shelling. All those poor dead. Let's hope it was for the last time. Peter said he hoped so too and went off to his room.


In the padded silence Catriona turned over in her mind the alternatives. Perhaps her interrogator really thought that she had been guilty of a mere slip of the tongue. He might read it as pointing to doubts or confusions in her mind, but if she were careful now when her interview – her debriefing – continued there was perhaps a hope that she might be given another chance. How she would use that chance would depend on many things, not all of which she could foresee. Clearly one thing she would be expected to do was to distance herself from the dream which people seemed to have had a century before, when it had not ended well if she understand the *Apology* properly. But it still lived on and drew her strongly. As it had Isabel, the daughter of Alita.

She could claim no such parentage, yet the fact that she was 'a child of the state' had only one meaning: that she had been removed from her parents or they from her. In the state boarding school where she had spent her childhood and where she had been taught to consider it an honour that the state was both father and mother, no one ever spoke of the missing parents and yet everyone knew that some secret was attached to their memories. Perhaps they too had dreamed the dream. And suffered for it. She would have to be clever. Even if she disowned the dream from now on she would be under observation and on her own. She did not wish to involve David – he would in any case ask no questions – because in her heart she suspected he could not in the end be trusted and because she could not bear to test that suspicion. Nor could she make contact with friends of Isabel's like the woman who had spoken to her on her way here. She wished only that her interrogator would come so that this moment of fear could be over and her doubts and hesitations resolved one way or another.

He re-entered quietly. 'Well, what have you been thinking?' he asked.

She looked up at him and said, 'It seems to have ended badly –the dream that lasted so many years.' He agreed – but did she understand why? She said she found a lot of what she had read difficult to understand and so it wasn't easy to put it into words, but the reason seemed to be that human beings were unable to live up to the dream and that they inevitably fell back into a kind of tyranny. It was a depressing thought. Her interrogator laughed and said it was indeed, but that to understand this was in a sense the beginning of wisdom. He was convinced however that she was sensible enough to draw the proper conclusions.

With that in mind he had talked to the appropriate authorities at the Control Commission and persuaded them to take a risk: it was this. If he were persuaded that she had taken the lesson to heart she would be allowed to return to her living-space and to wait there to be called for another reconnaissance. If she proved herself this time the incident would be closed, although naturally it would be entered in her records, and she would continue to be a valued member of the colony. If however she made any mistake, the consequences would be severe and there could be no question of mercy. The Control Commission was taking a calculated risk, as indeed was he, in recommending it. Had she anything she wanted to say?

198

She reflected for moment and asked whether she would be teamed with David again.

Yes, he said; was that a problem?

She shook her head. No not a problem. They had trained together and made good team.

'Right,' he said, 'in that case you can go back and wait for a signal. We expect to send out a scout-craft in a few hours. You had better try to rest.'

When at last she stood outside the building she was shaking. She hugged her arms round her chest and waited for the shaking to subside. As she walked off past the patrols, who made no attempt to challenge her, she knew already what she must do.

David was still sleeping, sprawled across the shelf. She took a duvet and curled up down below. Sleep approached and then eluded her. Her mind was full of the voice she had heard on her intercom and of images: of Isabel's face as she was led to the capsule and extrusion, of her face at other times too, alive, vivid, serious, joking. She had slept for a few hours when the signal rang and David woke above her. He showed no surprise at seeing her. Together they put on their gear and made their way to briefing where the intelligence officer was the familiar figure of their interrogator.

The situation, he said, had changed: the intruders had consolidated their positions and were beginning to build what looked to be a strongly defended locality. The scouts were to approach as close as possible and determine the exact nature of the defences, the armament deployed and the numbers of intruders involved. They would, he added, be fully aware of the serious nature of their task and the need to carry it out scrupulously as they had learned to do in training. They were to take particular care about signals procedures. He wished them good luck.

Perhaps, thought Catriona, he is not a bad man. It would be bad for him – bad for everybody – if things went wrong. Bad, too, for David whose hand she took briefly as they walked over to don their spacesuits. She smiled at him as she raised her helmet and drew it down over her face. They entered the capsule. As it accelerated away and turned towards their goal

Catriona felt a moment of excitement and fear. In her headset the voice of Control instructed her to set course and altitude. Once they were beyond the ridges it talked them down, instructed them to disembark and unship their snow-cats. As they moved forward their vehicles raised a fine thin cloud of dust. From a position overlooking the intruders' encampment they saw how small shelters had been constructed for people and machines. On the perimeter there were emplacements that might house laser weapons. But they appeared not to be manned.

Catriona reported back. David could hear her voice on his intercom, calm and measured. Her language was correct. Intruders, she called them. There was no interference by alien voices from the camp, little movement to be seen. 'You will return,' said Control, 'and dock as directed.' David switched on his engine and manoeuvred his snow-cat till it set course towards the capsule. He could see Catriona on his port side abreast with him. As he glanced over she raised her hand in what might have been a salute or a gesture of farewell then her snow-cat wheeled away heading back towards the intruders.

'Pursue and take under fire,' came the order over his headset. Obediently he turned in her wake. His laser-gun was ready for action. He found it difficult to bring her into the aiming circle and his finger shook as he found the firing button but he pressed it. Her snow-cat swerved, reared up and went cartwheeling across the grey dust, struck an outcrop and shot up out of control off the face of the planet. He managed to control his cat and make his way back to the capsule. His hands were shaking as he snapped down the roof and operated the jets. Control talked him through the procedure and docked him safely.

When he stepped from craft it was Peter Sinclair who welcomed him. 'It had to be done,' he said, 'for everyone's sake. The colony is grateful to you.'


It was not until he was in his flat that Peter re-read the account of Catriona's end which he had written at La Volpaia as he waited to be taken down to San Vito and on to the airport at Pisa. Once again he recognised in her the woman as victim but he could find no other logic for her end in daydreams fed by his own dark pessimism. He had by now phoned Will Brodie, chatting first about La Volpaia, saying Christopher Williams wished to be remembered to him, then giving a gossipy account of domestic drama and social tensions and the disintegration of the war-game. But when he had him on the phone could he ask Will for some advice – it was probably just hypochondria but he'd like to be sure – and the name of a good consultant? Private if necessary – which was a measure of how worried he had been. He wrote down a name and an address. When he had some news they must get together and have a drink, a meal or something. It had been too long. The phatic discourse of a dead friendship.

Now he was walking down into the autumnal park where children on bicycles pirouetted on the broad walks. From the Zoo a sudden trumpeting noise came across the grass, dampened by the distance. The house he sought would be solid, white-washed, confident in its age and dignity, perhaps furnished with a blue plaque commemorating some literary figure, some foreign statesman exiled by nineteenth-century tyranny or the fact that here in more recent times some special ops unit had had its London base. Today those who came out as he studied the bells were a family – Arab? Iranian? – a middle-aged man, plump, soberly dressed, a woman whose coat and hat were a tribute to her husband's wealth, a small boy with a bewildered air and the incongruous school uniform of the British middle classes. The woman was weeping but over whose fate he could not tell.

At the reception a woman in her forties was enthroned, with piled honey-blonde hair and red nails. Her sexuality bloomed in the house of death like a musk-scented plant in the rainforests. The waiting room she showed him into was dimly lit, heavily curtained and draped. On the walls, watercolours of Italy which he was examining when, from a quietly opened door, there issued the invitation to come in to where a rather short man with white hair and a sun-brown pointed face, light grey suit and army tie, extended a small pink hand.

201

'I was looking at your watercolours,' said Peter to fill the silence.

'Italy,' said the pointed face, 'lovely place. I have a villa there. Simply lovely. Know it?'

'Just back,' said Peter. 'You see,' he went on inconsequentially, 'I have this sort of mole on my chest and it seems to get bigger.'

'We shall have a look – shall we? If you will just strip to the waist.' His fingers were curiously light on Peter's skin, almost caressing. 'Any itching, pruritus. Bleeding?' A light directed on the black spot. A gentle pressure on the flesh. 'Right you can put on your things again.' Across the empty expanse of the fine, highly polished desk, they faced each other. 'I shall need to do a biopsy. I think I ought to tell you that it may well be serious.'

'A melanoma?' said Peter.

'Possibly,' said the brown pointed foxy face. 'I think the best thing would be for you to make an appointment with my receptionist. It is a very simple procedure. But we want to be sure, don't we?' He rose to conduct Peter to the door.

'San Vito?' said Peter pointing across the room at a watercolour.

'Yes, funny – do you know it?'

Peter nodded – he would have liked to talk, explain, but the other cut him with a 'good-day then,' and a shake from the delicate hand that responded to life and death like the wand of a diviner.

Garlinski was there as usual as Peter drove up to the gates in the gathering murk. Welcome back and he would find that the bothie was ready. There were logs if he wanted a fire, which Peter knelt to light and with remembered skills from his childhood coaxed into flame. It was a week since he had walked out of the consultant's and into the sunshine with no appointment made. He would have to look at his diary, he had said. He would ring and suggest a date. The receptionist had smiled from under her honey-hair as if she recognised the subterfuges of fear. When he rang, the Major was affable, of course he could come up – for how long? – no problem. Looking forward. So here he was once more confronting his fears in the bed where he and Ariel had lain together.

He remembered a conversation with Will Brodie in the common room about sex and ageing and the evanescent nature of the experience. Will, that man of the Enlightenment whose mode of thought was determinedly reductive, had quoted a physiology textbook he had used to recommend to his students. Coitus, it said, is accompanied by psychic excitement and must be regarded primarily as a cerebral phenomenon. To try to recall the experience was, he said, like shutting your eyes and trying to remember the patterns of summer lightning. If that electric storm had swept through him for the last time, Peter reflected as he drew up the duvet, he was glad it had been with Ariel, who had flown off not after summer merrily but to discharge some difficult, dangerous mission with that gesture of hers which was partly a salute and partly a farewell. He listened, as he lay, to stays of the yachts clattering in the wind, to the plashing of the water and the occasional cry of a bird. Tomorrow he would take out one of the boats and sail far up to the end of the loch, taking a deep breath, as it were, to master his fears, before setting course for the quay.

So he set a pattern for his days: walking, sailing, drawing some sort of balance sheet of his life, of his political efforts which had not been confined to the classroom or the study but included selling the Party paper on cold winter Saturdays outside tube stations in South London, and the long patient exhausting work of committees, planning, organising; learning from comrades from the Ford assembly line the difficult task of organising workers who were often backward, racist, dismissive of politics; finding the psychological levers to persuade them to see beyond the limits of conditions of work, rates of pay, and bonuses; speaking at meetings; facing the police cordons on picket lines. It had been a long, wearing endeavour which he could not bring himself to believe had been fruitless. Now he was engaged, he knew, on a rearguard action that must lead to a different kind of confrontation; for that appointment must be made and the outcome faced.

One morning he rose early. The sky had cleared overnight and the mist was thinning on Ben More. There was a flat calm; not a breath of wind to stir the thin layers of mist under the trees of the island. He took the oars from the back of the house and went down to the jetty. It was cool over the water but he would soon warm up with the rowing. He pushed the boat off. It listed and rocked a little as he settled on the seat and laid the oars in the rowlocks. Then he let them fall into the water and pulled away, listening to the gentle sound of the ripples raised by the stem of the boat and looking back towards the Big House where he was aware of a commotion on the steps that involved the Major, Garlinski, a woman who might be Mrs Garlinski and a confusion of dogs.

He back-watered and held the boat steady as he tried to read the scene before him. It was then that he saw in the water, in the shadow of the jetty, a white shape. It was difficult to raise her. All three men had to pull together – from the boat and from the jetty. She came up with her nightdress sticking to her slender body like cling-film. Over it she wore a dressing gown; the pockets were heavy with flat stones.


The image of the drowned woman no doubt raises several questions in the mind of a critical woman reader. To help you, let me say that this would be no pre-Raphaelite Ophelia with red, flower-decked hair floating downstream beneath a weeping willow, but a corpse whose face showed the cyanosis of asphyxiation, from whose lungs and throat there gushed water, snot and vomit. It may help you too to know that a drowned girl was one of the mysteries that haunted my childhood, fished up – as I gathered from snatches of conversation between by mother and her cleaning woman – from an amber pool just above the wooden suspension bridge from which we fished and watched the salmon run, leaping clean out of the water to shake off the sea-lice or drifting downstream trailing wisps of lethal fungus. That death by water was never explained to me; I was unable to interpret all the whispered sentences and only much later wondered what had led this young servant girl, daughter of some ploughman or farm labourer, to scramble down to the edge of the pool and launch herself into the cold, dark, nocturnal river. Did she have a breakdown – some unassuagable pain of the heart? Was she lonely? Desperate? Or pregnant by some young ploughman who had abandoned her, enlisted in the army, emigrated to Canada promising to write and never writing, gone into hiding in some great city where she could not hope to find him? I have no answer; but she has become for me a symbol of poor victimised womanhood, so much so that in my dreams and fantasies it has sometimes seemed to me that one woman I too abandoned will one day – at my death – rise up from the waters to confront me.

So in my imaginings she is a signifier that bears a meaning personal to me: but what does she signify in the fabric of the tale I am concocting?

Propp has one reference to death by drowning, under the rubric 'The Villain Causes Harm or Injury to a Member of the Family', eg, orders someone to be thrown into the sea. But who is the villain? Not in this case, I think, the Major, who – contrary to appearances perhaps – is a protector concerned to guard his sister from exposure to danger or to other people (men?).

But what of General Campbell, soldier and landowner, her father, the widower, who brought back from Bhutan the seedlings which grew into the delicately flowering shrubs behind the Big House? What of this man who – as he would admit to a very close circle of ex-army acquaintances – had used to spend his nights in the high Himalayas in the same sleeping bag as one of his young Gurkha bearers? Who had come home to be a grand figure at Highland games, at reviews of cadets and the Boys' Brigade, to be the patron of boxing clubs for boys from the slums, watching them strip and shower, dismissing them with a slap on the buttocks? Whose wife had died when his daughter was born? Did he find in the slim, slender-hipped girl – eleven years old when he retired in 1937 – a sexual object he could dominate, tyrannise, subject to his urgent and very direct sexual needs, so that he buggered her into subjection, shame, silence, withdrawal? A state diagnosed by the deferential family doctor as a breakdown to be cured in expensive nursing homes but one which yielded to no treatment. Not even when the old man died. For the young woman was no longer able to come out from behind her defences where the Major had kept her confined. Perhaps he feared what she might say if ever she overcame her aphasia, for he had guessed but did not dare admit even to himself the roots of her malady. So he had guarded her.

Question: was it the unbearable knowledge of the young woman's suffering and its cause that made Aunt Clotilde return to France?

Another question: did the sight of Lucy/Lucinda, slim, boyish in her leather gear, like some sort of page, awaken in Grizelle unbearable memories and fears, so that she had twice tried to warn her of danger – once years ago in that hurried whispered message beneath the stairs and more recently that evening when Lucy dined with the Major? Was that why she came looking for her in the bothie?

How you answer these questions will depend on your views on the tyranny of patriarchs, on the prison regime of the nuclear family, on the nature of male sexuality, on the springs and sources of evil.


Peter had always imagined the Major's ancestors were buried on the island in the loch with its gravestones sown in the grass like fossil teeth. But for Grizelle Campbell-Swinton there was no waterborne journey to her grave. Instead, her coffin was born away smoothly but with dispatch to an Episcopalian church near Stirling and on for burial in a graveyard where the Campbell-Swintons had a family vault – solid, but now rather dilapidated –in front of which a plaque marked the resting place of the mortal remains of Lieutenant General Lorne Campbell, KBE KCSI DSO MC who departed this life one day in June 1944, and was no doubt buried with full military honours and pall-bearers from the Home Guard, having served his country in India, in

206

Flanders, on the North West Frontier and explored the fast-nesses of Bhutan.

Peter Sinclair did not attend the funeral; he had, he felt, no place there; but some days later he drove over to find the churchyard at the foot of a steep rocky hill crowned by an Iron Age fort. Was it, he wondered, some sort of tact or merely the workings of patriarchal tradition which dictated that her grave (still unmarked by a cross but littered with brown, wilted 'floral tributes' on which the rain had smudged the inscriptions) was some distance away from the General, who in due course would be joined by the Major.

As he came away a heavy shower of rain swept over the hill, obscuring the fort and driving Peter to take refuge under the eaves of a shed along with a mild young man with a fuzz of beard who had been wheeling a barrow laden with decaying leaves and withered flowers along the gravel path between the graves towards the discreet, hedged-off rubbish dump. Was Peter looking for anyone in particular? he asked as he rolled a thin joint. A relative maybe? Not really, Peter said, just visiting the grave of an acquaintance. The young man offered the joint to Peter who declined politely; then they talked about his job as sexton – a good one, not cushy but not too tough either. One of these days they'd have to open up a new section.

The last big funeral had been of a woman who drowned in Lochmore. Quite a do, with a piper and a service by the graveside. There had been a funny military sort of chap in charge of things, a foreigner of some kind. Peter recognised a description of Garlinski. The chief mourner had been a biggish man with a bit of a limp. Titled apparently. A laird with a big house on the loch. There had been a good tip from the foreign guy – 'for a dram' – but he didn't actually drink alcohol. Preferred to smoke, which could be expensive. When the spring came round he was off to India. People said the stuff was great there. Though you had to be careful about hepatitis. Had Peter ever been in India? He himself got a lot of good vibrations from Indian things and he liked the idea of the burning ghats, or those other things, the towers of silence where some Indians apparently left the dead to be looked after by the birds of prey. It was a kind of way of going back to nature, didn't Peter agree?

Peter said he wasn't sure. 'Good luck in India,' he said and made his way back to the car, for the rain was now less heavy.

Since the morning when they had lifted Grizelle from the water he had seen little of the Major, who had no doubt been taken up with grief, or indeed of Garlinski who had been charged with supervising the practicalities of the funeral. There would, he felt, be no pressure from the Major either way – to go or to stay; over the waterlogged body they had struck a tacit truce. When he left it would be in his own time and by his own volition. But leave for where? There was an appointment to be kept in London to see once more the distinguished, sober-suited medical man in the lair where he uttered his sentences of life or death. But perhaps he would break the appointment; ring up the receptionist with her piled honey-blonde hair, her red nails, her hothouse sexuality, and plead some excuse, a bereavement, an indisposition.

He had some savings – not a huge amount but enough to finance a trip to the towers of silence and the burning ghats where he might recognise among the crowd a pale ascetic figure daubed with ash and marked on the brow with the scarlet pigment of the god Krishna: the young sexton and gravedigger. Or up into the hills to see the Himalayas lift themselves unimaginably above the clouds. Or along the motorways of America across the great plains, up and over the mountains and down to the ocean. And then? Then – why not? – swim as far and as long as possible beyond the rocks where the sea lions slipped into the Pacific surf towards the fabulous islands of the East?

But he did not know the answer to his own questions. What he did know was that he had a few days till he drove south and confronted his fate; it was not as if he had not done so before in his life, but now the rules of the game had changed. Meantime there were two things he had to do. He had to look again at his account of events on Andromeda but first, he had determined, he would write an apology for his life and beliefs – using the word apology naturally in the orginal Greek sense of 'an account, a history'; for while he might admit to mistakes, misjudgments, false hopes, there could be no question of disavowal or apology in the accepted sense. This is how his apology began:

I belong to that generation which grew up in the aftermath of one great war. We were convinced that another must come soon and that it would involve us . . .

The writing of the apology took him longer than he had expected, for it was a difficult and sometimes painful process to confront old hopes betrayed and dreams, aspirations unrealised. He was unsure for whom he was writing, perhaps only for himself, although the idea crossed his mind that he might send it to Orna to show that at least he had not been corrupted by the Establishment – as she had prophesied in a moment of anger he must inevitably be. She in turn might show it to Yoram who, although he had been exposed to the potent mixture of nationalism, religion, racism that fed the ideology of the Israeli state was still the son of a woman who had had the courage to break with Zionism and within the confines of her claustrophobic society to assert the rights of the people of Palestine.

So perhaps Yoram would recognise in the last pages of the *Apology* the politics his mother and father had shared in the days before the strains of cultural and (as she argued) class differences drove them apart; for to her he was a petty bourgeois intellectual tainted with the psychological and political shortcomings of his class. But she was the daughter of workers, of a Polish Bund Socialist and his Communist wife, who as a German citizen had been handed over by the Russians when the great dictatorships struck their bargain in the summer of 1939, who had survived the camps and had hoped to see in Israel not only a refuge from persecution but a new socialist state.

He wrote slowly, breaking off at the slightest excuse: to watch a wader probe with its long beak among the stones at the water's edge, to follow the shifting patterns of the clouds on the hills across the loch, to walk up to the gatehouse and enquire whether there was any mail; for he harboured the hope, the tenuous hope, that one day there might be a letter – a card even – the proverbial couple of lines, from Ariel. To say in so many words that she was well and indirectly that she still remembered and thought of him. But nothing came, only a letter from Urizen:

La Volpaia
San Vito
Provincia di Siena
30 October 1987

Dear Peter

I just wanted to thank you for your note, which I should have acknowledged long ago, but you will no doubt understand that things have not been easy for me since the day when summer exploded so to speak and scattered you all here and there and everywhere. I'm sorry our wargame ended the way it did. Are you still writing about Andromeda? I'd love to see how you brought it to a conclusion. Here we are, beginning to think of settling in for the winter which, as I am sure you know, can be quite chilly in these parts. Geraldine went through a bad patch but I am glad to say seems to have pulled through reasonably well. My wife has agreed at long last to divorce me. Once all that has gone through Geraldine and I will get married. I think it might give her the kind of security she otherwise lacks. When you saw her she was not at her best. Perhaps you will look in on us again in our matrimonial state and renew the acquaintance. I've rather lost my appetite for wargaming and am busy trying to set up a series of East-West seminars – not for you, I'm afraid – on democracy and the free market, very much in the spirit of glasnost. I wonder what you as an old communist – I think that is what you would call yourself – think of it all. To people like you who have committed their lives and risked them for a cause, a hope, a dream, whatever you care to call it, people like me must look very muddled and ineffectual. But I am as I am and must do the best I can.

All good wishes
Yours – no longer Urizen
but Christopher
Williams.

*Ciao.* Geraldine sends her regards.


He would indeed send Urizen the Andromeda story, thought Peter, once he had had time to think over its closure, about which he still had certain doubts. Meantime he would finish his *Apology* and post a copy off to La Volpaia. He could imagine Christopher reading it with care, grunting with approval or disapproval, annotating it and then putting it in a file marked *Politics: an Apology for*, along with all the other documentation that lined his study where he sat, listened to Geraldine's footsteps pass quietly through the empty house and wondered what she in her restless pacing was thinking, contemplating, how long she would submit to his kind and gentle prison regime.

On his screen Peter brought up the file *C:\ Apology* and ran the cursor down to the end of the last page. 'It will be a generation at least,' he read, 'before it will again be possible to discuss humanity's dream of something with the hope of being listened to, taken seriously.' So where did that leave him, he wondered, here and now, in such time as he could hope for? It was not till the next day that he felt able to pose the question to himself and felt his way towards an answer.

'Am I still a communist?' he wrote, 'or is the word too tarnished, too sullied by the crimes of Stalinism to be acceptable? First I want to pay homage to the courage and generosity of spirit of my comrades throughout the world who in the pursuit not of a dogma but of a noble and generous vision of human society gave their energies and often their lives. I do not believe that events – history – have proved that vision an illusion, merely that it is

**211**

infinitely more difficult to realise than we thought in our youth and optimism; that new strategies and tactics have to be discovered to realise it and that methods adapted to an underground, clandestine struggle are not those by which societies can be directed; that if communism cannot bring more than a drab basic security, cannot bring joy, pleasure into people's lives, it will fail; for it is one thing to ask for endurance in the struggle against great enemies and another to demand it as a way of life. But I do not believe that my life with all its mistakes has been wasted. Fascism was defeated. Certain liberties were asserted and defended. The long struggle of those peoples who are still exploited by old and new forms of colonialism goes on. It has its victories at the cost of a terrible price to victors and victims.

'I do not believe that capitalism has changed its spots and has suddenly become a beneficent force in the world economy. I do not believe that greed for profit is the only mainspring of human endeavour. I think that if we do not destroy the earth – that if we are not to do so – then we must embrace the old, heretical dream of a good society in which human beings live in peace and harmony, sharing the wealth of the planet, respecting not exploiting each other.'

The day of his departure Peter went up to the Big House, knocked and walked in. The Major was in his office, black-tied, rubicund.

'Ah,' he said, rising, 'so you're off. Haven't thanked you properly for your help that day. You'll understand what I mean. Will you take a drop for the road?' He poured a couple of glasses and raised his with a 'Sliant'. They drank in silence. Then in his oblique way the Major put the question: 'A very decent malt,' he said, 'the distillery's closed now but I have a few bottles left. By the way, any word of that niece of mine? Vanished, has she? Well, I expect she'll turn up one day as if nothing had happened and ask to be put up for the night. But maybe you know better?'

No, said Peter, he did not know any better. So they shook hands and he went down to his car. At the gate Garlinski saluted smartly and Peter raised a hand in reply.

On the motorway there was rain and water rising like a bow-wave from under the wheels of the great lorries. He played tapes, tired of Bob Dylan, tired of Brahms, tired of listening obsessively to a woman singing country and western about love and loss, and sent the tuner running up and down the wave-lengths: snatches of French, of German, local stations with local voices and local request programes, the bogus camaraderie of quiz masters and disc-jockeys and phone-ins. A newscast. But first the weather: deep depression, rain. The news headlines. The usual comings and goings of statesmen. The evasions of cabinet ministers. The triumphalism of Thatcher. A news item: 'In Cyprus there has been a terrorist attack on an Israeli yacht. Four people are known to have died in an explosion and an exchange of fire. Among the dead is the well-known Israeli poet, Itzak Peled. Responsibility for the attack has been claimed by a so-far unknown Palestinian organisation calling itself the Avengers, who claim that the yacht, an ocean-going vessel, was being used by Mossad – the Israeli intelligence organisation – to monitor Palestinian groups. The Israeli government has condemned this brutal attack on innocent civilians. The Cyprus police are holding a Palestinian and a British subject who have been charged with the murder.'

A British subject – but man or woman? Peter scoured the wavebands for more news. As he searched, his attention to the road faltered. A lorry with trailer towered alongside. His car swerved, buffeted by the slipstream and the thrown spray. He felt a spurt of fear and drew into a lay-by to resume his search of the airwaves, but there was no further information. By the time he had come level with Lincoln the item had dropped out of the bulletins. Turning on the television in his flat he waited in vain for an item, but these deaths were too marginal and the political realities of the war of which they were the victims too remote to displace items on flooding, on overturned lorries and the probable route of a deep depression approaching from the south-west. Next morning there was at least a brief item. 'The police in Cyprus are still attempting to establish the motives for yesterday's terrorist attack on an Israeli seagoing yacht in the course of which four people – two men and two women – were killed. Among the dead is the well-known Israeli poet, Itzak Peled. Two men have been arrested: an Arab whose identity is unknown and Duncan Hogg, thirty, who is believed to be a British subject. Both have been charged with murder. The security forces are anxious to trace a young woman, believed to be British, who appears to have been travelling with Hogg.'

So Duncan had at last found a cause and Lucy/Lucinda had brought him to it. What, he wondered with a sharp pang of jealousy, did 'travelling with' say about the relationship between the two of them? Or his own to her? He turned over the question in his mind all morning, taking it with him as he walked along the towpath by the Regents Park canal where he had used to walk with Orna and Yoram and on to the new, unfamiliar shops where the young and the tourists picked over the ethnic, the trendy and the fashionable, and styles were jumbled in an admirably postmodern confusion.

In Camden Town he looked at the Greek-language papers in the news-stands. On the front of one there was indeed a photograph of the *Sharon*; but having bought it he was unable to decipher more than the names of Duncan and Peled. On his way back he saw how mallards and seagulls disputed scraps of bread thrown to them by an old woman, laden with plastic bags, who looked up briefly when he stopped to watch the flurry of wings and webbed feet, her complexion ruddy from sleeping rough and from the booze she drank in her bivouac in doorways and under bridges; who once had been young, perhaps confident, perhaps happy, perhaps in love, perhaps loved. She shook the last crumbs from a bag, gathered her paraphernalia and walked off before him with a curious hurried gait as if she feared to be apprehended. Perhaps he should have called after her, found a sheltered place and over a bottle of red wine or flask of cider consulted her, the sibyl of Camden Town.

But what more could she tell him that he did not already know? That he must not feel jealousy, the corrosive agent which eats at heart and mind; not of Duncan nor whomever else Lucy

214

might travel with, sleep with, find moments of peace and shelter with, least of all of that Palestinian fighter whose name he did not even know, held incommunicado deep in the desert, without trial, without a term to his imprisonment, to whom she was in her own way steadfastly faithful.

It was later in the morning that he at last picked up the phone and heard the voice of the receptionist address him as if he were an old and valued friend. Yes, he could certainly make an appointment – for Monday next? Ten-thirty? 'Certainly, Mr Sinclair. Ten thirty then.'

He laid down the receiver and felt a certain relief. Monday – so, four days over which he scanned the papers daily but found no more mention of the attack on the *Sharon*; for it could only have been the *Sharon* which he had photographed with its quivering antennae and on which Peled had embarked at Santo Stefano. It was his restlessness that led him to the Tate where he lingered in a room full of great, muted, almost monochrome paintings from which he drew a sense of calm and peace that he would have been hard pressed to explain or justify in other than quasi-religious terms, and from them he shied away.

Much of the time Catriona, the courageous woman of his daydreaming, surfaced in his mind, submerging only to re-appear again unexpectedly when he was occupied with other things – in the tube, on a bus, when he was listening to music or quite simply busy by himself with the trivial tasks of house-keeping. Gradually he allowed her to emerge into his conscious-ness and to challenge the end he had imagined for her until he felt compelled to turn on his word-processor and by the green light of the screen to begin to type.


As they walked towards the capsule she reached out and took David's hand for a moment and smiled at him. It was a gesture she saw that he was unable to interpret or respond to. Then the routines of operational flight took over. As they left the exit port Catriona mastered her excitement and responded calmly as Control set their altitude and course. When they reached

Herringbone Ridge, the encampment of the intruders, she made no error in naming them, was clearly to be seen. Little movement. Emplacements that might contain laser weapons. Then came the command to unship the snow-cats and advance to within a kilometre of the intruders. As she moved off she was aware of David abreast and to starboard of her. They skimmed the uneven terrain, dodging to avoid outcrops and to make it difficult for the crews of the laser guns – if they were crewed – to hold them in their sights. This time there was no voice to break in and appeal to the two of them as brother and sister.

There was some movement now among the domed shelters which clustered round to form the nucleus of a colony that would, given time and peace, grow and establish itself. When they were at the limit of their prescribed advance the voice of Control told them to return to base. She saw David operate his reactors and manoeuvre to set course for the capsule. She did the same, skimming along close enough to see his face. When she turned away it was with a farewell gesture of her hand. The unexpectedness of her manoeuvre caught him and Control unawares. Before she heard over her head-set the command to David to pursue her and take her under fire she was already weaving and dodging among the hummocks of the outcrops, urging her snow-cat forward so that it shook and trembled.

She was aware of a laser beam flickering past her but she was now less than a kilometre from the encampment where she could see the new colonists move towards their emplacements. She had tuned to the frequency over which the woman's voice had come that other time and switched to transmission.

'Sisters and brothers,' she said, 'do not shoot. Clear for me to come in.'

As she skidded to a halt in the deep dust through which men and women hurried to meet her she saw David's snow-cat disappear in a fine white trail.

As she stepped out a woman of her own age came forward to embrace her and say, 'Welcome, sister, welcome.'

★

What was the ground, the underpinning for this romantically optimistic ending which must fall outside the Proppean categories since it is a heroine and not a hero who triumphs? Had the old powers fallen before a movement for freedom and liberation with, as its declared aim, new forms of social justice, new kinds of freedom, the will to create conditions in which a dream might be realised without puritanical tyranny and oppression? Possibly. But perhaps, Peter reflected, as he walked across the park to venture into another foxes' den as dangerous as La Volpaia had ever been, perhaps it was merely an expression of that residual optimism without which he would have been unable to face life and death.

The silver-haired man was dressed as before. His gestures and handshake were the same. But this time he said, 'I am afraid I have bad news for you.'

As he walked back across the park Peter saw with astonishment that nothing had changed, that the children with their bicycles still pirouetted on the broad walks, that a plane hung over the city, and understood that all this would continue without him.


I cannot find in Propp anything that casts light on the human condition.

30 | 7 | 98 | 4 0